Jodi

The
Greatest
Love Story
Ever
Told

Jodi

The Greatest Love Story Ever Told

BY RICHARD M. BRODSKY

TREBLOON PUBLICATIONS

A portion of the proceeds from each book sold
will be donated towards finding a cure for AIDS.

Trebloon Publications
P.O. Box 156
Lawrence, NY 11559

Edited by Irene Garbo
Jacket design by Dan Stoica
Book design by Abelardo Martínez
The text of this book is set in Palatino
Printed in TK

First Edition

2 4 6 8 10 9 8 7 6 5 4 3 2 1

Library of Congress Catalog-in-Publication Data
Brodsky, Richard M.
Jodi, The Greatest Love Story Ever Told /Richard M. Brodsky.—1st ed.
    p. cm.
LCCN 2001130873
ISBN 0-9715423-0-9
1. Brodsky, Richard M. 2. HIV-positive men—New York (State)—New
York—Biography. 3. Bisexual men—New York (State)—New York—
Biography. 4. Architects—New York (State)—New York—Biography
5. Runners (Sports)—New York (State)—New York—Biography.
6. Fathers—New York (State)—New York—Biography. 7. Bisexuality
in marriage. I. Title
RC607.A26A3 2002 362.1'969792
QBI33-214

To my best friend, Jodi

To Hillary, our firstborn, and after 18 years I've never felt closer to you

To Peri, truly Solomonesque and never without a kind and loving word for me

To Stacie; the spirit of the Brodsky family will never set as long as Stacie is near

To Anyone and Everyone whose heart is beating with a kind thought for Jodi and my family

"THE CREDIT BELONGS TO THE MAN WHO IS ACTUALLY IN THE ARENA . . . WHO STRIVES VALIANTLY, WHO KNOWS THE GREAT ENTHUSIASMS, THE GREAT DEVOTIONS, AND SPENDS HIMSELF IN WORTHY CAUSES. WHO, AT BEST, KNOWS THE TRIUMPH OF HIGH ACHIEVEMENT AND WHO, AT WORST, IF HE FAILS, FAILS WHILE DARING GREATNESS SO THAT HIS PLACE SHALL NEVER BE WITH THOSE COLD AND TIMID SOULS WHO KNOW NEITHER VICTORY NOR DEFEAT"

Theodore Roosevelt

DISCLAIMER

JODI, THE GREATEST LOVE STORY EVER TOLD is a love story. This book is not written with the intent to hurt anyone. If my story offends the public or any of the characters in my story then I apologize to those parties.

It was suggested I write in a pen name and change the names of my children. This book is about truth. Jodi, Hillary, Peri, Stacie and I will not hide or be ashamed of our commitment to family. We have been prisoners too long and we need to get out of our cage. Hoping my relatives and friends will accept and love us and embrace my family and my story is my goal. It may take time but I believe family forgives, and I pray the book is a rousing success someday, since that may have an impact on whether or not my next book is titled, *Writer Riding the Wave of Solitary Orphan.*

There were some business relationships and boyfriends that were referenced, and where these relationships ended negatively I chose to change their names. To those few people I thank you, and not in a sarcastic way, because you have taught me forgiveness. It is this group which has largely been responsible for my having discovered my mission in life. Professions and company names have not been changed. I wanted as much of my story to be true or at least as true as I remember it.

TABLE OF CONTENTS

INTRODUCTION

IMAGINE RIDING ON A TRAIN that could take you anywhere you wanted to go. Crossing beaches, oceans, flying above the tops of trees, even going back to another period in time, this train could go anywhere. The journey I am about to take you on is more fantastic, and I could not make it up if I tried. It is a true journey; it is the story of my family and me. I am a fairly successful architect, happily married with three teenage daughters, 18, 16 and 13. Relive with me the last four years of my life during which I sank to suicidal levels. Afterwards, you will understand why, despite my life-threatening illness, I would not trade places with anyone in the world.

At age forty-four I became HIV positive from having unprotected sex with an HIV positive man. August 4, 1997 was the worst day of my life, as that was the day I found out I was HIV positive, and I had to tell my wife I was both bisexual and HIV positive. I wrote Jodi, my wife, a poem, one of many I had recently written. As I gave Jodi the poem, I realized this might be the last bit of happiness she would ever receive from me. In my mind there were three choices which I subsequently related to Jodi:

1. She could divorce me and have everything. There was nothing I wanted. I would continue to support my family and live as frugally as possible. I'd take a small studio in New York and sell my car.

2. I would kill myself for hurting Jodi and bringing so much shame to my family. I don't know if I could have really done this since I have children. However, given my state of mind and my love for Jodi, I cannot say how this would have played out.
3. We would continue living together as a married couple and try to deal with the hurt and suffering I was causing.

I also told Jodi if she did not want me to come home that night because she needed time to sort things out, I understood.

Jodi never once wavered and we have been together ever since. Jodi understands that I am bisexual, and occasionally I am with men. Jodi and I do continue to have sex, although we use condoms so that she will not become infected with the AIDS virus.

My health is excellent. I exercise and work out at a gym, don't smoke, don't do drugs, don't drink except for a glass or two of wine a week, eat right, and have an excellent support system consisting of my wife and three daughters. I'm so healthy and strong, I run the New York City Marathon every year, and it's possible that my wife and I have the fastest combined times for our age group. Would it surprise you to learn that my fastest time was 3 hours 23 minutes, and that this was accomplished after being diagnosed HIV positive?

The main theme of the book is: **Let's get the medicine out to HIV positive people and encourage these people to live a healthy lifestyle.** If you have a dream, make it happen and don't let anyone keep you down. Keep your spirit flying and you can beat this illness. People, business, and government must unite and contribute towards finding a vaccine and a cure. People must speak out and say they are gay, bisexual or HIV positive, and not feel ashamed of who they are. All voices must be heard. We owe it to the 22,000,000 souls who have died from AIDS. They cannot speak, but their voices will be heard forever unless we forget them and the meaning of life. And what about those poor souls who are living and keeping all their secrets clogged up in their brain? Chances are, if you revealed your darkest secret to four people at a table, more than likely someone at the table would have a darker tale. Try eliminating whatever secrets you are hiding, and I guarantee you will be relieving yourself of a tremendous amount of stress. I believe stress is the #1 killer in this country, and that's just not how I am going to go.

There are few people in this world who can say there is justice in this world with respect to their family. I can. There is no one out there with whom I would like to trade places. My family loves me, and for that I love them a little more than the average father. I am well aware that the majority of families would have thrown me out, but maybe my wife and I showered so much love and affection on each other and the children over the years, that my story is the exception. Trust your wife, make her your best friend before it's too late, and together as a family you can get through anything. The worst mistake I ever made was not trusting Jodi and exposing her to my life-threatening illness. Any of my other flaws pale by comparison, and I will never forgive myself for not trusting Jodi.

I am not a religious person, but I have come to the realization that maybe God gave me this illness for a reason and maybe my purpose in life is to make a difference. The Jewish people did a great job in not letting the world forget that 6,000,000 Jews died during the Holocaust. I now pose the question: How will the 22nd century view us when the final count comes in at 50 million to 100 million dead from AIDS? Surely we will be called the darkest age. I can't accept these statistics. It is my hope that this book will contribute to diminishing these numbers. If I cause any pain and suffering to my family, as I am sure there will be people who disapprove of my lifestyle and book, then I apologize to my family. My family has been behind me and there is only one person who can stop my story from being told. I am Jewish, and believe it or not, it is not my mother, although she is not aware I am writing a book. How I tell her and her reaction could be a story in itself. The one person is my thirteen-year-old daughter. She suspects I am gay from conversations she has had with her sisters, although her sisters have denied any confirmation. My thirteen-year-old does not know I'm HIV positive, and if she is not ready to deal with this issue now, my story will be shelved for a few years. This child is such a kind, caring spirit that I am confident she will be proud of me and want my story told.

I find myself able to readily forgive people, because what I have done to my family has been far worse than what others have done to me. It feels great not to hold any grudges and not to be mad at people. If you hurt my child, my wife or my mother, however, then the rules change and you will not be forgiven so easily. If there is one episode that stands out as to what prompted me to make the commitment to chronicle my story, it might be when my daughter's ex-boyfriend threatened my daughter with announcing "the dark secret of the Brodskys that could ruin your life." I won't live my life in hiding anymore. My family loves me and I love them, and that's what's important to me.

I would also like to apologize to my mother, my brothers and their families, and Jodi's family. It was never my intent to hurt family or friends, and if I've said anything negative about any of you, I apologize. I love you all very much. I do believe in family and hope you will all forgive me.

Jodi, my wife, is truly an incredible woman. Passionate,

loving, intelligent, kind, decent, respected and being the best imaginable wife are only a few of her better qualities. I am clearly #2 in her life; the children come first. Jodi is the best mother in the world and through her kindness, love and wisdom she has molded this family into the type of family most people only dream about. My two oldest girls are each other's best friends and recently they have included my thirteen-year-old. Seeing my three daughters arm-in-arm on visiting day at camp in the summer of 2001 was the most beautiful sight in the world to me. Maybe I'm a little extra appreciative because I am not supposed to be a biological father by society's standards. Believe me, I do not take it for granted that my family chooses to keep me around.

Jodi, my story must be told from a humanitarian standpoint, but it must also be told for another reason. My story is my gift to you. I want the world to know this book is not about me. It's all about

JODI, THE GREATEST LOVE STORY EVER TOLD

Chapter I

A VERY DARK AUGUST

IT WAS MY 45TH BIRTHDAY and I was 'celebrating' it at the doctor's office. The blood tests were not supposed to be ready for another week, but my wife called the doctor on August 28th and he said he had the results. The doctor's policy was not to release the results of this test over the telephone. The test was to determine if Jodi would eventually become HIV positive. She had been exposed to it on numerous occasions over the past month or two. So we proceeded to the doctor's office for the 3:00 appointment.

We arrived about five minutes to three and you could hear our hearts pounding. Our blood pressure must have been through the roof. Finally we were ushered into the doctor's office and there we waited for him for another fifteen minutes. I shed a tear or two while waiting. Jodi and I repeatedly promised there would be no crying, whatever the results, especially not in the presence of the doctor. This I knew would be impossible for me because I had been crying quite a bit since August 4th. So here we were now, waiting for results that would forever change our lives, although we both knew our lives would never be the same no matter what the test results revealed.

Since you bought, borrowed or bargained for this book at a garage sale, you are the reader, the customer, and you are allowed to ask questions. I'm not there to answer them nor do I have an 800 number, but I know a few questions you must have on your mind. If the roles were reversed, Richard, wouldn't you dump Jodi in a second? Would a man be more or less likely to leave his wife than a woman leave her husband? Think about it for a minute. I mean really think about it. How did this whole mess start? What really happened... and what about the test?

The last question is the easiest. The doctor came in and said my wife was fine and that it was almost certain she would not become HIV positive, provided we practiced safe sex. Naturally I started to cry, but this time it was a positive emotional release.

You've heard of surprise endings, so how about surprise upbringings? Everything I've told you so far has been the truth although I owe you some explanations about August 4th and the 45-some-odd years leading up to August 4, 1997.

I was born August 29, 1952 to Herbert and Gladys Brodsky. I am the middle son of three boys. My parents had a great marriage and they loved each other dearly. I had some middle child syndromes growing up. I remember my father being impatient with me. He used to say, "Why must you always have the last word?" I would reply, "What are you talking about?" In fairness to my father, he was a nice man, a kind husband and a caring father. It was a little difficult for him to be warm or emotional with my brothers and me. My parents belonged to a generation which believed that affection was not something to be expressed in public. As I think back I don't have any recollection of them holding hands or giving each other a big hug, although I do remember my parents dancing together and my father taking on a warm glow after a few drinks. I never saw my father cry. Just like me... yeah, right. We are total opposites.

I love to hug my daughters and wife in public or private and tell them how much I love them and how proud I am of them. If I died tomorrow I would want my family to think of the 1,001 times I hugged them, including the last few times which will remain etched in their hearts as if it were yesterday. I remember being in a store with my father one day and he saw this jacket that he had to have. My mother told him he had one very similar, so he told me to try it on. He bought me the jacket; it was one of those moments I'll never forget. I wish I had the confidence I have now to have given my father a hug. My father died at 57 from a heart attack and I wish I had a hug to remember him by. I was 30 at the time and had been married a few years. It was during the last few years of my father's life that I began to feel his warmer side. He loved my wife. Even now I can vividly see him sitting on the steps with Jodi, talking to her. He never did that with me. It was a terrible shock when my father died. I was naturally very sad. I remember crying, but somehow you go on. No one in our family went for therapy or felt unable to cope with his death. However, there's something about losing a parent that makes people feel compassionate towards others. But when my friends said, "I know how you must be feeling, I'm so sorry," I would think, How can they possibly know? They still have both parents.

I didn't realize it at the time, but when my mother lost her soulmate for life, her children, friends and relatives became extremely protective and considerate. This is an example of human instinct at its finest moment. Wasn't the kindness offered to make my mother feel good? Or do people offer their kindness to feel better about themselves? I think it is a combination of both. To anyone who's been a little kinder to my mother since my father died, I'd like to say thank you. This thank you is actually extended to everyone my mother knew, except for just a few individuals.

The night my father died he had a heart attack and fell in the bathroom and did some damage to the toilet. The next day my mother called a plumber named Saul. Saul had been doing thousands of dollars of work with my cousin who owned a factory. Saul got the account directly because of my mother who had introduced him to my cousin. Saul promptly repaired the toilet and sent my mother a bill. I found this to be extremely insensitive of the plumber, and though it will be twenty years this December since my father passed away, I still cannot forget Saul's callousness.

I feel like a newspaper editor reporting morbid news because bad news sells, not good news. Let me correct that image. From the time of my father's passing to this day, everyone who has been in contact with my mother has been quite kind to her. Those few who have not I'll deal with later. Nobody who hurts my mother or family can expect me to remain silent.

I still remember the first dinner we went out for as a family after my father died. We dined at a local restaurant, La Viola; my parents had frequented it often. The setting was very elegant. It was my mother's birthday, and my mother always likes for things to be smooth and perfect. My mother, brothers, and Jodi and I had just been seated at the table when the waiter walked by and asked, "Aren't we waiting for someone else?" I was proud of my mother as she just held her head high. We all felt her grief, but she did not cry. It has never been my mother's style to display tears in public.

About my mother. She's still around. She's 74 and still going strong, very strong. She looks great. It must have been hard for her growing up. Her sister was absolutely gorgeous. She had another sister who died in her early 20s. My mother is kind and loving although she criticizes incessantly, and this has always been tremendously stressful for me. She has a good heart. I know she loves me and probably even more so as the years go by, but I've always felt she likes my older brother Stuart the most. My mother always thought of me as silly, whereas my wife and friends realized I had a great sense of humor. I can be quite humorous at times, and I love making people laugh or just getting a response from them. In recent years my mother's sister Ronnie and I have gotten a little closer. She appreciates my witty ways, perhaps because she has a wonderful, whimsical wit herself.

Aunt Ronnie is one of my favorite people. She's gotten a little heavier in her later years, but she is still beautiful. Even as a child, I noticed how all eyes turned to her when she walked into a room. Her personality and smile and stories are legendary. She has a dark private side, however. Her son Steven died in a car accident fifteen years ago, and since then she has never quite been the same. Sometimes she can be mean and critical, but I love her and empathize with her, and I often wonder how parents can go on living after their child dies.

There is a certain sadness about our family which I feel. Since I am the one who opened this chapter, perhaps it will be me who closes the chapter. All of my parents' brothers and sisters who had children have had to bury a child, a fate no parent deserves. My first cousins, David, Alan and Steven, all died before they were 40. Only my parents have had the good fortune not to lose a child, although who knows when this story will be published? Perhaps in death I will be saying, "See, I told you so." Actually I'm really not that morbid; I'm just looking for a little sympathy.

I could go on about my adolescence and life in general before I met Jodi, but I will not bore you. Suffice it to say that my life began, truly began, the day I met Jodi.

I am one of those people who believe in fate and that things happen for a reason. I have to believe this because my wife is so kind and loving, and I am not the easiest person to live with. If I hadn't met Jodi and married someone else, more than likely I would not have remained married.

I met Jodi in Houston in the late 1970s while Jodi was attending law school. I went to a seminar one day at my synagogue to hear about the exploits of someone returning from Iran. In the back of my mind I can still hear my parents telling me to introduce myself to the rabbi. That is what I mean about fate. My parents were not religious and the comment had been made only in passing, but some things you remember. I weighed this statement in my brain and decided it was worth holding onto. So after the lecture I introduced myself to the rabbi. He asked me what had brought me to the synagogue, and I explained that I had worked in Iran for fifteen months after graduating architecture school and that I was curious to hear the stories of a fellow traveler. The rabbi asked me if I'd like to meet a nice Jewish girl and I said, "sure." The rabbi gave me Jodi's name first and then struggled to come up with a few other names. Thank you, Rabbi Segal, for a wonderful wife and family.

When I graduated from college in 1975, there were no jobs in architecture in New York for *RAGS* (recent architectural graduates) so I traveled to Iran to try to find a job. That was probably the most courageous thing I had ever done in my life, and it remains an accomplishment I am still proud of. Considering I never even went to camp or lived in a dorm, this was quite an adventure for me. I felt good that I was doing something positive with my life, really taking control. My mother tells the familiar story of how she sobbed so incessantly for a week after I left, that my younger brother Victor threatened to leave home. In some ways my mother isn't overly emotional or affectionate. I wish I could have been there to see her reaction. It's sort of like me wanting to be at my own funeral, just to hear what people think of me and what they say about me. Did I really have a purpose on earth? Would somebody stand up and say something nice about me? How many people would attend? Oh, why are we even discussing this now? I'm going to be around for a while. Don't come to my funeral; I don't want to go to yours. When I tell you about my father-in-law, we can talk more about funerals and attendance.

To be fair to my father-in-law Jules, I must first list his good points. He adored my mother-in-law and took care of her, always being there for her, especially during her four-year bout with ovarian cancer. He was a hard worker and did quite well financially. Jules was clearly the favorite son of three children. The sun rose and set around Jules. Jules was a first rate son and if I were to utter one negative comment about Jules' mother, I would never be forgiven. If I were to comment on Grandma Helen in a negative manner, I would be hard pressed to write a three-sentence essay. Maybe she cooked with too much salt. Maybe she cooked with too little salt. If you can love your grandchildren too much then Grandma is guilty. This little woman towered above all of us in her commitment to family. Jules has four children of his own, who are all married and reasonably happy, and he is blessed with eleven grandchildren. The best thing I can say about him is that he helped create my wife. We are all prod-ucts of both our genes and environment. There must be some very good genes in my wife's family because the environ-ment she grew up in was lacking. By environment I am not talking about their neighborhood, cars or clothes. I'm talking about being loved, being told your parents are proud of you, getting help with your homework, having a parent there for you when you come home from school, that type of thing.

It's interesting I call Jules 'Dad', even though he is far from my favorite person. He still is my wife's father and he deserves to be treated with respect. But what about children? Don't they deserve to be treated with respect? Isn't it the parents' obligation to give their children self-confidence so that they can go out and face the world? I always tell my children, "I'm here for you, you're not here for me. It's my responsibility to take care of you. You didn't ask to be born into this world."

One day while Jodi was visiting me in Texas, before we were married, Jules called apparently just to lecture her. Jodi cried for a full twenty minutes while he droned on, but she never once interrupted.

There have been numerous incidents over the years, each one worse than the previous. My wife does not look forward to her weekly calls to her father because he is always mad at her for something. Jodi is so loved by everyone in New York and so misunderstood by her own family. I think her family is jealous of her. They know she is as near to perfect as anyone who has ever jogged on this planet, so anytime she does something wrong they are ready to pounce on her, or hide her running shoes for life!

Get on your Nikes. You're joining Jodi and me in Houston's Memorial Park, a popular jogging trail, for our first date. I was a little nervous because we were going to run five miles and I had been used to running only three miles. Jodi looked great. She wore a beautiful smile. A woman's beauty is showcased in her smile. Why else is a bride always beautiful? A laugh can go a long way, too. Jodi's laugh must be genetic because my middle daughter Peri is blessed with her hearty laugh. It's something you don't expect from a 5'-1" girl.

There are so many things I did not know about Jodi at the time. In tune with the song that declares, "The only thing constant is change," discovery has been our journey. My wife has clearly changed for the better and our marriage has become stronger with every passing year.

From day one I was attracted to Jodi and made plans to see her again and again. I knew I liked her a lot but never realized how much until two and a half months later when I visited my family in New York. My parents picked me up at the airport and all I did on the ride home was talk about Jodi. It was as if I had to stop and sit back and listen—then the voice, my voice would crest into another monologue about Jodi. My week's vacation passed, slowly. My flight back to Texas was late and Jodi picked me up at 1:45 a.m. That night Jodi stayed over and we made love. It was not the first time we had made love, and I began to realize how much I had missed her and that I wanted to share the rest of my life with her, to hold her and see the love in her eyes. She had missed me, too, and everything seemed so right.

I asked Jodi to marry me that very night. Many years later I made a startling confession to Jodi during a visit to our kids' camp. I hadn't planned to ask Jodi to marry me. The words had escaped spontaneously. After I proposed I was in shock for that moment. Who was this person inside me proposing and did I mean what I was saying? I immediately realized yes, this was something I wanted more than anything in my life, and if it took a moment of spontaneity to realize this, then maybe we should have a holiday called Spontaneity Day. On Spontaneity Day everyone would have to do something that would be totally out of character, and the act would require an element of kindness or compassion.

So what do you think Jodi said? She said she needed time to think about it. I forgot to tell you my wife has always been very indecisive (although on August 4th, 1997 she was anything but indecisive). A few days passed; okay, so it was only a few hours during which I asked Jodi about a dozen times to marry me. I can be very persistent and don't take "no" or "maybe" very easily. It was right about this time we were driving to Corpus Christi to visit Jodi's brother Neal and sister-in-law Elaine. We must have been an hour into the ride when Jodi started to tell me in a roundabout way that she was agreeing to be my wife.

We recently had a good laugh about my proposal and her acceptance when we discussed this openly and honestly a few months ago. Jodi never knew I had asked her spontaneously and I think that bothered her slightly. My wife is more of a planner. I asked her when it was that she decided to marry me and she said it was before we started the trip to Corpus Christi. I argued with her. Where was her passion, and why did she wait until an hour into the trip, since this was such an important moment in our life? The moment we commited to spending the rest of our lives together, truly the happiest day of my life. I guess I'm in favor of spontaneous passion, a blessing at the time and a tragedy waiting to happen.

So we were finally engaged. Both our families were surprised because we had both been told our whole lives that we were difficult people. I don't think that's fair to say about Jodi, and I'm not so sure about myself, either. Right now I'm a little confused and I might ask you, the reader, to come to your own conclusion. So far I seem pretty focused in all my thoughts and I suppose organized, or at least organized enough to write this book, but everyone has a hidden side. Didn't Romeo and Juliet each have a tragic flaw of character?

Jodi and I were ecstatic. Relatives and friends commented on how happy and great we looked together. This was a true love affair if ever there was one. I adored Jodi. She was so loving and affectionate. My family adored her too. Everyone she met she touched, even my four-year-old niece. Friends of mine in Texas made us a beautiful engagement party at their home. Thanks again, Bruce, Lynn and Amalie. I'll never forget that party. There were candles aglow all over the house. It was so romantic. In my heart it reminds me of a timeless, tranquil setting that Thomas Kinkade might create if he were to paint an interior, although don't get me started about him because I think he is so talented the way he creates those romantic architectural landscapes, that I long to be a part of the life he envisions. I find him more creative than 99% of all architects; plus, he has a truly luminescent spirit and a wonderful sense of perfect realism of how people should live in rural America.

Jodi and I were disappointed that her parents didn't come to Texas to meet me. If it were me and my daughter, I'd lace up my Nikes, race to the airport and hop on the next flight. Who is this young whippersnapper who is planning to steal my daughter and be the #1 man in her life? I have been numero uno for 20-some odd years and I will not relinquish that post easily. I've got one question: Do you love my daughter?

If you do not look me squarely in the eyes and answer with a resounding "yes", then you have failed the test and you are history. Profess your love with all your heart and I will embrace you, my son.

I, Jodi's fiancé, needed that hug, but without her parents' visit there would be no acceptance or hug. How could this be happening? Here was Jodi, their eldest daughter planning to spend the rest of her life with a man they had never met. We needed that visit.

The next several months of our engagement were not pleasant, to say the least. Our love and commitment to each other was constantly and severely tested. Jodi and I wanted a big wedding to celebrate our love. Jodi's parents did not want a big wedding. Finally, we decided to have the wedding in Jodi's parents' hotel in Florida. It was a nice enough place by Florida standards and could easily accommodate 200 people, which is probably how many people would have attended. All my parents' friends and cousins would have flown to Orlando. When Jules heard that, he nixed the idea pretty fast. In the end, we had a small wedding, 53 people. Jodi and I realized it was either this or nothing, so we accepted. We were both hurt in later years when her two younger sisters were given ballroom weddings which 200 guests attended to share their special day. Jodi and I swore we would never hurt our children like that. We started planning our firstborn daughter's Bat Mitzvah even before she was born. We knew her gala would become the wedding we never had.

So the years passed for us and our three beautiful girls, Hillary, Peri and Stacie. Hillary was conceived right after my dad died. We had been married almost two years when he died and although we never discussed when we would have children, we both knew we wanted a family. We decided to plan a family, and shortly after, Hillary was born. Hillary brought new meaning to our life and I saw a side of Jodi that I had never seen. Motherhood and Jodi were made for each other. Jodi has a tremendous need to right everything that was wrong in her life. I don't know if Jodi is clearly aware of this, but it's a beautiful thing. If Jodi was deprived of a balloon at a birthday party, you can be sure my kid would never leave a party without a balloon. I never saw such care and love, although it shouldn't have surprised me, the way our relationship was growing.

After six months Jodi was ready for another baby. Jodi never complained it was too much work. I told Jodi it was too soon. So we waited a little and our second daughter Peri was born 23 months after Hillary. Peri was such a doll and she adored Hillary. Peri became the 'Solomon' of the family. One time we were in Orlando when Peri was ten. We saw a beautiful blanket in a store that said, "Grandmothers make life's journeys a little more pleasant." We knew we had to buy the blanket. I asked my family if we should give it to my Grandma Clara or my mother. Peri instinctively said to give it to Grandma Clara to make up for all the times we didn't see her. Another time, when Hillary was six or seven, she wrote a note that said, "I wish I could be as good a sister to Peri as Peri is to me." This is all to Jodi's credit for bringing up our daughters in the manner she has always seen fit to.

Three years later, Stacie, our youngest, was born. She was named after my cousin Steven and immediately captured everyone's heart, especially Aunt Ronnie's. My children understand that she is Aunt Ronnie's favorite because she is named for her son Steven, who had died so young. We all accept this. Aunt Ronnie has been like a mother to Jodi and a grandmother to the girls. Stacie is an incredible athlete, very intelligent, a talented singer, artist, and a tomboy if ever there was one. Her only weakness is that her attention span can be limited and her behavior needs improvement. However, to know Stacie is to love her.

As the kids were growing there were the normal financial concerns. I'm an architect and fortunately I made a decent living so that Jodi could stay home with the kids. I never wanted Jodi to work and she made a full-time career out of caring for our family. Only recently did I find out that Jodi thought I may have wanted her to work or resented her for not working. I never knew Jodi felt this way or that I acted this way in the least. If I did, I honestly never meant to. I was content to have Jodi stay at home and I felt fulfilled being able to take care of our family.

Our expenses ran quite high so we did not save as much money as we would have liked to. Jodi would buy the kids new clothes before buying for herself, although she always looked great, and don't get me wrong; she bought clothes. Cars didn't interest her, unlike my children and my brothers. Her Volvo was approaching its tenth birthday and she couldn't care less. She loved the wedding band I had bought her. It was enough for her. Women love jewelry. They especially love the idea that someone who loves them bought them the jewelry.

Jodi placed so few demands on me over the years. She loved me unequivocally and for me this was truly a reciprocal love affair. However, she also loved her jogging and never missed a day. I mean never, unless you count Yom Kippur. Jogging was a part of her life and I made it a part of mine. It was our special time together. In our early years of marriage before the children, we ran a marathon or two together. There's nothing more exciting than running the New York City Marathon. As the years passed my running subsided and my weight went up. I had gone from 150 to close to 170 in a few years and I felt helpless that I couldn't control my weight. Diets were useless as they might work for a day or two at best. I was approaching 40 and I began to forgive my father for having a heart attack despite repeated warnings to watch his weight. How could I be mad at my father if I couldn't do any better?

It was about this time at age 40 that I decided to try to get in shape and back into running. Running 10 miles a week just wasn't cutting it so I decided to increase my mileage and begin weight training. In a seven-month period I dropped twenty pounds and begin to look at myself as a suitable match for my wife, and not her chubby husband. My running mileage increased to 35 miles per week and I decided I could run the 1992 New York City Marathon. I ran it and completed it in approximately 4 hours 20 minutes, the same time I had accomplished ten years before. I had to walk the last few miles, but the same thing had happened in the past.

I continued the weight training very diligently and continued running after the marathon. It was about this time I began to actually like how my body looked. I never took drugs or food supplements to get in shape, but something about my body chemistry and sexuality was taking place. I would read exercise magazines to learn new exercise routines and my body was responding as it became toned and firm. I started admiring the male models. They really looked quite hot.

I had always admired a woman's body with her curves, softness and shapeliness, and now here I was admiring the firmness and muscles of a man. Both are beautiful sights. My admiration for the male body and desire to touch and hold a male body began to consume me. It was about this time that I had my first homosexual experience as a married man. It wasn't overly memorable but it left me feeling really hot. Needless to say I felt ashamed and guilty. (How could I do this? I'm a happily married man. I love my wife and children and I love making love to my wife. I'm a success in life with a wonderful family. What am I doing?)

Several sexual scenes with men flashed before my eyes as I recalled a few isolated incidents that occurred in my early 20s while working in Iran. But wasn't I just experimenting then? Or was that what my mind had been directing my body to believe? After fifteen months in Iran, I returned to America. The next stage in my life would obviously be marriage. Clearly, sexual encounters with men and a marriage made in heaven did not fit the mold for a successful life, especially true in the late 1970s more so than today. These gay feelings would be buried and sealed, but obviously not deep or tight enough. My only hope was that I might outgrow this gay side of my sexuality. This was not too much for me to wish for. I had managed to bury these feelings once; so couldn't I do it again? This time was clearly different. I was consumed with a need to be with men. In Iran, my sex life with women had not been very active so perhaps I thought, okay, let's try guys. But here I was, fifteen years later, happily married with a great sex life. My wife and I loved making love, often and passionately. And just as passionately I was seeking out the company of men.

Usually for about a week I'd control these feelings and then after the week was up, a similar encounter would occur. I felt helpless. (I'm not a cigarette smoker, alcoholic, drug abuser or any kind of addict. I don't have any vices. What's wrong with me?)

This continued for several years. I no longer had control over my body and I had no interest in things right or wrong or how much I would hurt my wife. I blocked everything out and cared only about my sexual needs. Somebody forgot to tell my body that sex is supposed to become less, not more important as you get older.

The summer of '96 was approaching and for the first time all three kids were going to be at sleep-away camp. My wife was going to come to work with me for the whole summer. I was thrilled because I love my wife very much. It may be hard for you to understand, but I did not want these bisexual feelings and I kept hoping I would outgrow them. At the very least my wife would be spending the whole summer with me, so hopefully, I would not have the opportunity or inclination to seek out men. This actually worked for the summer and I thought perhaps I had finally outgrown this stage of my sexuality.

The kids came back from camp on August 18th and now that Jodi was home with them once more, my bisexual feelings surfaced stronger than ever. I refer to these feelings as bisexual, but they were really gay feelings. I had, after all, never cheated on my wife with another woman. I couldn't do that. Don't get me wrong. I am attracted to other women and I love making love to my wife, but if it were a question of making love to another woman or a hot guy with a firm body, there would be no question; I would prefer the company of a man.

My encounters with men became more frequent. My sexuality seemed to be peaking. I loved going for walks and feeling the sun on my body. Massaging oil on my body and having the sun bestow its fire on me became my addiction. I rejoiced in the presence of my sun, knowing full well that my reward would be a tan. My tan would be the physical proof that I had seized the sun's energy. This new-found energy powered my body into overdrive. Everything seemed so sensual and my body was so alive. As I said, my encounters became more frequent and I could not stop or even control my feelings. I wanted to tell Jodi and came close on one or two occasions during the summer of '97, but by this time it was too late.

I was still somewhat naive about HIV and AIDS. Okay, so I was completely naive or did not want to know. Besides, I was feeling invincible and very strong. One day in late April '97 I met a guy named James. After a few minutes we proceeded to his apartment and things moved along a little too far. James had piercing blue eyes, a decent body, a handsome face and a slight sense of depression about him, although he had a nice smile. We got together a few times in the next few weeks, and then he told me he was HIV positive. He reassured me that whatever we were doing would not cause me to become HIV positive. I had a need to believe him so my trust was placed in him. Of course I took an HIV test, and to my tremendous relief it turned up negative. I trusted James and needed him and continued seeing him, but in a safe manner.

It was at this time I was confronted with a major decision. Do I tell Jodi? I was confident she would forgive me, but it would break her heart forever. I was a coward and wasn't 100% sure of Jodi's commitment to me, so I chose not to tell her. Upon taking the test I was informed that it takes three to six months for the virus to become detectable. I didn't know it at the time, but I could have taken a test a month later to determine if I would become HIV positive. Had I been aware of such a test I would have taken the test, and if the results were positive I'd have told Jodi then.

May, June and July passed. I was a little uptight during this time and despite the fact that Jodi was spending the summer with me, my sexual feelings and needs were out of control and I continued seeing men. The three months finally passed and it was time to take the HIV test again. I proceeded to the doctor's office which was just a block away from my office, and paid the medical technician $30 cash so there would be no record of my being tested. I asked the nurse if the doctor had told anyone that day they were HIV positive. She replied 'no'. I asked her how many people she had tested that day. She replied 'thirty' and at that point I began to feel at ease. The blood was taken and then I was ushered back to the reception room where I had to wait fifteen minutes for the results. Needless to say, it was the longest fifteen minutes of my life. The nurse finally ushered me back into the doctor's office just as I had remembered three months earlier. A few minutes later the doctor entered and started mumbling about the reliability of the test. I remember him saying there was a possibility I was HIV positive. I was wondering what had gone wrong with the test and if a possibility meant 10% or 30%. He did say possibility and not probability. The doctor continued speaking and gradually, after having him repeat what he was saying on four occasions, it finally sank in. It was 99.4% certain I was HIV positive.

I started crying and explaining to the doctor that I was married and loved my wife and family. He suggested not telling my wife for 48 hours until a more conclusive test was done. 99.4% is pretty certain and I decided I had to tell Jodi then.

Do you ever watch the evening news and see some immigrant who doesn't speak English, and the only thing you can understand is the universal language of tears and crying? His face is lined with pain and his sobbing is so real you might nominate him for an Academy Award, except you're forgetting for the moment that his anguish is real. His entire family was just killed by a man paroled that very day for previously running over a nun who was on her way to her niece's wedding, only this time the drunken driver managed to wipe out an entire family. Sure the father is left, but he wishes they had taken him too. How do these people go on? Can they sink any deeper in their abyssmal sorrow? Imagine looking at me then as I had to confront my wife and you will find the only person on this planet in lower spirits than those poor people. Maybe if I'm lucky I'll get run over by a drunken driver, I thought, and the poem I just wrote Jodi will fall out of my pocket and will be glued to my body by my blood that has cascaded from my wound and formed a red heart on the street, and the headline will read,

ARCHITECT TRAGICALLY DIES HOLDING LOVE POEM WRITTEN TO JODI

I had thought about how I would tell Jodi as I crossed the only intersection heading back to my office, for there were no cars to save me from living. I would have to face Jodi and the total betrayal of the person I was to Jodi. It would have been so much easier if I had confessed to murdering eight people who did not concur that Jodi was the best mother on earth. How could I tell Jodi the previous four years of my life I had been doing things that I can't even put into print? Maybe this book will make a great movie because I can't imagine a more tragic scene if I had to make one up. Emotionally I was caving by the second into a fog of despair that could have produced a cloud over every desert on earth, only the darkening clouds were consuming me as fast as I was losing control of my life. What right did I have to destroy myself?

I didn't even deserve to have crossed the street safely.

No, I take that back. The dialog in me continued:

Die a hero, you coward. No, I won't hear it. Suffer and look inside Jodi's heart and feel the poisoned arrow you, Richard, have driven into her soul. Tell Jodi, break her heart and maybe after telling her you will slip on an oil patch, and some wooden sticks will ignite a flame and you will burn and you will feel the pain for hours, days, months, until you die, and then you can go straight to hell. But before that happens I have one more agonizing moment for you. That's right, you still have to look your wife in the eye and tell her you are the lowest creature on this planet. Do you have a plan, Richard? Because I don't think that poem is going to help you.

Of course I had a plan. I was always smart but there are just some things in life even a smart architect cannot plan, so come with me now as I plan to sit Jodi down quietly in our living room and tell her what had happened. It's fine to plan but suddenly the reality was here and I could not wait until we arrived home. This day, August 4, 1997 was the worst day of my life. I got back to the office about 5:00 and I was told Jodi was downstairs. The building I work in has a gym for the employees of the building. I went downstairs and found Jodi there. My heart felt like it was carrying the weight of the world, only it was worse. It was carrying the burden of my betrayal of Jodi.

It's painful for me to relate the next few minutes so I will digress for a moment. I had become an accomplished poet during the summer. My three daughters had been away at camp for the past five weeks and they desperately needed mail from their parents. I understood this well because I remember years ago when I lived in Iran I didn't receive a letter from my father for three months. I just wanted him to say anything, maybe two or three lines and "Love, Dad." It's a funny thing about being a child. Whether you're two years old or forty-five you still need your parents' love. Anyhow, I started falling into the trap of not writing because I had nothing to say. Yeah right, you find that hard to believe. What was I supposed to say? "I went to work, had lunch and saw a hot guy today." Great letter! What actually happened was I saw a mattress fly off a car in the middle of the Van Wyck Expressway. It was really funny. Read the poem I wrote. Hopefully, you'll agree.

Dear Stacie,

As Mom and I were driving home
I decided to write you this poem

I began to think what I might say
When this big thing blew away

It all began on the Van Wyck
And it happened oh so quick

A mattress flew into the sky
And oh did it fly so high

I was never so surprised
And then all at once I realized

A car was backing up
As Mom and I were cracking up

Now I'd like to turn to another matter
The house seems so quiet without the chatter

Stacie, you really are a special child
Even though at times you are wild

No one can say you are boring
And you certainly are very adoring

You have always been very caring
And one who always believes in sharing

It's especially nice that you've been writing
And you three sisters are not fighting

I hope you don't find this letter pathetic
Perhaps I should be apologetic

I guess it's time to say good bye
Even though you may wonder why

I miss you with all my heart
From each and every part

So I'm sending you this kiss
So you'll know how much I miss

That special little girl of mine
Who's still my baby at age nine

Love, Dad

This poem launched my career as the poet laureate of the camp and about eight or nine poems followed. Read them, if you like, and you will see a pattern developing. The main theme is to reassure my children I love them and always will.

THROUGH THE EYES OF A DAD

I've come to watch you grow year after year
Through your eyes I've become so aware

The love and respect you show for each other
Is comparable to a child and a mother

Summer after summer you watch the sun rise
I wish I could be there to see it through your eyes

I love sneaking into camp the night before
I know the rules, but some things I ignore

If Sue ever caught me I'd have some explaining to do
It's just I couldn't wait another day without seeing all of you

I'm not good on names and forgetful at times
I'm trying to say I'm not perfect, not even my rhymes

To us, you kids are the greatest gifts in life
If you don't believe me just ask my wife

We love you, adore you and miss you when you're away
For me there's no better day than visiting day

And the love in your eyes when I first see you
I wish I had a mirror, you'd see it too

Being young is truly fun
Running, jumping, swimming, playing in the sun

But being a parent is really the best
Someday I hope, I pray I pass the test

Give each other a hug from me
Through my eyes each of you I see

A day older, a day wiser and another day to be so proud of you
I love you Hillary and all your friends too

Love, Dad

Dear Peri,

The years seem to be going by too fast
I wish your childhood could last and last

I remember when you had a yellow blanket
And I would always try to yank it

I remember you asked, "Was I invited?"
If I said yes you were so excited

Your smile and laugh could brighten any day
I hope you won't change, please say okay

I miss our rides on the boardwalk
I remember we had a very long talk

You pedaled for eighteen miles, do you remember?
Promise me we can do it again, before September

Perhaps the best thing about you
Is watching you develop into

The kind of person that makes me proud
To say I'm Peri's dad, and I say it loud

I hear from people you are very kind
This is a trait that's hard to find

When a person can truly share
This is a wonderful gift, I hope you're aware

I hope I am making a big enough fuss
Because to our family you are one big plus

I wish you a long life where all your dreams come true
And only good things happen to you

So Peri, think of me when you close your eyes tonight
Because to me you're one kid that's out of sight

Love, Dad

Dear Hillary and Bunk Thirty-Two,
I am good, so how are you?

It's great you kids are having fun
Being outside every day in the sun

You girls fill your parents with so much pride
On this we all stand side by side

We all want you to succeed in whatever your endeavor
And this we wish for today and forever

Sometimes it's hard to say the things we should
But we always mean for all things good

So sometimes if we try to hold your hand
Or need an extra hug, please understand

We miss you all a lot
And one more thing I almost forgot

We parents are all astonished
At how much you've accomplished

This feeling is very strong and real
It's something that we all feel

You kids seem to be one step above
And even if you weren't, our love

For you each day since your birth
Has grown so much due to your worth

In your goals and in your dreams
And friendships and everything it seems

That you've learned the value of a friend
Is someone you can count on and always depend on

To share a laugh or a cry
And someone who will always try

To be there for you yearly
And care for you very sincerely

You kids really are the best
North and south, east and west

So try for us parents to enjoy your youth
And this we mean, this is the truth

So reach for the sky this very minute
Think of something and try to win it

We parents miss you all
And can hardly wait till fall

Play hard, play fair and be strong
You kids are great, I'm not wrong

Gotta go I'm out of time
And if all these verses didn't rhyme

I'm really just an architect
So how much can you really expect

Love you all,
Richard Brodsky

Dear Stacie,

Right from the start you had a special glow
When you were born I loved you so

Over the years I've come to love everything about you
I could not imagine how I lived without you

I always loved being close to you
It's something always that you knew

As the years pass by so fast
There are some moments I wish could last

Forever and forever in my heart
It's so difficult when we're apart

I pass your room each summer night
And wish that one night I might

Open your window and enter a balloon
And hold you close and fly across the moon

And tell you all about my wildest dreams
And all my secrets and my schemes

For being the most caring and kindest dad
Any child in the world ever had

I'd tell you about a child who continues to amaze
Me and her family with her special ways

She's beautiful, fun, a super kid and a tennis star
She's artistic and can even design a car

Playing, jumping, hockey and basketball
Animals, friends, family, she wants it all

And indeed this special child of mine
Is super and turning out so fine

So close your eyes and imagine hugging me
I wish tonight this wish could be

In your sleep I will always be your light
I love you Stacie, think of me this night

Love, Dad

The last poem to Stacie became very surrealistic to me. I had needed to escape the pressures of my real world, my bisexuality and my fear of becoming HIV positive, and my conflict of whether or not to confide in Jodi about the double life I was living.

Jodi had been reading my poems and I was getting a lot of recognition at camp. Just as children need reassurance, so do parents. The kids in camp loved my poems and on visiting day I was hailed as a great poet.

Jodi had wanted me to write her a poem and I kept meaning to, but I sensed the kids needed the poems more. Finally in the doctor's office, to help pass the fifteen minutes waiting for the HIV test results, I decided to write Jodi a poem. It doesn't sound terribly romantic but let me reassure you, I never stopped loving Jodi deeply with my whole heart. I knew that if the test came back positive, my life, love and relationship with Jodi would need far more than a poem. Anyhow, here's the poem I wrote:

Through the years I've come to love everything about you
I could not imagine life for a moment without you

You have brought true happiness to my life
This you must know, you are the best wife

A man could ever hope for
I've come to know this more and more

My only regret is not saying so before
I love you, I worship you, it's you I adore

I know I may not always be right
But I hope you agree with me tonight

There is no other person like you
And everyone who knows you knows this too

You have captured the moment, the spirit and the heart
Of me and the children when we are apart

From your love, warmth, kindness and caring ways
This is true, yesterday, today and always

Jodi, in my wildest dreams beyond and forever
Promise me we will always be together

Love Richard

I don't know how I managed not to cry immediately upon seeing Jodi. I gave her the poem and turned away because I could not look at her. I knew this poem would bring her happiness; it just might be the last morsel of cheer Jodi would have to remember me by. Jodi loved the poem and saw the sadness and tears in my eyes. I couldn't speak and she became frantic. Was it our parents, aunts or worse yet, had something happened to the girls? I assured her in my shaky voice they were all fine and that she'd better sit down. Jodi was shaking and I was in no position to reassure her. I finally told her part of the bad news. I told her I was bisexual. She sobbed bitterly and was so afraid that I would leave her. I told her I never wanted to leave her and that my bisexuality was something I couldn't help, something inside me, and that I'd been this way for the past three or four years. I then told her there was more. I was HIV positive. She took that much better than my bisexuality, although she was still crying. Why shouldn't she cry? I was Jodi's pillar of support. We were such a respectable family. We were the picture of health. Our children were overachievers. I was a financial success. None of this made sense to me, so how could this make sense to Jodi? Our love life and the affection we had for each other were thriving and growing. I adored Jodi and Jodi adored me as much or more. This wasn't fair. This could not be happening.

I wasn't sure how Jodi would deal with this. I thought in the end she would probably keep me, but the odds were only marginal in my favor. I gave Jodi three choices:

1. She could divorce me and have everything. There was nothing I wanted. I would continue to support my family and live as frugally as possible. I'd take a small studio in New York and sell my car.
2. I would kill myself for hurting Jodi and bringing so much shame to my family. (I don't know if I could have really done this since I have children. However, given my state of mind and my love for Jodi, I cannot say how this would have played out.)
3. We would continue living together as a married couple and try to deal with the hurt and suffering I was causing.

I started to cry, which over the next few weeks would become a common occurrence. I could not deal with the pain I was causing Jodi. She never deserved this. I was her life and she was my life. To everyone we were the perfect couple. I loved Jodi so much. My passion for Jodi was so strong! Yet I could not control my feelings towards men. I did not want to have these feelings for men. I was a married man and I loved my wife and family. I felt so weak and helpless. I could not accept this bisexual side of me. I'm often considered to be intolerant and I just could not accept my behavior. If I could not accept my actions, how could I expect Jodi to accept me or understand me, like me, or love me?

But this is exactly what Jodi did. She never wavered, continued to be supportive of me, and never asked me to leave.

Chapter II

THE REALITY SETS IN

WE BECAME CLOSER. I BEGAN to really appreciate Jodi because now we had real problems we had to deal with. The medical aspect was inconsequential at this point as I had no symptoms or ailments. For about a ten-day period my mood would mostly be depressed although at times I would be in a good mood. If I saw Jodi was sad I would cry. If I found myself in a good mood I would feel guilty, become depressed and have a good cry. If Jodi told me a sad story from a book she was reading, I would start to cry. We were still working together while the kids were at camp. Thank God we had this time to accept my illness. Accept is not the right word. You never accept it and you always wake up thinking it was just a nightmare, and you cannot exist for more than sixty minutes without realizing you are HIV positive. In looking back, I realize having Jodi with me every day while the kids were at camp was both a blessing and a curse. I needed Jodi near me, for it was her love and affection that got me through those days. However, being with her constantly made me sad to see what I had done to her.

Each day ushered in a new emotional crisis. Driving time was the worst. There was always time for an argument or a good cry. Work was the best therapy, as it took my mind off my problem. What choices and options did I face? There were too many unknowns and that became frightening. How sick was I? Would Jodi get the virus? How was I going to deal with the guilt I currently felt and how would I deal with the guilt if Jodi ever became HIV positive? Would Jodi eventually ask me to leave? How could she ever trust me again and what would that do to our marriage?

Jodi was not pleased with the clinic I had chosen to determine if I was HIV positive. She decided this partly because she did not like the results and partly because they advertised in the *Village Voice*. Besides, a *clinic* does not sound the same as a *doctor's office*. I felt the doctor at the clinic was very competent. He had explained that based on the test results he was 99.4% sure I was HIV positive and a further test would be required for 100% confirmation. Jodi decided it would be best if she saw her obstetrician, and she told me to come along. Dr. Roseff treated me not at all disrespectfully, but it was very awkward for me to be there. He had delivered my three girls, and Jodi and he had always enjoyed a close relationship. I felt like a kid being sent to the principal's office for something minor, like burning down the school and 16 people died. So the day doesn't sound so good so far? (Not to worry; it only gets worse.) After waiting in Dr. Roseff's office for over an hour, Jodi took a blood test to determine if she was HIV positive. It would be several days before we could get the results. The clinic I went to had given me the results in fifteen minutes. Jodi decided I should see a *real doctor* and have my test redone. I couldn't exactly call my own doctor. My doctor had always had a great deal of respect for me. But he was in a suburban office, and the nurses would probably don rubber gloves when they found out I was HIV positive. I still couldn't accept it. You know how they always ask you a million medical questions. I've always been so healthy, I answer no to all of them. Besides, by the millionth question what jerk feels like answering the familiar question, 'Have you ever experienced a prolonged period of impotence in the past 25 years?' I suppose question number one million one would illogically follow: Have you ever been exposed to the AIDS virus or are you now HIV positive? I would say 'yes', and one million sirens would sound off.

Back to reality and Dr. Roseff. He referred me to a doctor on 75th Street off Madison or 5th. We arrived at his office, not very impressive, professional or busy for the address. We waited only a few minutes before the new doctor saw us. He proceeded to take my blood and felt my body for lymph nodes and found several which he said was not promising since lymph nodes develop when your body is fighting a virus or infection. Up until then I didn't have much of a problem with the doctor. He was probably about my age and had a pleasant look about him although he seemed a little sterile, green, innocent, young, inexperienced or some combination of the above. Maybe he needed glasses or a beard or a receptionist who gave you the feeling she had worked there for the last 150 years.

The doctor said to me, "I hope you have life insurance." What a thing to say in front of my wife. He proceeded to paint a very bleak picture for Jodi and me. I had done some reading the past few days and was aware of the remarkable progress made in combating AIDS in the past two years. I asked the doctor to say something encouraging to my wife who was now in tears. He said that people are living longer with HIV now. Truly inspirational!

It is essential for people who are HIV positive to reduce their stress levels as much as possible. HIV is now being treated as a chronic condition like diabetes, but I guess nobody had told my fancy Eastside doctor that. The doctor fumbled around with the HIV forms I needed to sign, and it became obvious that I was the first person he had ever known or met who was HIV positive. If it was up to me I would be the last person that ever visited his office.

Needless to say I was feeling depressed. I found myself drifting back in time to my childhood when things seemed so much simpler. Recalling a neighbor who lived in a big house near my apartment building landed me safely in the year 1958. My neighbor Meyer Glick must have been about 60. That seemed so old back then. Meyer had a big garden, since his attached home was at the end of a row of twelve identical houses. I don't recall how I met him, but I was a friendly kid, like Stacie, and I might have introduced myself. We became pals and I would sit on his porch looking out on Kings Highway. I knew the year and model of all the cars that passed by. Life seemed so simple watching cars go by on Kings Highway. There must have been a million a day. It was coming up on my 6th birthday and we were moving to North Woodmere, a sub-urb on Long Island. I still remember the date we moved. It was August 20th, nine days before my birthday. A day or two before we moved, Meyer bought me a red scooter. I wish I still had that little scooter and everything it symbolized to me.

I was six and playing in the street
Not with my brother because I couldn't compete

I found an old man who was very kind to me
He bought me a present, it was something to see

It was a week before September
Some things you'll always remember

This is one memory that could never be erased
Some things in life can never be replaced

A red scooter is such a thing
If only I had it beside me it might bring

A memory of a day gone by
When things were simple and I never asked why

Please bring my red scooter to me
It's something I just have to see

It's something I've lost
It can't be replaced at any cost

I grew older day by day
But some things never go away

The days were very sad
I lost everything I had

At night I wanted only to sleep
Perhaps privately I could weep

I cannot accept what I have done
I cannot escape, I cannot run

Today (September 18, 1997) I was scheduled to do a 20-mile run, the last long training run before the marathon. The 20-mile runs are always very difficult mentally and physically and are probably a little more so this year. Well, I did it. I finished the run and felt pretty good. Sunday I ran 7 miles and worked out at the gym that night. Not bad for someone who is HIV positive! In case you haven't realized I've been feeling a lot better lately. I haven't been depressed and the medicine has been working. I firmly believe there will be a cure coming out in a few years or perhaps the current medicine will be the cure.

The September 18th run was a little extra special for me. That day my mother told Jodi that she wanted to watch me in the marathon next year. This year she would be out of town at a wedding. I felt like a kid at a little league game whose father always worked; then the father finally takes off to watch his son play. Similarly my mother's interest really meant a lot to me. I'm still a child and need my mother's encouragement and support.

Sunday I had a setback. It was hard enough jogging the day after the 20-mile run, but it became even harder when Jodi started getting upset with me. As I said, I've been feeling better and that's because I don't think about my illness constantly. Also, the medicine is working and I feel strong. But during the run Jodi decided to rehash the entire two months. Jodi needs to talk about my illness and I need not to talk about it. A definite conflict. When she finally realized how upset and troubled I was becoming, she backed off. By the end of the run I had a terrible headache. Fortunately it went away in about thirty minutes and I enjoyed the rest of the day. I think Jodi finally realizes we have to go forward and be grateful for what we have now. It sounds selfish of me and it probably is, but I can't live with the guilt and the constant minute-by-minute reminder of my illness. As I said, this may be selfish of me, but as you know, I've done far worse things.

I am not so sure that I'm the bottom rung on the ladder of humanity's uphill climb called Life. Perhaps I'm not so boring, but a colorful, daring character. Okay, let's not get carried away, Richard. Well, my feelings about myself are changing and I guess I honestly like myself.

The weeks moved along and the last week in September wasn't the worst, nor was it the best. On the positive side I ran 15 miles Saturday, 7 on Sunday and went to the gym Sunday night. I also read Greg Louganis's book over the weekend. It was a very touching story. It makes you realize how important your upbringing is. Your upbringing is your foundation and without a solid foundation a person will grow to a certain size and fall down. What a great story, what an athlete! He's a true Olympic hero, a great inspiration for me. I always feel like a gold medalist when I make that final turn into Central Park to complete the marathon. The crowds are cheering wildly and it's easy to imagine they are cheering for you. I usually cry when I finish the race. It's such a physical and emotional release. All Olympiads and non-Olympic athletes have their goals and the goal is usually the same. Just do the best you can, and if you have done your best, then you've won. It sounds like the Nike commercial, "Just do it."

I guess you can see I've been in a pretty good mood despite the fact that I've developed a rash that's very itchy. Dr. Brook prescribed an over-the-counter medication which has been fair at best. I'm reluctant to insist on seeing him because if I complain too much he might send me to a specialist. I simply don't have the time. It's difficult and costly to take time off from work. Tomorrow I'm scheduled to have an electrocardiogram. It's routine only because I run a lot and I'm HIV positive. 70% of doctors who have examined me over the past twenty years have detected some kind of heart murmur. There are two types and mine is the type that is not harmful, but it should be checked out.

My mother has been quite good and seems to be making an effort not to upset me or cause me stress. She has even been quite considerate of Jodi, although today she made a big fuss about our serving Rosh Hashanah dinner at seven o'clock instead of six. It was such utter nonsense. We were having the dinner at seven to accommodate Aunt Ronnie because she and Uncle Joe could not be at our house by six. I used the excuse that I had to work late and could not be home by six. If my brothers or their wives knew that Aunt Ronnie was the reason for the later invite, they would have jumped all over me. This is exactly the kind of stress and nonsense nobody should be subjected to.

Jodi as always continues to be very kind and supportive. I wrote Jodi a few lines one night and she reacted as if I had written a book devoted to her. She was very appreciative. Sometimes I think she may wake up one day and throw me out. I guess I don't really believe that. Maybe I'm just grateful, and since I know Jodi reads my journal it's just another chance to say, "Thanks, Jodi, I love you." Jodi has a way of making me feel special because I know 99 out of 100 women would never speak to their husband again except to finalize their divorce settlement. The love is equally returned although you, the reader, may be thinking: Why is she still stuck with him? I do love and adore Jodi very much. I've never been an alcoholic or drug abuser, nor have I ever hit my wife. Yes, we've had arguments and we still argue, but Jodi is my best friend, and the longer we are together the closer we become. The arguments tend to occur less often and the intensity seems to have decreased over the years. There exists a nice comfort level between us. The words, "It's your turn to..." have never come up between us over the years. We are always there for each other, even when I make bad mistakes. Thanks again, Jodi.

October 1st was the first night of Rosh Hashanah, the Jewish New Year. We had a nice family dinner at our house.

It was a nice evening. I don't know if I will ever tell my brother Stuart about my illness. Sometimes I wish he would ask me about myself. The conversation always focuses on Stuart and his business. My brother Victor was friendly to me and said he would be going to my temple. My mother told me the same thing the other day. Things like that make me feel good.

Jodi and I went out to dinner Saturday night. It was one of those nights we were undecided about going out. Jodi was tired from having taken the kids into New York. It had been a long weekend with the kids, and we made the mistake of going out. In the back of my mind I felt uncomfortable leaving Peri and Stacie alone. Stacie had been a little difficult this long weekend and it was the first time we punished her. Jodi is great with the kids, but I think they need more discipline, especially Stacie.

Anyhow, I was lying in bed Saturday night after dinner when I heard Peri crying downstairs. Teenage girls are often prone to weepiness so this episode didn't require a response from me since I was tired and Jodi was already downstairs with Peri. Jodi called up and said, "Richard, I think we have a problem." I knew Peri hadn't broken an arm or anything, or Jodi would have told me to come downstairs immediately. It was probably about a sleep-over that wouldn't work out because of plans the family had that day, or perhaps Peri had forgotten to do her homework. These were the important issues that tears were normally shed over; consequently, I was not overly alarmed.

Jodi started coming up the stairs with Peri and this time I began to feel it was more serious. I briefly thought Peri might have recognized some of my medication, but the names were so scientific and technical, how could she know? And besides, I had been taking the medicine right in front of the kids.

I already take several vitamins and am sort of a health nut so taking a few extra vitamins would seem perfectly normal. You must think it's pretty depressing having to take this medicine a few times a day. Sometimes I swallow my medicine in the middle of a busy intersection or Times Square. Listen, You up there. You may have won the battle, but You have not won the war. I'm still alive, talking, walking, running, writing and promoting my book, and You will not get me down.

So getting back to Peri, here I am wondering for a second or two at the most what the problem could be and Jodi says, "She knows." My heart suddenly felt so heavy. Only the fact that I was tired dulled my senses. Peri explained she had read part of my journal. We quickly realized she had not read any part about my bisexuality. I was relieved, but I still had to deal with her question about my HIV status.

I should have lied and told her I was writing a novel but, as I said, I was tired. I reassured her for about thirty minutes that my health was fine and I was strong. She understood this and I explained that I had become HIV positive from using a bloody towel that wasn't mine when I had an open cut. I am ashamed of myself for lying, but under the circumstances I had no choice. This is one of the few times I will allow myself to fast forward my life and realize that this lie was a serious mistake.

Jodi felt helpless and betrayed by life. Telling our children about my illness was something Jodi and I agreed would occur, but not at this time. Now our strategy crumbled before us as the time continuum of our life's journey was broken. Jodi was totally unprepared for this. Jodi's usually sharp mind was now blurred, unfocused, and disoriented. I was still what she valued most in the world after the children. I was Jodi's second love, symbolized in her cherished engagement and wedding rings. Umpteen million dollars in love went down the drain when Jodi inadvertently misplaced her prized rings, never to be found. The loss of her jewelry wounded me deeply for I can still remember Jodi's passion the day I presented these rings to her. Only now the memory of her passion would be replaced with the finality of my guilt. I should not have become HIV positive, nor should I have kept a personal journal where my child could find it.

My favorite saying has become, "We are where we are now." Jodi loved her jewelry. Perhaps someday I will be able to replace the rings.

Today is December 27th and it's been about ten weeks since I've done any writing. The fact that Peri found my journal was almost enough of a reason to burn the journal. However, writing is a form of creativity and anything that expresses feelings can no more be destroyed than a child's unfaltering love for her father can. Unsurprisingly Peri has accepted both me and my illness. Who's sick? I just ran a marathon and I go to the gym twice a week. I can outrun 99% of the population. My positive outlook has left Peri in a strong emotional state. We asked her if she wanted to discuss any of this with Hillary and she emphatically said, "No."

Overall the last two months have been pretty good. I haven't been entirely faithful and I admitted this to Jodi one Sunday morning. We discussed it at great length and Jodi decided it was okay for me to be with men. The following evening I was with James, and Jodi was upset. Her mind was telling her it was okay but her heart was telling her other-wise. This would become a recurring theme for the next few weeks until gradually Jodi accepted my sexuality and my needs. I have been trying to control my needs and I've been very busy at work, so work has been a good diversion.

The last three or four Saturday nights Jodi and I have been going to the West Village for dinner. We seem to have a stronger feeling of love, warmth, honesty, affection and sexuality than we've ever had. We both look forward to our Saturday nights and sharing each other's company. The Village is so alive with angled streets, plazas, restaurants, stores, people that there is an aura of invincibility and eternity—the pride of the Village, its symbolism for artistic freedom and expression, passionately recognizing and pursuing its role for future generations, thus safeguarding its landmarked past.

Let me go back a few weeks and I'll tell you about the '97 marathon. Okay, so let's go back to '93 for a brief history of my running times. In '93 I ran about the same as '92, 04:20. I was disappointed because I knew I could run faster.

Jodi had been running with me in the '94, '95 and '96 marathons, and each time Jodi was cutting her time substantially. I was so proud of her. Her '96 time was 04:03 and this year I'm sure she will break 4 hours.

In '94 I ran the marathon in 03:53. I finally broke 4 hours and I was so proud of myself. I'm surprised you haven't heard, because I told strangers in elevators all over New York City about my accomplishment. '95 was a disaster, as the weather was terrible and I had to call it quits after 17 miles. I was so depressed. It's really demoralizing to set a goal for yourself, then not achieve it. '96 for me was a do-or-die year. Was I aging or had '95 just been a bad year? In '96 I ran the marathon in 03:37. I was invincible. I felt great. My body was stronger than anytime in my life and my kids' friends thought I looked pretty hot. I was getting older and getting better. Now I would be getting ready to run the '97 marathon and my goal was an improved time, although frankly I'd be glad if I could just maintain the same time as the previous year.

Hey, wait a minute! What happened to getting older and getting better?

Give me a break. I am HIV positive and I wasn't sure if that would slow me down. As it turned out, it did not and it never will. It's sort of like the driver who has a handicapped license plate for life. We all know the majority of those plates are not legit. Sure, you were in a cast for a few months, and the day the cast came off you jogged over to the Department of Motor Vehicles and were the first one on line to return the handicapped plate. Face it. You don't have a disability any more than I do.

Welcome to the 1997 New York City Marathon where 30,000 of the scrawniest bodies you have ever seen congregate to torture themselves and perform some of the unkindest acts of human sacrifice to their body. And for one day only *cruel and unusual, self-inflicted punishment* is permitted. Pound the pavement with me and join me in my annual pilgrimage across the five boroughs or imagine you were fated to deliver a message in Greece in ancient times and your message had to be delivered at all costs. Thrill to the sound of your name being chanted as you become the local hero, the legend of the day on this one day only. For just this once, there is no *home* or *away* team and everyone is on the *winning* team. Parade around New York after the race with your mylar cape to keep you warm. Relish your victory because it will be another year, and in some cases it will seem like a lifetime, until next year's marathon. Be proud of your accomplishment, because for those of you who do not run, you have no idea of the mental and physical training that is involved. With that said, save a place on the podium for me and let the band herald the words of our national anthem.

If you are expecting me to tell you the sun shone over New York just a little brighter than ever and the warmth filled my body with energetic waves pressing my muscles forward, then let me stop right now. Let's cut to the chase. It was a cold, dreary day, the dreariest of days. The weather was terrible and for the last 11 miles it was raining; the last 8 it was coming down in buckets. My shoes were damnably waterlogged to the gills. Every step was a squishy-like sound since my shoes were gifted in receiving an extra layer of insulation, thanks to my rain-soaked shoes combined with any remnants of what the horses had left behind in their daily buggy rides around the park. It was the aching of every joint in my body that would not let me quit. My mind kept telling my joints, "I don't care how tired you are; your job is to finish." This brain refused to walk 6 miles on a cold, rainy day and that is what got me through the race. I finished one minute slower than last year. Jodi finished two minutes faster. I was beginning to feel that as long as I kept up my exercise routine, running and weight training, my body would stay strong and I could fight off this disease. I'm so tired of people complaining about their health when 98% of these people need only to eat properly, exercise and lose weight. Sometimes I listen to two or three people talking about their health, medications, various counts, and doctors, and I feel like saying, "Look at me, aren't I the picture of perfect health? Surprise! I'm sicker than all of you." I feel health is a personal issue; it's a private thing.

Thanksgiving was approaching and the family would be getting together. I had a need to tell my older brother Stuart about my illness. I could never tell my younger brother Victor and his wife. They and their home are so sterile. They even once made fun of a married friend who was bisexual. You can just imagine how they would embrace me and my illness. I asked Stuart on Thanksgiving and on one or two other occasions to meet me at the health club. I wanted him to see I was strong and healthy, strong enough to run marathons and also lift weights. He always declined. He was too busy either playing golf, going to the Hamptons, or doing whatever else he does.

So here we all were at Victor's and Susan's celebrating what should have been a perfect Thanksgiving. I managed to get Stuart alone, but it was difficult to initiate the conversation. He kept thinking I was going to criticize him and/or his lack of interest in my family. It's hard for me to judge people after what I've done. That's not entirely true. I do know the difference between right and wrong, and in some ways I can understand why people do things that are wrong, but I certainly didn't arrange to meet Stuart to discuss what he does wrong. Stuart was shocked, dismayed and very upset for my family and me. His mood clearly showed and Liz, his wife, kept asking what was wrong. Eventually he told her and in some ways we all felt a little closer. I hugged Liz good-bye instead of just kissing her and she didn't back off as if I were contagious. A week or two later we had dinner in New York for their birthdays and by this time I had received an excellent bill of health. My viral load was down to 67, almost undetectable by standard tests, and my T-cells were at 694. 694 would be a normal count for a person who was not HIV positive. Even my doctor was surprised. Unfortunately I'd had a few colds and a scratchy throat during the past three months. None of this had affected my jogging or workouts, however.

As I mentioned, Jodi and I were growing closer. We have always cherished our Saturday nights together and our weekend jogs together. We were always affectionate in private and in public, and now we found our affection towards each other was increasing.

Chapter III

GUESS WHO'S COMING TO VISIT?

THE COMBINED STRESS OF MY illness and the fact that Jodi's family was coming to town for Jodi's cousin's bat mitzvah brought Jodi and me closer together. We never know what to expect from my wife's family. This weekend in December proved to be no exception. As usual, Jodi picked up my father-in-law at LaGuardia Airport, along with his sister who was flying in from Ohio at the same time. First stop, where else but the cemeteries? That's right, two cemeteries. This way we're assured of about 50% of the weekend's conversation. If you get tired of hearing about cemeteries and how some cousins don't take care of their parents' graves, you can always see a video of 35 years of my in-laws' marriage. That's great entertainment when you plan a dinner party for 30 people and only one person wants to see this tape.

Join us for our dinner party. Have a nosh. It's on me. We're also serving sweaters and hand-me-downs. If it's not nailed down, it's yours. A spirit of love and family togetherness permeates the room. You can't purchase it, but you can cut it with a knife and savor it for a lifetime... and then POW, you're down for the count!

1. You didn't get the money.
2. We did. (Neal, Suzie, Patti)

3. Five thousand bucks.
4. Five months ago.
5. We weren't allowed to tell you. We were sworn to secrecy.
6. We kept the secret.
7. You didn't go to Uncle Julie's funeral.
8. You should've listened to Dad.
9. You are not so perfect after all, Jodi.
10. And we siblings never say we're wrong.

Approximately five months earlier my father-in-law had given each child $5,000 and told Jodi's siblings not to say anything to Jodi, because she would not be getting this money now. You see, Jules was mad at Jodi for not going to Uncle Julie's funeral. Uncle Julie was Jules' uncle who died at age 85. He had been in a nursing home and had shown no interest in living since he was about 40, or so I was told. Jodi and I were extremely upset with her father and brother and sisters. We could not accept the reality that we had been slighted again and no one had spoken up for us. Everyone had managed to keep the silly secret. What a loving, supportive family! Just what my wife and I needed then.

1997 was coming to a close. New Year's Eve I found to be depressing. On the one hand I was glad to be around for another year, but on the other, it was just a chance to remember the worst year of my life. I remember crying a little, but I was also secretly thrilled that 1997 was over.

The early months of 1998 have been pretty good for Jodi and me. There were a few troubling times regarding my bisexuality. I think Jodi is slowly accepting me for who I am while I continue to struggle with my guilt. Jodi genuinely wants me to be happy, but her feelings of jealousy, not rejection, continue to be present. I understand this and do not blame or resent her because I am the one who has caused the problem. Jodi continues to be as loving as ever and perhaps even more so. I spoke about Jodi at Peri's Bat Mitzvah. However, the shining star of the day was my Peri. Peri and the girls were absolutely beautiful and Peri's poise, grace, charm and maturity were noted by everyone. She really has developed into a beautiful young lady. I liked my speech and I don't think there was a person there who didn't have a tear or two in their eye or didn't compliment me. Yes, you're going to have to hear my speech and I will preface it by saying Jodi is always late and Stacie is a great hockey player.

Rabbi, cantor, friends and relatives. I'd like to thank everyone for coming today and sharing in Peri's Bat Mitzvah. To Rabbi Ginsburg and Cantor Shechter I am especially grateful that my children have been guided by you over the years, and on the occasions I have been in the synagogue I have always been impressed by your extreme patience and understanding of the children.

Peri, you have always been a delightful, talented, articulate, fun-loving, popular kid. You are fortunate to have two sisters close in age who love and adore you. Peri, you know what I really admire about you? Whenever Mom and I say no to Hillary or Stacie, you are always on their side pleading their case. Per, don't think for a moment these things are not remembered. I remember when Hillary was six and you were four, Hillary said that she wished she was as good a sister to you as you were to her. I hope I am as good a father to you as you are a daughter to me. It hasn't always been easy growing up in a house with four women. In fact, it's never been easy. It's certainly not boring. The girls are still working on coordinating my clothes and I think they've about given up on my sense of humor. But despite all my faults they still keep bringing their friends over. Oh, and one more thing, whoever is making those phone calls after eleven at night, please stop. It gets pretty annoying when 98% of the calls are not for me and the other 2% are from my mother, who usually doesn't want to talk to me, either.

Per, sorry about this speech but I did ask you to help me. I think you were out shopping that day. It's very rare to see a child work so hard in school that even the teachers have commented, "you should lighten up." On the other hand, it's rare to see Peri without her friends. You've developed some pretty strong friendships. It's very gratifying to see you're also friends with your sisters and even their friends.

To Hillary and Stacie, I'd like to thank both of you for being great kids and always being there for Peri. Stacie, maybe you might even consider letting Peri win at hockey once in a while.

Jodi, I remember saying a few words at the funeral for your mother, whom we all miss very much. I remember your sister Suzie wondering if I was ever going to stop talking about you. Suzie, I guess I'm not ever going to stop talking about Jodi. I'm crazy about her. She's always been there for the kids and me and seems to have an endless sense of love, energy and patience for her family. Jodi, I love you so much. And thanks for being on time today.

Peri, the greatest gift your mother and I can give you is our love for you. On this special day I'd like to say how fortunate and proud I feel being your father. I wish you a long, happy lifetime where all your dreams, goals and desires come true, and may you always know how much I love you. I love you, Peri.

I felt good being a little funny and especially good confirming my love for Jodi and my family. It was kind of like being married again or renewing my wedding vows. Jodi even got her rings back and the second ring arrived at the bat mitzvah. Once or twice I had a tear or two in my eye, particularly when they hoisted me on a chair for the traditional Hora dance. It would have shocked our guests to be aware of my sexuality and health. Jodi and I, along with our girls, appear to be the absolute perfect couple and family, and in many ways we are. I seem to accept my health a little more each day, although taking the medicine three times a day is a very strong reminder. However, Jodi is always there for me. I've gotten a little closer to my brother Stuart and his wife Liz. They know and understand my emotional turmoil. How can one person be so happy and proud of a truly perfect family and live with a condition that is so totally unpredictable? I feel pretty confident I'll be around for a long time, but it's like crossing the desert with blindfolds. Perhaps only one car will travel the road in a single day, and if you are the one on that road that day, you've had it! I say 'you' because it's hard to say 'me'.

The bat mitzvah weekend was not too stressful. Even Jules and all the brothers and sisters got along. My mother was especially supportive that weekend. My mother took Jodi's father for a drive, bought some paper goods for a house party, attended both family dinners, and just showed up early on the day of the bat mitzvah. These may seem like little things but collectively it meant a lot to me. Thanks, Mom. I still do not deal well with stress or criticism, and when I spoke to Aunt Ronnie about my dissatisfaction with the DJ, I felt I was being yelled at for being stupid. It's extremely uncomfortable being spoken to as if you're a stupid child. I must learn to choose my conversations with Aunt Ronnie more carefully. It's not that I want anyone's sympathy; it's just that I can't deal with negative comments which only cause stress. This has been true my whole life and I realize it more now. My feelings and emotions are a little more exaggerated, and in many ways I've become more aware of myself. I may even appear to be selfish at times, but I have to do what is good for me. I'm not looking forward to going to Orlando or North Carolina because it's difficult being around Jules so long. Even when he's not difficult, it seems like an invasion of privacy, compared to the Saturday nights spent alone with Jodi.

I feel as if we are dating again; there is a spark of magic in the air this night. Somewhere afar there is a star above. This brightest light in the galaxy is gazing upon us. The star has just one question:

WILL ETERNITY REMEMBER MY SPARKLE OR RICHARD'S PASSION FOR JODI?

The star has seen many of its neighbors destroyed over millions of years. Random heavenly bodies have crushed and fragmented glowing stars into nothingness, leaving a void. But a void implies that something existed previously. Maybe it did, maybe it didn't. No one can say for certain since no one was present. However, my present to my wife will be this story. My story is the affirmation of my undying love. Nothing can destroy the greatest love story ever told. It has become my passion to share it. May the epic of Jodi and Richard endure forever.

Chapter IV

BROTHER, CAN YOU SPARE A DIME?

IT'S NOW APRIL **20, 2000** and it's been almost a year since I've written in my journal. Financially things have gotten very bad. In many ways this has been a great distraction to my constant thinking about my illness, but the financial situation is extremely stressful and depressing. It basically began when the building owners sold the building for which I had been the architectural consultant during the past 17 years. There were two active partners and I handled the architectural and construction work for the company. Sometimes tenants in the building hired me directly for various projects. It was a fairly active office and it was very profitable. I had other clients but this was always a good base income. My relationship with one of the partners, however, became abusive over the years. He began to call me a moron and an idiot in front of my employees, which was very embarrassing and demoralizing. Most people had little respect for this partner and it was mostly shameful for him. It was embarrassing for me because people would wonder why I still worked there. Over the years there had been a minimal turnover of employees, consultants, contractors, etc. We sort of bonded like a family, a family that often had brothers and sisters not talking for years, but we were a family. We spent more time with our work family than our real family. I once referred to one of our employees as a prima donna, and he didn't speak to me at all for two or three years. The next two or three years he spoke to me minimally, and about five years later, when the building was sold, there were tears in my eyes when I said good-bye to this individual, Mike. There are tears in my eyes even now as I type this story more than a year later. Relationships had developed with numerous people, and the severed relationships were so abrupt, I don't think I was prepared to deal with such an emotional upheaval.

Simultaneous with the selling of the building, I needed to rent an office and buy equipment, pay security, pack my belongings and set up the new office. Finding a space took weeks and the whole process was very stressful, time consuming and expensive. I still had some good clients at this time and the new building owner was giving me a little work, too. However, my new office has not brought me financial success; in fact, quite the opposite has occurred. It became so bad that I was suicidal for a few days. I love my wife and family too much and don't think I could ever kill myself, although I was very depressed. Financially, things are extremely difficult now and we are dipping substantially into savings. There are a few opportunities and potential clients that could effect a turnaround, so my mental outlook is more optimistic than it was a week or two ago. I'm actually becoming computer literate and have learned the basics of Autocad 14, a computer-aided drafting program. I thought I could go through life without becoming computer literate but I was wrong. I haven't mentioned the other client I lost this month. The company's name is AGT and I took this loss very personally. AGT is a publicly owned company for whom I have been actively working for about two years. There were constant and endless changes of who was coordinating the project and how the space would be developed. We did manage to renovate 13,000 square feet of space at their New Jersey facility and the space turned out great. Everyone seemed pleased with the renovation although lurking quietly in the foreground was an individual named John. John was upset that his contractor friend had not gotten the contract for the 13,000-square-foot space.

As I reflect back on the past few months, I realize there have been a few incidents that have affected me and my emotional well-being. Work, success, respect and supporting my family are all very important to me. My new landlord has been a terrific client, not so much because I'm making huge amounts of money, but rather because of the respect and trust he shows me. He probably doesn't even realize it, but I was very touched when he agreed to provide me with an air-conditioning unit at no cost. I even told him that if there was a charge, I would pay it, as it is unquestionably my responsibility to pay for the unit. However, $1,000 one way or the other to cement a long-term relationship is not important to either of us. Thanks, Ed. This relationship was especially important to me as I was coming to the end of my business dealings with Lloyd and Ivan at Midtown Realty.

In the past, every four or five months there would be a disagreement of $500 to $1,000 with Midtown Realty and it was never settled in my favor, although I always put up a good fight. It wasn't worth losing the account because the average monthly invoice was $12,000. When I received my final payment from Midtown Realty I was glad this chapter of my life was over, but no. Ivan managed to screw me and embarrass himself, and he even dragged Lloyd into the shameful fray. Several months before the building was transferred to the new owners, Warner Chappell, a tenant who was moving into the building (1775 Broadway) retained my services to do some work. I had overheard some discussion that Warner Chappell might be paying Midtown Realty for this work and Midtown would then pay me; however, it was only a discussion of something that might occur and it was something that I only overheard and I was not included in the discussion. What eventually happened was that Warner Chappell did pay Midtown for work on which I had a contract with Warner Chappell to execute, but no one ever informed me that Midtown received payment for the work that I had invoiced Warner Chappell for. I only found out about Midtown snagging money that was due me when I contacted Warner Chappell and advised them they owed me a balance of $1,250. Warner Chappell obviously did not want to pay the invoice a second time, so they contacted Midtown. Midtown informed Warner Chappell that I had been paid for this work. Warner Chappell asked me to send them copies of all the invoices that Midtown had paid me. It would soon be clear to Warner Chappell that Midtown had not paid me the $1,250. I discussed the situation with Lloyd, the senior partner, and I told Lloyd that the only way I could get paid was if I sent Warner Chappell copies of the invoices that Midtown paid me. Lloyd immediately realized this would be embarrassing for him because Midtown was charging Warner Chappell $15,000 for work that was executed by me, but Midtown was not paying me $15,000. Warner Chapell finally realized that I wasn't paid the $1,250, but they still were not going to pay the $1,250 a second time. The $1,250 was too small an amount to sue for. I spoke with their agent Mike, who was pleased with my work. I suggested that if he hired me in the future and gave me a project within a year, and that if my fee was $2,500 or more, this would void the $1,250 invoice. If he did not get me work, then Warner Chappell would be responsible for the $1,250 fee. Warner Chapell would not agree to this arrangement. The Warner Chappell fee was resolved late in 2000, which I will tell you about shortly.

What was very disturbing to me was that although my relationship with Ivan and Lloyd was terminated, there was one item that still needed to be concluded. I had given Lloyd a letter stating that he was my client and all professional discounts and courtesies should be extended to him. I didn't exactly give Lloyd the letter. He had Carol, his secretary (whom I truly miss and shed a tear or two for when I said good-bye), type the letter on my stationery. Lloyd then presented it to me for my signature. I was not happy about signing the letter because if he dropped dead or was not pleased with the finish on an item that he ordered, I could be held liable. Even if I won in court it would cost me thousands of dollars in legal fees. So instead, I sent Lloyd a certified letter advising him that he was no longer a client of mine. Such notice would officially end our twenty-year union.

Divorce, what an ugly word. Yet it reared its ugly head as the separation between Midtown Realty and me was finalized. There would be no future conversations between Lloyd and me, or Ivan and me, unless of course it concerned 'our children', the tenants of Midtown's building.

My other family was also at a major crossroads. Trails on the homefront were becoming muddy and difficult to traverse. Mucking up the waters was my daughter Hillary, who was dating a guy named Bruce. In the beginning we all liked Bruce, but after seven or eight months it was unanimous: Bruce had to go. We could not accept his lying ways, and Hillary was starting to weave her own web of lies. Yes, it's true, I've told a few whoppers of my own; but does that mean I must abandon my responsibility as a parent if I see my child lie? Besides, I hate lying. I have always hated myself whenever I've had to lie. And I hated the change in Hillary. I was losing my daughter to a rogue and would not allow my daughter to be taken from me right before my eyes.

I finally told Hillary if she didn't break up with her new-found scoundrel, she was to leave the house on her 18th birthday and not expect to receive any spending money or payments towards her college education. Her reaction hurt me, as she did not even acknowledge what I was saying. I would have expected her to cry or plead with me to give her relationship another chance. This was the boy she was planning to marry even though he was mentally very abusive to her. The truth of the matter was that Hillary had been thinking about breaking up with Bruce for days, ever since she found out that he had kissed another girl. Bruce's betrayal hurt Hillary deeply and she could not accept this or trust him anymore. Hillary was very sad for a few days but recovered quickly and became her old self.

The break-up spread like wildfire at school. It seems as if everyone knew Bruce was cheating on Hillary and that many people just assumed that Hillary was aware of this. Bruce really wanted to get back together, but Hillary realized this young man was not for her. I suppose I need to fill you in on something I forgot to tell you about. I guess it even deserves its own paragraph.

Sometime within the last six to twelve months Hillary and Peri became aware of my journal and the gay magazines I was reading, and I could no longer continue lying to them. Yes, your father is bisexual and that's how he became HIV positive. Jodi and I reassured the girls that we were not getting divorced, that I was in good health, and that my viral load was undetectable. Hillary was more troubled by this than Peri and shortly after, Hillary began to talk to a therapist. Hillary and Peri gradually accepted this bizarre situation and I think Hillary would have stopped seeing the therapist except that her relationship with Bruce had been so abusive that she continued her therapy.

Getting back to Bruce and the breakup: Bruce started telling people he knew Hillary's secrets and could ruin her life. He did in fact know about my being both HIV positive and bisexual. It had happened during a weak moment in Hillary's life, but she had no right to discuss this with her boyfriend without first talking to me. I don't resent her in any way. I love her and all my girls very much. I spoke with Jodi and Hillary and we are all at a loss as to how to proceed. I think some rumors may have begun to spread. Tonight Hillary asked the $64,000 question. What should she say if people ask her if her father is HIV positive and bisexual? I had my thoughts but could not finalize them and Hillary was not sure either, although whatever she said would have to be agreed upon by Jodi and me. I finally deferred to Jodi who stands to be hurt the most. I really have no voice or vote. I have caused the problem and if Jodi chooses to tell Hillary to deny the story then I will do the same. My preference would be to tell my story and the truth when I am good and ready, and not be pressured by a spurned boyfriend.

I do not like this boy, Bruce, although I do not wish him any harm. I think he is going through a difficult time in his life. Adolescence is never an easy time. However, I am troubled he will not be able to deal with the consequences of blowing the whistle on my family and me. Nobody likes or respects a tattle-tale, especially in my case where I have not hurt anyone.

My copy editor, Irene, posed the question, "What does it matter whether Bruce is able to deal with the consequences or not, since he is out of the picture now?" This brought me into a dialog with myself. 'I know I made my share of big mistakes when I was Bruce's age. Some of my tales I would not even repeat, as I would not want to bring unnecessary shame or embarrassment to myself, let alone others. I wish they sold extra-large erasers so that I could erase all the mistakes in my life. No, life would be boring, Richard, and you would have nothing to write about. Admit it, your adolescence was boring. What did you learn about compassion? Nobody had any fights. You never even argued with your brothers over who got the keys to the folks' car. What challenges did you face growing up, Richard? So now you have a challenge. You might be ostracized by the community, but here you are, looking back now, and so far nobody has blown a whistle, but how did you feel at the time you were being threatened, Richard?'

I didn't know if I would be ostracized by the community and I hoped my story would not be too painful for my family and my mother. I never wanted to hurt either, but Mother, you and the world must understand a person cannot train himself to prefer men or women sexually. If there is a lesson to be learned here, mine is to trust my wife and not keep secrets from her. I should have had the courage to admit my bisexual side. I want to thank those few friends and relatives with whom I've shared my story for being such good listeners. Most of all, whatever happens, I apologize to my daughters for not living up to their image of what a perfect father is. I may not be perfect, but I love my family as much or more than the next guy, and this added love results from the acceptance my family has shown me.

Irene read the above paragraph and commented that it sounded like the end of the book. That's close, but coping with Bruce's threat made me feel as if this was the end of my life as a respectable family man. The fear of being exposed was overwhelming. This was probably the one episode I stated in the introduction that drove me to writing this book. At the time I felt as if my life was ending. I was sentenced to a life term without parole, given the fact that my behavior was unpardonable. Imprisoned by *His Wardenship, Brucifer* confined me to a 6' x 6' cell that *dungeoned* deeper my feeling of impending doom. My *morselic* crusts from feeding-time were littered just outside my padlocked cage and I longed for these crumbs or just... even one last sunrise. Yet somehow out of my dark cell, a pulsating light *laserly* beamed its way to my brain cells. Escaping from solitary I sought the refuge of my doctor's chambers where my life was being examined. The sanctity of my doctor's office, my haven, my embassy, where I was protected by diplomatic, *doctoratic* immunity was *nestlingly, cocoonic* and comforting, in contrast to the masses that would devour me. I couldn't weather the angst of my community throwing their *boulderous* comments and thrashing, *hailike*, stinging criticisms my way. Targeting and marketing me would give rise to dartboard and video games sinisterly labeled "Kill the Fag." The toy and video industry would make a killing. Ahhhhhhh... sweet revenge for the video game industry whose artful thievery of our children's minds should be punished by video *morbicide*. But even through these *morbidlike* times I knew that things had to change for the better; there had to be a reason for my existence, I hoped. And I continued writing entries in my diary, hoping one day I would tell my story.

Maybe I'm being depressingly reflective at this time because I don't know what lies ahead. There are a few good things that have come out of my illness, and one of them is the increased love for my wife and family. Another is I honestly look forward to getting older each year and I relish aging, *gustofliably* so. Not growing old is not a great option for me, so think of me every August 29th and write me two or three lines wishing me well.

My life is not easy and I am continuously burdened by guilt. It's easy to say a person cannot control his sexuality, but what about commitment and love? That is my conflict and that is the part that keeps me in turmoil. If I didn't love my wife and family so much, the conflict would not weigh on me so heavily. I pray my family will never be hurt by my indiscretions. I also pray for a change in my life. I'm in a rut.

Things have not been going so well lately. I've run into a string of bad luck, although I do believe people make their own destiny. I've been faced with many confrontational situations and in some I volunteered to be the wimp; in some I wanted to fight vigorously but was talked out of it. There is a new pattern developing and I'm beginning to understand myself a little better. In some ways I prefer the person I'm becoming. I like the sense of caring and feeling but sometimes it's emotionally draining. I think I have to be a little tougher and find a consistency. My breaking point this week was a business setback and this prompted a visit to GMHC (Gay Men's Health Crisis). I wasn't sure why I was going there and I almost turned around. Before my visit I walked into a Bonsai store and got refreshed and invigorated. I love being around plants and could never understand why bonsai plants are so undervalued compared to paintings. Even if I had $60,000,000 I would never spend it on a painting, but a bonsai? Maybe. Nature is the perfect art form, and what is more graceful and sculptural and ever-changing than a 500-year-old bonsai that grows and evolves and needs caring, compared to an inanimate painting? There is a certain tension about ~~owning~~ nurturing (Nature cannot be bought) a bonsai worth $50,000 to $1,000,000. If you don't love the bonsai and care for it, the bonsai will die. I would never want to have that on my conscience, that I killed a plant that had been cared for by generations of people who never knew each other. This book takes on a similar theme. Caring for people so they may live a normal life span will become my goal. I have so many exciting ideas that are just bursting out of me! But the thought process is also important. In writing my story, sometimes new or modified thoughts come my way. But my goals remain constant, so much so that the pieces of the puzzle and what's important in my life have begun to evolve in a very clear vision.

So I visited GMHC and was sent to the eighth floor. I explained that I wasn't sure why I was there and maybe I would like to talk to someone. The receptionist wasn't sure where to send me and finally sent me to the sixth floor. The receptionist there introduced me to Michael, a volunteer counselor. At first glance I could see Michael had a very bad physical disability and had a difficult time walking. He seemed rather young and I was feeling a little unsure. I was concerned about his disability and he thanked me for asking, although I was saddened when he told me it was permanent. In hindsight, I think his disability made him more compassionate. He never looked at his watch and always seemed very attentive to what I was saying. The session lasted for about ninety minutes. It started off by my shedding a few tears and just feeling sad. People had been disappointing me in a big way lately and maybe I didn't realize it until I listened to myself for ninety minutes.

Since finding out I was HIV positive almost three years ago, I have confided my secret to only a few people I felt I could count on for emotional support. In all cases, except for my wife, they have not come through for me. My mother refuses to accept the fact that I'm bisexual and credits it to curiosity or a phase that she has decided is over. She has told Jodi that my father would never have been able to deal with this situation. I confided in my older brother Stuart and specifically asked that he not mention this to his wife. He did tell Liz, however. Although it's not a big deal, I would like it if he called me more often than once a month. And when he does call, why can't he seem more interested in me? The conversation always revolves around his business. I never told my younger brother Victor, because in the past he had made fun of a bisexual married friend of his. Aunt Ronnie found out through my mother and although I've never discussed my personal situation with Aunt Ronnie, her belief is lie, lie, lie and deny everything. I hate lying and people who lie. This will be discussed later. I told my friend George, and he told Jodi that she should offer me an ultimatum: stop my bisexual ways or get out. I told Charlie who I thought was a better friend, but now I never hear from him. Strangers I've told have turned out to be some of my best listeners. I also told Monica, a part-time secretary. She's a hot 45-year-old black woman with tremendous energy, kindness and sensitivity, and I always enjoy being around her. My reason for telling Monica is I sensed her caring ways and I think she saw me as a perfect husband and father. I felt that I was creating an untruthful image of myself. Although we speak only on a monthly basis, our conversations somehow always pick up where we left off. Thanks, Monica.

As I stated earlier, people have let me down lately. Peri's best friend's father, Jason, asked me on two occasions to design his kitchen. He's a successful cabinetmaker. After his second request I said okay. He asked me what I would charge and I stupidly said, "I can't charge friends," to which his wife Lisa said, "Don't worry about it; we will take care of you." "Great, I said." The design came out really great and the family praised my talents. I completed the drawings several months ago and have not received a penny. I paid my employee $3,500 in salary and benefits, plus I had spent a considerable amount of my own time. I find it inexcusable that he has not paid me anything, and when the kitchen is complete I will tell him he did not do the right thing. I suppose he will offer me $500. I cannot accept the fact that this pattern of people looking to beat other people is becoming so prevalent. We are talking here about a kitchen renovation that cost well over $100,000. I started working on it the day after I had a hernia operation. I gave up being with my family for hours on end on Sundays. Sundays were spent agonizing over details and finishes, and extending the concept into their living and dining rooms. Improving the quality of my friends' environment was my goal; sacrificing quality time with my family was the result.

My next favorite client is a lifelong friend of my father-in-law. Jules visited New York several months ago. Jules, his friend Sabrina and her husband Nathan, and Jodi and I all had dinner together in a very fancy restaurant. Fancy, expensive and overrated, just like Sabrina. Sabrina is quite wealthy and was in the process of buying a $1,000,000 + apartment. It came out at dinner that Jodi and I were going through a rough financial time and Sabrina said that she would like me to be the architect for her apartment renovation. She already had a designer whom I subsequently invited to breakfast at my apartment. Both the designer and Sabrina seemed pleased to be working with me. Sabrina's husband Nathan had no involvement in the project except to say how much he trusted me. I felt the same way when I made purchaces from his appliance store, as I knew he would steer me in the right direction. Sabrina was anxious to begin the 'planning and drawings' for her new Park Avenue 'lifestyle and maison'. For you see, madame and her mutts, pardon me, pure-bred greyhounds had 'arrived'; living in her current prestigious Eastside penthouse would be but a memory of slummier days. I explained to Sabrina the drawings would take about three months to complete, approximately the same amount of time it would take for *Her Worthiness* to be reviewed and approved by the co-op board. I made it very clear to Sabrina that if the deal fell through after I started on the drawings, I would still have to be paid for my work. Sabrina understood this, or at least she said she understood this, and authorized me to proceed with the drawings. She had me work on two apartments in a seven or eight-day period, but then the sale of both apartments fell through, and she told me to send her a bill. The bill was for approximately $3,400. I received a telephone call from her husband Nathan saying that his wife was extremely upset. She could not believe I would send a bill after all she went through. Mistakenly I told him to forget it. I cannot stand petty people. I had sensed this project was not for me. I did not want to work with these people. I felt they would take advantage of me since they were friends of the family. We will probably never see them again. Ironically Sabrina never even called to thank me. If she ever asks me to help her on another apartment I will decline politely, or perhaps not so politely.

The lying issue is starting to burn inside me. It is not so much the outright lying that people do in life; it is the misrepresentations and avoidance of telling the truth. I find all this hard to accept and I think the next story basically ties together most of my conflicts.

My older brother Stuart is in the sweater business and my mother has worked for him for the last eleven years. My younger brother Victor has been their accountant and his wife has worked for them over the years. Everyone has made a lot of money, but now the business is faltering. A Chinese company, basically the government of China, will be taking over his company. The name of the company is Sunbird. My contacts at the company were Peter and his wife Carly. Sunbird had hired me to design their offices eight months earlier, before there was any takeover or planned takeover of Stuart's sweater company. I did some preliminary design work for Sunbird and sent them a bill for $3,300, which they paid. Upon paying this invoice, Sunbird decided they needed more space. This involved more of my time as I had to survey the additional space and redesign the entire space based on the new concept. This also involved meetings with the Landlord and strategy planning with Sunbird on how to deal with the Landlord's unwillingness to conclude a deal and his inconsistencies with respect to the base rent. Subsequent to the $3,300 invoice, I sent Sunbird two invoices, one in February and one in March. Neither invoice was paid. I tried to contact Peter on numerous occasions and on two or three occasions I got through to his wife Carly. I spoke to Carly in early June and the conversation got rather heated, although it ended up on a civil note and she agreed to pay the unpaid invoices. Three weeks later we had another conversation and I informed Carly that the February and March invoices had still not been paid.

For the past two months Sunbird has been trying to buy my brother's company, though it is sort of a friendly takeover merger wherein my brother will still have some ownership. The takeover is essential to my brother, and if it does not go through it will be disastrous for him. Peter and Carly will probably be recalled to China in shame, so the deal must go through for them as well. My mother is now working for Sunbird, doing work for Stuart's company even though the deal has not been finalized. My mother spoke to Peter, who explained to her why Sunbird would not be paying me any more money, and that the $3,800 they had paid me was all I was entitled to. My mother began explaining this to me and I went through the ceiling. For months I had been trying to reach Peter to resolve the unpaid invoices. Now he was basically telling my mother I was a crook. My mother defended him and I had to explain the situation all over again to her. If I sent out monthly invoices for two separate months and Sunbird had no intention of paying the invoices, they were obligated to tell me promptly and not have me continue working on the project. Furthermore, I had been paid only $3,300, not $3,800. My mother and I got into a disagreement. I discussed the situation with Victor and he said I should definitely sue them. My mother wanted me to come up to the showroom to talk to Peter, but I was tired of wasting my time and being lied to. I'm tired of being told what to do by others, and I'm still upset with my mother who seems concerned more about my older brother than with what is right. I agreed not to sue them for two weeks because my mother believes the papers will be signed by then. I am not so certain, and I have a feeling Peter and Carly will be recalled to China. Good-bye, Sunbird and my money. Sometimes I don't control things in my life and the idea of waiting two weeks because my mother asks me to really bothers me, just in principle. It's getting to be like everything else in my life. Yes, I understand why this has to be done but I am tired of understanding. I just hope my family understands why I had to write this book! Anybody want to adopt a writer whose family may disown him? Actually I have more confidence in family, but every family has a 'black sheep' somewhere on their farm.

Okay, so maybe I'm rambling again. This 'understanding' is beginning to take a toll on me and is pushing me towards new goals and directions. Ironically the above mentioned cast of business characters that have caused me grief are pushing me towards some very worthy goals. If these ideals do materialize, my life will have meant something. Perhaps I am a dreamer, but at least I am beginning to formulate a plan where my life and time spent will make a positive difference to many people.

This entry in my journal is written on my father's birthday, July 17ᵗʰ. I miss him very much though we weren't very close. He used to be impatient with me. I don't think I was an easy child, and I haven't gotten any easier as I've grown older. I feel especially sad for my mother, but I'm also happy to see she is with a man who is really kind and loving. I was a little harsh on my mother yesterday and for that I apologize. Sorry, Mom. Sometimes it's difficult for me to always have to understand. Things just aren't so easy now. I could have eliminated the entry from yesterday but a person can't apologize for how he feels, and that is how I was feeling yesterday. I'm sorry I can't eliminate how I feel. Perhaps this journal is my therapy since I don't go to a therapist. I would also like to say my mother was very kind and offered to pay me the $1,800 that Sunbird owed me, but on principle alone I can't accept the money from her. This entry is probably uninteresting, but I did write a good poem to Stacie this weekend. That's a good sign and it means my creativity is not dead and I am not totally consumed with my current problems, even if this is a long run-on sentence.

The year 2000 continued to cause me great stress, but on a few occasions I felt so victorious that I was on top of the world. The emotional roller coaster of the ups and downs was getting to me. I had to decide on which "issues" I would stand firmly, on principle, and which ones I would bypass. Stress can be a killer for HIV positive people. If I let everyone have his way with me, I wouldn't be able to live with myself, so I had to strike a balance I could live with.

Issue #1. Sunbird and I went to small claims court and that issue was resolved and finalized.

Issue #2. I told Jodi to forget about getting paid from Lisa and Jason for their kitchen renovation. We shouldn't waste our time and energy. Jodi was extremely upset and felt this was very unfair. When Lisa sensed Jodi's coolness and asked what was wrong, Jodi told her. This went back and forth and I asked Jason just to pay what he thought my services were worth. He said $700, which was a tremendous insult. In the end Lisa told Jodi that Jason would like to build Peri some cabinets for her bedroom that would be worth $3,500. This occurred at the end of the summer of 2000. Financially things were quite tight and we had no plans to renovate Peri's bedroom for $3,500. However, since it was this or nothing, we said, "Fine." Jason said he would design the cabinetry and meet with Peri. If we ever receive a visit from Jason or see any cabinetry I will add a footnote to the epilogue, but my intuition tells me we will get zippo.

Issue #3. Newmark & Company were the new managing agents at 1775 Broadway. When Midtown Realty sold the property, Newmark needed my services as there were a few projects in transition. For the first few months of 2000 I sent Newmark invoices totaling approximately $7,000. It is common knowledge in the industry that Newmark is a slow payer, but that they eventually pay their bills. However, by the spring of that year I had completed my work. From Newmark's point of view, my services were no longer required, so why should they pay me? At the very least it would cost me a small fortune to hire an attorney, plus endless hours on my part, and surely I would opt to settle for fifty cents on the dollar. Wrong! They were not going to beat the little guy, not this time. My spirit was all I had left. My family pitied me as I became obsessed with one more battle that I'd never win. And even if I won, these fights were becoming quite stressful. Newmark finally agreed to pay me $5,000, plus they would give me future work. We agreed to this at the end of the summer of 2000. In the two months that followed I never received any work or the $5,000 check.

Issue #4. Warner Chappell, whose parent company is Time Warner, also was not paying me the money they owed me. I ended up writing letters to *The New York Times*, my New York State senator, my congressman, and the top brass at America Online and Time Warner. This was all happening when both companies were staging their blockbuster mega-merger. At the same time Warner Chappell received notice to appear in small claims court. They quickly settled and we agreed on $1,975, approximately $700 more than they originally owed me. That same week I received a $5,000 check from Newmark, although Newmark felt I had extorted the money from them because I had threatened to report them to the Buildings Department for performing work without a permit. Anyhow, that week I felt like a million dollars. I beat Time Warner. They couldn't beat the little guy and neither could Newmark & Company, probably one of the top three realty companies in New York. It was about this time that I started doing work for AGT again, and I felt good about that because I liked the people I was working with.

Issue #5. Things didn't go so well with Sabrina and her million dollar apartment. I received only a token payment from her husband. Considering I would not get a dime from Sabrina and would not initiate a lawsuit against Jules' friend, something was better than nothing.

Chapter V

A ROLLER COASTER OF EMOTIONS

OUR CHILDREN ALL HAVE A spirit of adventure and creativity and a penchant for getting into trouble. I wonder where they got that gene from. In some ways Peri gives us the least trouble at this stage in her life and gets the best grades, but that doesn't mean I love her more or less, nor does it mean she is incapable of making some bad decisions and dragging the family along for the ride. In fairness to Peri, her choice of Jeff as a boyfriend didn't seem like such a bad choice at the time. Peri and Jeff started going out probably around January 2000 or a little earlier. They were inseparable from the start and seemed to like each other a lot. In many ways they were opposites. Peri does well in school; Jeff does not. Peri has a very sweet side and Jeff can be the tough guy. They made a handsome couple. Jeff's toughness developed into a protectiveness towards Peri and her sisters. My girls are all extremely close, especially Hillary and Peri who are each other's best friend and share each other's friends. Add Stacie to the package, and you get a wonderful, close set of kids with a super, fun-loving, youthful, spirited mom. Jeff, as well as Bruce and other boys, have loved Peri and Hillary respectively, but they also loved our family. There have even been a few spurned boyfriends who have turned to Stacie for advice. Our family is very tight. We're very caring towards one another with no exceptions. Jodi has set the tone for this closeness and caring. Back to Jeff. Jeff took a liking to our family, and as long as Peri liked him, he was welcome in our home. As the summer of 2000 was approaching Peri and Jeff seemed to be getting closer. Peri did not have the heart to tell me (and I found out from Hillary only after Peri left for camp) that she really did not want to go to camp that summer but preferred to spend her vacation with Jeff. For that reason alone I would have definitely sent her to camp, because she was too young to be that serious about a boy. Peri needed a poem and a visit from Jeff. Here's the poem:

In a faraway place
There was a mountain and the sky it did grace

With silhouettes of orange yellow and golden honey
I traveled the road and the sky filled my car with rays oh so sunny

The hours, the days drifted by
Without meals and water, I began to wonder why

I was here and you were there
And wouldn't it be great
For you and me to eliminate the wait

Of being together on visiting day
And then the car began to laugh and say

If you wish it hard enough
And fill me with candy, balloons, dreams and lots of good stuff

And wish in your heart and dream of all the colors in the rainbow
And close your eyes and remember back a day ago

As I hugged you and held you tight
And made your world seem oh so right

So close your eyes and count to a zillion
And I promise to be there before you reach a million

Love, Dad

I followed this poem up with another poem. Yeah, you have to read this one, too.

Think of me flying alone
Up above this giant ice-cream cone

I dreamed of many new flavors
To share with my new neighbors

The stars and planets, my new friends
This is only true, it depends

If you reach out, reach out, more,
Higher and higher, into my world you can soar

To higher heights
With new sights

Of places where water flows upstream
And gardens blossom in your dreams

Birds have legs and animals sing
People take flight when they dream of a wing

To fly them into levels of higher moods called the moodosphere
Where birds, animals and people have not a single care

Live a life of merriment
And live a life of Periment

Named after someone loved by all
Whose name is graced on every Perimall

She loves to shop and laugh
And is even loved by a giraffe

And sea lions and a penguin
And so many others I failed to mention

So go to sleep tonight
And in the darkness find the light

To follow your dreams
You are very much loved it seems

By all who know you
And so many others too

You're in my thoughts tonight
You're truly such a delight

So dream your dreams and fly in your balloon
And I can't wait to see you soon

Love, Dad

We did bring Jeff up for visiting weekend and it was quite a scene at Point O' Pines. Point O' Pines is an all-girls camp for 300 girls. I could swear we were the poorest ones in the camp, but it is possibly the best camp for girls in the country, which is why Jodi and I chose to send our girls there. Even though the camp had rather strict rules, there was no rule against having a boyfriend visit. I'll bet that Jeff was the first. There was a twenty-foot banner welcoming Jeff. Since he is a handsome young man, he immediately became a teen idol at the camp. The owners, Sue and Jim, are fairly strict and had the girls take the banner down immediately. I think that only brought more attention to him. It's like telling children not to do something, so of course they will try it. After a while I think the owners got to like Jeff because he was so affable and appeared to be relatively harmless. Peri was thrilled to see him and I was happy for her. When the summer ended they started going out again, only this time there was a lot of fighting and making up. Hillary did not like Jeff anymore, although at times she would tolerate him, and then Peri's best girl friends started not to like him. The arguments between Peri and Jeff were escalating, as well. Jeff began lying, which got Peri so upset that she decided in December of 2000 that she did not want to see him ever again. Jeff was very convincing in promoting himself, however. He even called Jodi to say that when Peri needed someone to talk to, he would always be there, and that now he just wanted to speak with her.

Every time I open my mouth in social settings it is usually to put my foot in. This time would prove to be no different. I told Peri that she should tell Jeff her feelings in person, since by this time he was already in our living room. I brought the two of them together in Peri's room and became the referee. The two of them were extremely emotional. I just wanted them to end the relationship since that is what Peri wanted. I stressed that it should be ended civilly. They did have many of the same friends and it would be much easier if this all ended peacefully. Things seemed to work out finally after the shouting ended, and Peri had explained that she did not want to go out with Jeff anymore and that if she ever had a change of heart, she would call him. Although Jeff seemed to accept this, I couldn't help but feel a certain sadness for both of them. They had been very close and both had been hurt in the relationship. Jeff had not been faithful to Peri and there had been too many lies. In the end Peri emphatically said, "I don't ever want to see you again." So this affair of the heart was over. Peri's heart mended quickly, as she is extremely resilient; but I felt a loss. My children were growing up and becoming involved in adult relationships too early in life. It seemed as if they needed me less each day.

It was around this time, mid-December that I telephoned my best friend Joel and his wife Ronnie. I told them my family would be accepting their invitation to visit them for Chanukah and Christmas. That holiday weekend there was a lot of bonding going on among Hillary, Peri, Stacie and me. They all started to really enjoy having me around. For a father of teenagers this is no small feat. Teenagers and their relationships with parents: you could write volumes about them, as there have been scores of novels, short stories, essays and psychologists weighing in on the subject, but that weekend was a very positive experience. One evening while we were all together I told Jodi I was going to tell Joel and Ronnie what was going on in my life, but somehow I could not get the words out. Jodi was getting sleepy and excused herself. I still couldn't bring myself to begin my story and the only way I could begin sharing the last few years of my life was when Ronnie said she was going up to bed. I asked her to wait as I had something to share with her and Joel. Now there was no turning back. I wished Jodi were there beside me. I think she falsely assumed I'd prefer to tell them in private, but nothing could be further from the truth. Jodi was my wife, my best friend and pillar of support, and over the years I have come to respect her more and more for her logic and clear way of thinking, her solutions to problems, and her patience. Now I was on my own and I proceeded to give a one-hour monologue on my last few years. A very interesting thing happened during that hour. I saw a large outpouring of sadness from Ronnie and very little reaction from Joel. I should not have been surprised because Ronnie was facing many personal issues that have plagued her throughout her life and a few new ones. She was clearly going through a troubling time. As for Joel, I have never seen him lose his temper, nor have I ever had an argument with him. He is basically very easy-going, and things do not bother him. After my monologue Ronnie said, "Thank you, that must have taken a lot of courage." She was visibly upset and could relate to the turmoil in my life. I don't even remember Joel's response, if he had any. We talked a little afterwards; then Joel's flaw became apparent.

Joel is one of those people who are perfect. He cooks and caters his own parties for fifty or more people; his home is perfectly designed by him, as were all of his earlier homes. He is a perfect son and a perfect host and his parties are always perfect. Because he never loses his temper he can't have an argument with his wife, so he is also a perfect husband. So where does this leave Ronnie? Ronnie has some personal issues she has been dealing with her whole life and she would like to turn to Joel, but Joel is perfect and cannot relate to people with problems, because anything short of immediately life-threatening really isn't a problem. Joel's emotional state is so balanced that he has no arguments. He will be there and is an excellent listener and will not interrupt, but don't expect buckets of tears from him. I know Joel was listening and genuinely cared, and that was enough for me. All I really look for when I tell a friend about my health is maybe an extra telephone call or any kind word or two. Joel gave me a hug when he said good-bye on the next occasion we were together, and that's the sort of thing I need from people. Thanks, Joel, and thank you, Ronnie for your compassion and for relating to how I was feeling.

A hug and a kind word go a long way. Friends should be more generous with both those items. The same is true of compliments, making people laugh, or just making someone feel good about himself. They all have one common denominator: they all cost nothing and the person that bestows them usually gets the reward of feeling good about himself. As far as a hug or touching goes, guys should be able to be more affectionate with each other in public, whether it's hugging a brother, uncle, friend or father. I wish my father were around now, because when this book is published I'll need all the hugs I can get. Children never grow up. We're always craving our parents' love and acceptance.

Another interesting event in parenting happened that weekend. We got invited to a Christmas party at Ronnie's best friend, Carol's. Carol is a sweet girl who never married and has a slight disability. However, I'm convinced that God has given people with disabilities an extra gene of kindness and understanding, making them more tenderhearted. They have a need to care for others who are in greater need than themselves, and they often don't view their disability as a disability at all. Carol still lives with her 93-year-old father. That evening there were about twenty people at the party and we congregated in the sunroom. Hillary and Peri took comfort in each other and were shy about participating in conversations. Stacie, by contrast, was the star of the evening, proudly wearing her new pink beret which was a present from Joel and Ronnie.

I will digress for a moment and add that earlier we were invited to Joel's and Ronnie's for a Chanukah party where they must have spent about $100 in gifts for my family, all perfect gifts, especially Stacie's pink beret. After she received the beret, every word out of Stacie's mouth that weekend had a French accent, so here we were at the Christmas party with our little Parisienne.

Stacie parked herself in the middle of the room and the discussion turned to skiing. Stacie had gone skiing once in her life when she was two, but somehow Stacie became the moderator of the skiing discussion. Everyone started directing their comments to Stacie, waiting for Stacie to ask the next question. Stacie knows absolutely nothing about ski resorts, yet she was engaged in the debate over which resort is the best.

This is a trait Stacie has easily cultivated over the years. She talks to Japanese people to discuss sushi, even though they don't speak English, and she often leads Herb, my mother's boyfriend, into discussions about what he does in Florida. She really is quite the conversationalist and doesn't shy away from any subject. Her range of knowledge and interests includes sports, art, sushi, French, cooking, tennis, animals, car design, automobiles, astronomy and computers.

2000 is coming to a close and during the last week of the year, my 1990 BMW convertible died. I need a new car. I have lost my dollar bet with Stacie that I would be driving this car to her wedding. We were going to go double or nothing that I would be driving this car for another thirty years until I was 78. We were predicting that my car would be a classic like the '56 Thunderbird. I still believe it could have been, but when the engine died, so did my interest in caring for the car. I do believe a car is an extension of one's self, and a little of me died when I said farewell to my car. Farewell, car, the year 2000, and the sadness my illness caused my family and me this year. In some ways it doesn't get easier living with this illness. You have to fear the unknown and ask what happens when the medicine stops working. As far as another year coming to a close, I have to feel grateful for Jodi's love, my three wonderful daughters, and my relatively good health.

It's June 10, 2001. I haven't written in quite a while, so here we go.

I've been continuing to see my doctor every three months and I've come to accept the fact that the medicine I've been taking will keep me healthy. I've considered seeing the doctor every four months, but that has not come to pass. At my last visit a few weeks ago, I learned that while my T-cells have remained relatively constant for the last few years, my viral load has become detectable, and the doctor wants to see me in another week. This three-week period is causing a great deal of anxiety. I ran 15 miles today and the run was pretty easy so it's hard to comprehend the medicine may not be working anymore. Dr. Brook explained this may not be the case, and that's why he wants to retest my blood.

Newsweek came out with a cover story marking the 20th anniversary of the AIDS outbreak. I would have written the story differently, but I suppose if there were 100 writers there would be 100 stories. Perhaps the cover story should be written 100 years from now, when the world looks back at how 25, 50, 100 or 200 million people died from AIDS. The Jewish people are constantly reminding the world to feel guilty about how six million Jews perished during the Holocaust. We have been quite successful. But how will future generations view the people of this century when the final count for AIDS is tallied? The medicine is here, but somehow it is not being distributed. This cannot happen. It is unacceptable. The medicine must be distributed and money must be spent to find a vaccine and a cure. Compare this to eminent domain: If a town needed a road the local government would buy the obstructing house and tear it down. Human lives need saving. Doesn't the government have the right to buy the patents on the current drugs for the good of humankind? We can build roads, but aren't lives more important? Maybe the courts will shoot down this theory, but somebody must think of something. At present almost everyone knows someone who has lost a loved one through AIDS. The suffering and dying must stop.

The *Newsweek* article also revealed the depressing news that it appears the 'three-drug cocktail' does not work after a while, but this isn't true in all cases. The author should have offered more hope to people like me who don't smoke, don't drink, don't do drugs, do exercise, have good diets and enjoy good support systems in friends and family. I personally hate referring to this medication as a 'cocktail'. Do people think we are having fun taking this medicine? For those of you fortunate enough not to be HIV positive, 'the cocktail' must be taken either with or without food, depending on which specific medicine you are taking. The various side effects include diarrhea, nausea, numbness, and dizziness. The long term effects are not yet known. Moreover, taking the medication on a rigid schedule is a constant reminder of your illness.

It is commonly assumed by the public that all people who are HIV positive practice unsafe sex and lead an unhealthy lifestyle, but this is not true. There are lots of people who lead healthy lifestyles, practice safe sex, and run marathons. But are there any statistics on us? Probably not, given that we are in the minority. The public must realize that there are HIV positive people running both marathons and successful businesses. This fact might inspire all people to realize that HIV positive people are not on death's doorstep, and that we continue to be productive, participating members of society. On the other hand, if the purpose of the *Newsweek* article was to show there is no hope, that's okay too, providing this hopelessness is directed to the world at large. 22,000,000 people have died. Wake up! Spend whatever money it takes for a cure and get the medicine to those who need it. As for myself, I'm very uneasy. I realize there is probably a 50/50 chance the medicine is not working for me anymore and that I will have to take other medication and hope that it works. Perhaps I can change medicine every four or five years for the next ten to twenty years, and by that time there will be a cure. I'm probably too optimistic, but I do believe a cure is possible. It could happen at any time with a stroke of luck.

American know-how and brainpower will generate the cure. We will remain the true superpower in mind and might that we were destined to be. Our greatest resource can never be depleted, but can only augment itself and spread its word and wings, elevating itself to a place where others only dream of going. We walk there with our eyes wide open, for our life is but a dream to others. Thus we celebrate our ever-increasing greatest resource: the American people and our undying spirit. For it is this spirit that brought our founding fathers to America's shores a few centuries ago that still dwells in our hearts a few centuries later. Those early patriots, much like those of today, fought tyranny and oppression with a passion as though they were fighting for their very lives. They were and they still are. Their goals have remained constant: freedom and achieving a better quality of life for their family and for future generations. To that end they have succeeded remarkably: thwarting enemies for centuries, for no sacrifice would be worth the loss of our freedom; discoveries or inventions, or just opening up new playing fields for humankind: baseball, 'three strikes and you're out', or 'step-up to the plate'; the light bulb, that very image signifying an idea, or 'have you seen the light'; and rockets, a generation of songs and movies about space travel that have rocketed our economy skyward. New frontiers have been opened that only dreamers of earlier generations might have dared to dream. Now, we can direct rockets to the moon and outer space that travel at several miles per second. We have tiny computer chips that contain entire encyclopedias. Let's just find a chemical, enzyme, hormone, plant, mineral, something that can trick the body into removing the AIDS virus from the body. If somebody had asked me years ago if such a thing as a fax or computer could operate the way it does, I would have said no with 95% certainty. Obviously I was wrong about technology. Now I believe with 95% certainty that two things are possible. I believe at some point inanimate objects will be able to be demolecularized and sent over a cable line and remolecularized, or whatever the correct word is, and appear at the new site. What that means is that you would be able to send a refrigerator from Florida to New York in seconds. The next step would be sending people over computer lines and that would follow with sending people to a different time period. For the purpose of curing AIDS, that might mean sending a person back in time to the moment the sexual encounter occurred that caused the AIDS infection and then have him relive that day without the sexual experience. Alternately, we could send someone to the future and retrieve the cure which may be discovered within five to a hundred years. While all this may sound fantastic and science fiction-like, I have not lost my mind. I have always been a dreamer with the belief that anything is possible. However, even a dreamer has to occasionally return to reality.

Stacie had her bat mitzvah a few weeks ago and there was a lot of love that went into the party. Jodi and I were not really in a financial position to make the same extravaganza we did for Hillary and Peri. But since we were both scarred by not having the same type of wedding Jodi's sisters had, and I didn't have the same type of bar mitzvah my brothers had, we knew what we had to do. Begging, borrowing or stealing would not be beneath us. There could be no do-overs. This day would be a lifetime memory for Stacie. And what a day it was. We even had a few more guests than planned, as Stacie wanted to invite the world. Of course I have to thank Jodi for all the work she put into the party. I wanted my last bat mitzvah speech to be special, but I also didn't want to get too sentimental. During my speeches at Hillary's and Peri's parties I thanked the grandparents, and if I could have planted a tree in the middle of my speeches honoring and commemorating our love for each other and the lessons learned in life and so on and so on, I would have planted a forest. I recollect at Hillary's Bat Mitzvah I even thanked her third grade teacher and stopped short of thanking the school crossing guard.

So find your seat and listen to the proudest dad in the land. Drum roll, please! And you'd better read this speech, since I practically went bankrupt paying for this party. But, I would do it again. You have to understand this is one of the few moments in life when people are truly listening to me, and it is a chance to make a statement about my family and let everyone know what a lucky guy I am. You have already read enough to know how true that is, although I was not about to share my story with 240 people on that day. And now the speech:

This is great. I can't believe you all have to listen to me now. Even my family.

Rabbi, cantor, friends and relatives. I'd like to thank everyone for coming today and sharing in Stacie's Bat Mitzvah. To Rabbi Ginsburg and Cantor Shechter I'm especially grateful my children have been guided by you over the years.

Stacie, I'm so proud of you today. You did a great job as I knew you would. It isn't easy being the baby in the family when you have such a tough act to follow. Parents, myself included, make the mistake of comparing siblings, and the only comparison I will make today is to say you are definitely, definitely your own person. Your interests vary from animals to tennis, astronomy to hockey, car design to football, French to art and sushi. Unfortunately Hebrew was not one of your stronger interests. It wasn't easy for you to sit still in school, but somehow you learned more in Hebrew class about life and a sense of history and the Jewish people than you realized. Stacie, you told me the story about Esther saving the Jewish people and we talked about stories of how the Jewish people were oppressed over the centuries. I still remember the day you got yelled at in school for standing up and telling a teacher not to blame another student for doing something that he did not do. That took guts, and I admire you for standing up for people when they are not treated fairly.

Stacie: Mom and I count our blessings that you are such a beautiful, popular, athletic, intelligent child. You have a gift in that you can relate to people big and small, old and young, and they don't even have to be able to speak English. You even get along with your sisters' friends and their boyfriends. I get a kick out of you screening these boys. Keep reminding them of the rules: no calls after midnight, and Dad likes white chocolate.

Hillary and Peri: you girls are great and you've taught me a lot about family and compromise and that I can't always have my way. Thanks, girls. Hillary, do you think I can borrow my car tomorrow?

I know you are all tired of my telling you about the most perfect person in the world, so I won't talk anymore about my mother, uh, I mean my wife. I'm not going to mention how Jodi's understanding, kindness, energy and passion are what keep our family flourishing year after year. One thing I'll say about Jodi is that someday I hope Stacie finds as much happiness in life as Jodi and I have found with each other and our family. Stacie, my greatest wish for you is that you live up to your potential which is limited only by how far you dare to dream, and then challenge yourself to fulfill your dreams by imagination, hard work and creativity. Stacie, whatever your dreams, desires and goals are, your mother and I will always be your proud and loving parents. I love you, Stacie.

I have a tendency to write about people who have hurt me, but now I'd like to write something nice about Mikey Mike, our DJ. He was great and his dancers were excellent and extremely energetic. Financially he worked with us very graciously, even though we didn't cry poverty. He was a class act and we enjoyed this party perhaps a little more than the previous two. Our pictures told the story; I never saw my family look more beautiful. Jodi had her dress made by Holly of Infinity. Holly is a legend in the area and Holly takes a personal interest in our family because Holly, like everyone, loves Jodi. The dress was pure magic. The girls also looked the best they had ever looked. Stacie's dress was also made by Holly, and with the dress, her poise and energy, she was 100% Stacie. When Hillary and Peri made a toast to Stacie, you would have thought they were actresses flown in from Hollywood. I even photographed well that day. It was the first time I entertained the thought of having a cameo role featuring me solo in '*A Bat Mitzvah Album*'. I couldn't wait to stop into Holly's store to give her a big hug and thank her.

To Holly and Mikey Mike, I hope this book sells umpteen million copies, as this will be my way of saying thanks. And if you have to fight off the masses for a day off, so be it, as that is the price one pays for excellence. It is so gratifying for me to hope that 10 or 1,000 or 1,000,000 people might read this book and meet in these pages some really nice, talented, creative people out there, like Mikey Mike and Holly. I love people who are artistic in their field. I have a lot of respect for talent, especially when it is accompanied by caring and enthusiasm.

Stacie was aglow, thanks to the teaching, caring and enthusiasm offered by the rabbi, cantor, Holly and Mikey Mike. Even though Hebrew school was not really her thing, Stacie somehow managed the day quite successfully. There was one major flaw, however: she forgot to thank her parents in her bat mitzvah speech. That hurt Jodi to no end. No one deserves more thanks from our children and me than my wife does. Jodi was hurt, more hurt than she let on. Stacie sensed this and the following day wrote a note which I have inserted here. It would have brought tears to our guests' eyes.

I know you think you had to yank teeth to get this out of me but you really didn't. I just wanted to put it in the right words, and I wouldn't be able to do that just five minutes before my party. Maybe I don't express my feelings that well, because you think I didn't enjoy or appreciate the party, but I really did. Thinking back on it, every penny Dad spent on me, I felt so bad. I know that Peri did not ask for that much at her bat mitzvah, but I guess I'm not like that. I'm the kind of person that has money on her mind every second of the day. I think of how my house is going to be, and if I am going to have a bowling alley in my house, and an indoor pool. I think you know what I'm talking about because you don't hear many kids saying they always wanted a McLaren F1 which is 1.5 million. I used to worry if when I grew up I would be able to afford things from Hammacher Schlemmer or if I would live in a brownstone. I guess I always think "The seaweed is always greener in somebody else's lake." And then the line goes I dream about swimming there, but that is a big mistake. I think that is what I learned from you and Dad. That money isn't everything, but generosity, loyalty, respect and trust is. I think these are some of the many things that you taught me. I think my bat mitzvah was based on generosity. Dad was so generous to put his hard-earned money into me. I guess you guys really make sure that there is no middle child syndrome, or favorites. I know I ask for a lot, like a new computer and all sorts of things, but I don't think I could've asked for anything more. I mean, what else can you want from the Sands Beach Club, Dazzling Parties, and Mikey Mike! I don't want to spend any more of your money by buying a compass, but I think that is what the bat mitzvah stands for, a guide to keep our family traveling in the right direction forever. I am really sorry I didn't make any of this clear to you earlier, but I guess it took a while to find the perfect words. I love you.

Okay, I'll stop for a second while you get the box of Kleenex. Stacie really does have thoughts and feelings. I explained to Stacie that sometimes in life there are no second chances, no do-overs. This was one of those times. Stacie had also been practicing to sing a medley of songs, but she came down with a case of stage fright and opted not to sing. I could have encouraged her but I knew my words would not comfort her as she often chose to disagree with me. I had probably spent $1,000 on singing lessons in the last few months but Stacie's not singing was something I was not overly upset about, unless Stacie would regret it later in life. However, the incident passed and Stacie quickly forgot it. I could not fault her for not singing. I threw up at my bar mitzvah right after my haftorah, so I would be the last person in the world to encourage her to perform.

I was a very different child from my children, but I still find myself comparing them to me. I was extremely independent, financially and personally. I feel they lack both these qualities and the sensitivity I had for my parents. It goes beyond that and too much has to do with the times they are growing up in. There is no longer calling a neighbor Mr. or Mrs. Stone. Now everyone is Jayne or Steve. Computers, America Online and video games have all but robbed my memory of playing outside and kicking a ball. Calculators have replaced math and everyone gets tutored for certain subjects, even the smart kids. Let's not forget about MTV and the casual sex that's portrayed on television. I feel as if I'm living in a time I don't belong in; the Renaissance, that's my time. My friends would be Brunelleschi, Ghiberti, Cellini, Magellan and Michelangelo, and I would be living in Florence. I would be jogging across the Ponte Vecchio at five in the morning, inhaling the aroma of freshly baked bread. Sculptors inmortalizing nude models, and painters, artists, jewelers and masons beginning their sixteen-hour days and reveling in their creativity would eagerly greet each new dawn and question, "What are you always running from?" I found an old card that I must have written Jodi in those Florentine days.

Sweetheart,

There were times I'd see a painting, perhaps of Florence in the 1500s or a timeless country scene in France or perhaps simply a bird in flight—flying, soaring to heights and places it would never see again, or a child walking along the shores of Nova Scotia...

Was I meant for another age, another place... a Renaissance architect, philosopher, writer, poet with side interests in theology, botany, astronomy, and fencing to stay in shape? Or was I a loyal soldier to Alexander the Great longing to return to Persia?

How often I could see myself in an artist's painting, or beside a portrait by one of the great masters. Was her smile for me? Of course it was... For that very morning I remember waking up to the sights and smells of Florence. Upon awakening I washed and put my watch on and left hurriedly, forgetting my perspective plans.

My watch was an antique. My great Uncle Magellan gave it to me before he set sail around the world six years ago. He said the watch was mine forever until I made a wish that came true. And so for six years I have treasured the watch and loved the story and legend of this timepiece.

Today was not your typical day. My friend Filippo Brunelleschi and I were to announce to the world we had discovered the art of constructing perspectives. For fifteen years we had been working out our calculations and today was to be truly the most exciting day in the history of the art world. This would even surpass Ghiberti's magnificent doors and the De Medici Chapel. Naturally, of course, the entire art world of Florence—painters, sculptors, architects, masons, goldsmiths—even those apprenticing for the arts would be given a half-day off to witness the first mechanical perspective drawings. And then, as I crossed the Ponte Vecchio, hearing the sounds of the world's fore-most jewelers whittle away at jade from the Orient, turquoise from Persia, Florentine gold and diamonds, I began to wish I did not have to go to this opening, but instead could be lying beside the world's most desirable woman. But then I realized this could only be a dream... And I awoke. I reached for my watch that was no longer there, and all I could think of was how lucky I was to be beside you.

I love you so much.

Love

Richard

Today is Saturday, June 23rd. I received a good report from Dr. Brook this week. My HIV viral load has become unde-tectable. There is nothing worse for me than fearing the unknown, and not knowing if the viral load would spiral upward or become undetectable was pure torture. I heard the news a few days ago and cried a few tears. The week was very emotional for me. Hillary and Peri were both going to the senior prom, and Hillary was graduating from high school. It isn't easy for adolescents growing up in today's world. Hillary had a particularly tough time in school. Kids can be extremely hard, competitive, insensitive, selfish and spoiled, and these are the good kids. The bad ones lie and manipulate. I'm just glad Hillary finished high school on a relatively positive note. I think the turning point for Hillary was Bruce betraying her trust. My illness also took a toll on her, but I think she has resolved both issues, and now she is excited about starting college at the University of Florida at Gainesville. Go, Gators!

Peri's prom date was Gil, an extremely affable guy who captured my heart. Instead of bringing Peri a corsage, Gil brought Peri a dozen long stem roses with white flowers and wrote her a very sweet romantic note. Sorry Gil, I won't print the note. Looks like your phone won't be ringing off the hook with eligible young ladies calling. Peri looked like a million dollars; her smile confirmed her worth. I admired Gil for having the courage and creativity to bestow this huge arrangement of flowers upon Peri in a roomful of Peri's friends and family, plus four other prom dates and all their entourage. It was a real class act. Anything that makes Peri feel good is magnified in me tenfold. Jodi, my mother, Aunt Ronnie and Hillary all shared the same feeling. Thanks, Gil.

And now, Hillary's prom dates! Hillary dated a few boys during her senior year, although none too seriously. There was a young man named Harry who adored Hillary. Hillary liked him as a friend and agreed to go to the prom with him. Harry was extremely happy that Hillary accepted. He seemed to follow her around like a puppy dog. In fact, he had genuinely had a crush on her for many years. Hillary can be insensitive at times and this was one of those times. Hillary had been going out with this new guy, Al for a few months and wanted to go to the prom with Al. Our family repeatedly advised her it would not be right to cancel with Harry, who would be very hurt. I put myself in his position and told Hillary it was not the right thing to do, reminding her that Harry had never done anything mean to her. Guess what! No kidding, she told Harry she would be going to the prom with Al. I felt bad for Harry. Hillary has since tried speaking with Harry on occasion, but he has no interest in speaking with her now. I don't blame him. I just wish Hillary had believed me. I'm an expert on being hurt, but I guess Hillary will have to develop her own sensitivity level. Now, she was going to the prom with Al, so he went out and rented a tuxedo. Guess what? Yeah, you probably figured it out, but this time Hillary was right to cancel her date with Al. Apparently Al had been saying things about Hillary that were not so nice. So Hillary dropped him and decided to ask someone who had graduated from Lawrence the previous year to be her date. Peter, her third and final choice for prom date, and Hillary made an elegant couple. We took tons of pictures of Hillary and Peter, and Peri and Gil. A *Kodak Moment* if ever there was one! What a beautiful sight, all these children grown up and looking so handsome and elegant on their special day! "Where had the years gone?" I sighed, as I drove my convertible into the sunset.

I think I told you earlier I had to buy a new convertible since my topless BMW had died. I bought a Mazda Miata, British racing green with a tan top and tan interior. It's a five-speed. I really have a good time with the car and have quickly forgotten about my BMW (although I do miss it sometimes). I would like to thank Richard, the car salesman who made buying the Mazda a pleasant experience. Thanks, Richard and thanks, Mazda. I really like the car. Hillary and I fight for the car on weekends and I usually lose. When a daughter asks for a favor like borrowing a car, she knows it's an imposition; that's why we call it a *favor*, and it's hard for me to say no. I just wish she wouldn't ask me for the car so often. (Maybe I will tear this page out and leave it in Hillary's room accidentally).

Cars. It seemed like just yesterday that Hillary was still in diapers. My next trip back to yesteryear is even nastier, but before I tell you about Hope and Martin, I'd like to mention two special ladies who were born on the same day, Alice and Aunt Helaine. Alice is a very kind and sweet lady whom I have known since I was two years old. I always told my mother how much I liked Alice, and for the past six years, my mother has been working with Alice on a daily basis. Alice consistently remembers my children's birthdays and graduations and she's always upbeat. Aunt Helaine was married to Uncle Ernie who was Jules' brother and a really sweet guy. The two brothers were very close but Ernie could never understand why Jules didn't make *the big wedding* for Jodi and me. Aunt Helaine and Uncle Ernie would do anything and go anywhere for their two girls. Aunt Helaine has been very kind to Jodi and me over the years and we share a soft spot for each other. We both know the best kept secret of the Slansky (my wife's maiden name) family. It's the in-laws. We were at Aunt Helaine's daughter's house a few weeks ago, celebrating her granddaughter's bat mitzvah. There were about twenty-five people in the room and probably six or seven discussions going on. I commenced speaking in a loud voice about underrated ballplayers. My comments had nothing to do with any conversation in the room and after repeating my trivia about five or six times, I finally had everyone's attention. I proceeded to say that Aunt Helaine is like an underrated ballplayer and her true value has never been fully appreciated. I gave her a hug and told her I love her. Why can't more of us make others feel a little extra special? Thanks, Aunt Helaine and Alice, for being there for my family and me.

The couple I now want to introduce are Hope and Martin. Martin is an extremely successful coal trader. Initially, in 1985 he commissioned me to design his office. Over the next five or six years I designed three rather grand renovations for their apartments and they all came out quite well. I suppose that's why they continued to call me back. They were a little difficult but they always paid their bills, although not always in a timely manner. Hope constantly flirted with me, and I think it was a little more than just flirting on her part. For example, while we were working on a project that involved adding a balcony to her living room, she would call me into her bedroom which was all the way at the back of the apartment. I felt a little awkward, but I followed her into her bedroom. There she would be lying on her bed, fully clothed, with her checkbook, getting ready to write me a check. It was all a little too suggestive for me. I was attracted to her personality but there was no physical attraction. Besides, I would never have an affair with a woman. All this predates my involvement with men by a few years and I can say with 80% certainty that even if Hope had been Miss America at the time, I would not have looked to have an affair. I'm only human and I'd like to say 100% sure, but since I have never been asked to have an affair with Miss America, what can I say? Ten years ago I would have said there was a 0% chance I would ever be involved with a man. Anyhow, getting back to Hope, I would say the likelihood I could have had sex with her that day was 75% and another 25% that she would have been flattered by my advances. I think not showing an interest in her is what cost me dearly later on. Women do not like to be rejected.

A few years later, in 1994, Hope called me and told me she was buying a brownstone and would be gutting all six stories of it. I would be their architect. It was a very exciting project and it should have been very profitable. All four of the past projects I had worked on with Hope and Martin had been profitable and interesting ones, all in the range of $125,000 to $200,000. This project would be close to $1,000,000. I gave Hope and Martin a preliminary timetable for the project: from start to finish, the project would take one year. I also provided an estimate of what my fee would run. The estimate was only a rough one, based on a percentage of the construction costs. With these projections in mind they said, "Let's get started." It would take months for the drawings to be completed and to get the final prices from the contractors. It was agreed I would be sending monthly invoices for the work I performed each month. If the value of my time spent on the project exceeded the fixed percent of construction costs that I had estimated my fee to be, I probably could convince Hope and Martin to pay me the difference or at least part of the difference. If the value of my time added up to less than the fixed percent of construction costs, I would have a very appreciative client. I started sending Hope and Martin monthly statements. They found my time charges to be excessive. However, the project became much more involved than originally planned. For example, instead of six bathrooms there would be 9! And the bathrooms would not stack vertically. This became a problem for running the plumbing lines, the air conditioning ducts and return lines. I tried to discourage Hope from locating the nine bathrooms without regard to the economics of the plumbing and heating and air conditioning systems. I informed her this would substantially increase the construction costs as well as prove extremely difficult for my engineers and me to coordinate. Hope's standard answer was, "This is what I want. Make it work." Since my fee was based on a percentage of the construction costs, who was I to argue if she wanted 100 bathrooms and none of them lined up?

Hope and Martin and I decided a formal agreement for architectural services should be executed. This was the first time I had ever entered into a signed agreement with them, and I wound up making a costly mistake. My intent of the agreement was to indicate what my fee would be and when payments were due. I never expected the project to end up in a lawsuit, but that is exactly what happened. In January 1995, we finally signed a contract, although the terms were substantially negotiated in Hope's and Martin's favor. At the time of the contract signing they already owed me close to $30,000, so I had little choice but to sign this contract whose terms had been mostly dictated to me. Even with the slightly discounted fee, the project still should have been profitable. Wrong again! As the architect, I had the job to send a complete set of drawings out for competitive bids and then review the bids with my client. Then they would select one of the bids and I would formalize it into a standard American Institute of Architects agreement. This was how all four of the previous projects were done and there was no reason for me to believe this project would be any different. Wrong again! Hope was anxious to move the project along and have it done as cheaply as possible, so she hired a contractor who was not licensed by the Department of Consumer Affairs. Hope began construction work before the drawings were completed and without obtaining permits as mandated by city law. Consequently, I never knew the cost of the project. Several months passed and Hope stopped making payments to me, so I terminated my contract. It took Hope an additional 27 months to complete the project. I had scheduled her move-in date to be November 1995. Hope did not obtain the final certificate of occupancy until August 1997. Considering I was only one week late in obtaining the permit, Martin's and Hope's decision to withhold my payments would cost them a delay of almost two years in completing their project. At the time I was losing interest in their project for a number of reasons:

1. The contractor Hope selected was not competent and eventually she fired him.
2. Hope was not being honorable. It was my job to

send a complete set of drawings out for competitive bids so that I would know how much the project cost. Obviously, this did not occur.

3. Hope was doing work illegally, such as removing asbestos and not dumping it in a legal manner. Other work was performed before the necessary permits were obtained.

4. Hope was not paying her invoices in accordance with the contract.

In May of 1995 I terminated my agreement and in 2001 the case was finally tried. It was an unusual case for a couple of reasons:

1. These types of cases are generally settled and never go to trial. However, Martin and Hope never even offered a dime.

2. I found it very awkward initiating the lawsuit, but a six-year delay did seem quite excessive. I remembered they had been at Stacie's baby-naming ceremony; surely, this case should have been settled without going to court.

The lawsuit and preparation for the trial were extremely time-consuming, and while I did receive a substantial payment of $19,000, it was still less than I expected. The judge got both sides to accept the settlement and I know Hope was not happy, either. She was suing me for an amount to be determined, because she believed I had delayed the project completion date. It must have cost Martin and Hope $25,000 in legal fees plus a few thousand dollars in transcripts and witnesses, not to mention days of lost time for her and her husband. I found the case to be emotionally draining. It was so difficult to have to sue people who had been close family friends. There was a lot of wasted time and energy put into this case by both parties and their attorneys. If one good thing came out of this lawsuit, it was that my attorney became quite close to Jodi and me, and Jodi is now working for him on a part-time basis. It was a relief to have this six-year chapter of my life over when this case finally came to a close.

Chapter VI

A DEAFENING SILENCE

I THINK I ALREADY MENTIONED to you that Hillary will be going to school in Florida. Jodi took Hillary and the girls to see the school in May of 2001 and then visited her dad and her sister Patti in Orlando. Jodi was feeling close to Patti and told her and her husband Bruce about me. They have been genuinely concerned about us and have come to understand and love Jodi considerably more. All the garbage of judging Jodi for what she did or did not do was just that, garbage to be thrown out. Patti seemed to develop a tremendous sense of respect and caring towards Jodi and was also concerned about me. Telling Patti was good for Jodi because now Jodi comes across as a saint and I come across obviously as not a saint.

We did tell one couple, Mitch and Michelle, who are local friends of ours. I think they were as shocked as Bruce and Patti were. As I said earlier, if you were to list 100 couples and eliminate them one by one, Jodi and I would be the couple least likely to have a bisexual spouse or any marital problem.

Bisexuality, homosexuality and AIDS are phenomena that are not limited to the cities and black population, despite how the media portray AIDS. The reality that I have found from telling my story to strangers differs sharply from the media's take. My listeners confided in me truths they would otherwise not reveal. But as I have bared my soul, they have responded in kind. Recovered alcoholics, alcoholics, drug abusers, strangers who have suffered bouts of depression, young adults who were abused, gay, lesbian, and bisexual people have all told me their dark tales. It is my belief from listening to these scores of people that all men and women have both a heterosexual and a homosexual side to their sexuality. That includes straight, married folk as well as gay people. And to those few who choose not to be aware of both sides of their sexuality: you have simply chosen to block your true sexual identity from your mind. Let me take this one step further. Guys, go to a bookstore and take a peek at Greg Louganis's book, *Breaking the Surface*. You need only glance at the cover that is graced by his lithe, tight, fluid body. His body and lines define perfection. Okay, I understand you can't exactly go to your local bookstore and ask for a book focusing on the life of a gay man. Hmmmmm... wear dark glasses or go to a bookstore where no one will recognize you. Better yet, just ask for the autobiography of the all-time greatest diver. I think you will agree with me that a sculptor would have a hard time creating a more perfect form. Curious to touch and feel it, the book cover? Of course you are, just as you would like to run your hand across a sculpture in a museum where the sign says, "Do not touch." Yet you touch the forbidden fruit. Unfortunately, you are probably the macho-type guy who wouldn't be caught dead reading my book. Women, if I've described your husband to a T, show him a picture of a hot guy at a tender moment. You know, after sex; see if he can confide in you that some actor or model is incredibly handsome. And guys, don't be so uptight; women are forgiving.

Did you ever wonder why so many artists, designers, musicians, actors, writers and other creative folk are gay or lesbian, yet so few accountants and stockbrokers are? It's because the first group consists of people who have chosen to live their life in a more creative field, people who can be more open-minded and can explore their sexuality without being afraid of the rules and taboos of society. I am not saying there are no gay or lesbian accountants or stockbrokers, and they may be just as creative in what they do, but I think account-ants and stockbrokers tend to play more by the rules of soci-ety than those who work in the arts. For this reason I cannot be ashamed of my sexuality. My only problem is that I'm married and that I made a vow to my wife the day we were wed, yet I cannot keep the vow of being faithful.

I will be discussing the prospects of writing this book with Hillary and Peri tomorrow. Stacie will be leaving for camp and I have chosen not to burden her with my illness at this time. Whether this book I am writing ever goes into publica-tion will ultimately be my decision. However, my wife's and children's opinion will strongly affect my decision. One of my major reasons for publishing the book is for preventive and educational purposes. Perhaps people will realize that AIDS is not limited to some nameless, faceless person without a family, that it can happen to the guy next door, even a married one who lives in the suburbs. The main purpose of my story is to reassure you through love and support, diet and strict adherence to taking medicine, you can beat AIDS. My message applies to all people all over the world. It cannot be a question of money if 22,000,000 people have died. It has to be a question of priorities. Do we appropriate money for keeping people alive or spend billions sending rockets into outer space?

I'm getting sleepy so off I drifted
To another time where my spirit was lifted

Only downward in reverse
As I thought of AIDS and its curse

And then the phone awakened me
And said you have been selected to see

The most powerful force on Earth
Greater than life, death and birth

A thousand of the most brilliant men
Have created a rocket that is more powerful than

Any force ever felt or known
'Big deal' I said and hung up the phone

And then the room started to rumble
Perhaps I must learn to be more humble

The next thing I saw
Was a rocket coming through the floor

The rocket invited me inside
And said 'I'm taking you for a ride'

I climbed aboard through a tiny ladder
For me only one thing would matter

I would travel to another time
Where I could solve our planet's greatest crime

For I will bring back a suitcase full
Of diamonds, rubies and jewels until

I have enough money to buy the cure
This is something I couldn't ignore

Fly with me in the darkness to find the light
And off we flew for mankind this night

As the rocket went soaring through the sky
It said 'I apologize for the lie

I have no power, I cannot even feel
I have no heart and I cannot heal

I am driven by the creation of 1,000 brains
Of 1,000 men whose accomplishments and gains

Depend upon convincing man and womankind alike
That the space program should not take a hike'

I said 'okay I'll give you a chance
Perhaps I could learn to change my stance

Listen to me and stay the course
I direct you on for today I'm the boss

I want you to find a place where a heart does not beat
Flying at supersonic speeds oh what a feat

Your engines will deafen any other sound
From here to heaven and back to the ground'

The engines roared and a sound could not be heard
Not a laugh, not a cry, not a single word

And then I heard a beat of a heart call
Slowering, quietening as it began to fall

And fade away into nothingness but the beat
In my soul grew louder and it would repeat

A deafening silence was inside me roaring
Within me was violence and it was pouring

From my heart and all parts of me
I felt death and knew this was to be

An unpleasant tragic event
The rocket began its descent
And shortly after we touched down on cement

And there before us I understood why
I had the urge I had to try

To bring life to this child who had just died
But his beat was still in my soul and I cried

I told the rocket 'your force is not as strong
As the silence of a heartbeat and you were wrong all along

It is the power of the silencing of a heart
That has a force that tears me apart

And others I hope and I pray
Will vote their conscience and will say

The money, energy and love must find a place
That will save lives and not conquer space

Go to the 1,000 brains that conjured up this space scheme
Rechannel your efforts and dare to dream

Of saving lives on this planet Earth
And then you can be proud your brain has worth'

Just then the rocket seemed to hear
And for a moment perhaps it learned to care

For in that flash the rocket turned to dust
And 1,000 brains realized they must

Redirect their energy toward finding a cure
And the world would echo its sentiments, I was sure

If only I had the power to make my poems and dreams come true you wouldn't have to read another poem about my flying around in rockets and balloons. I could then dedicate my life to writing poems that would cure all diseases. That would be something to write Stacie about while she was away at summer camp.

On June 24th, we said good-bye to Stacie as she left for camp. Last night we went out for dinner and I discovered an interesting talent that Stacie possesses. Stacie has a knack for imitating people's voices with a comical twist. I could see her becoming an actress or comedian. When we said good-bye this morning the family was in tears, especially me. I started giving Stacie a few last minute instructions such as: don't forget to put on suntan lotion, but this conversation was going nowhere fast. Stacie had obviously heard it all before. Usually Jodi and I stress that she should eat healthy stuff during the summer, but this time I told her to have three doughnuts with every meal in case they run out of doughnuts that day, to make sure her bagel is perfectly buttered a quarter-inch thick all around, to always ask for a doggie bag after dinner in case she gets hungry in the middle of the night, and to make sure the 24-hour deli is listed as an emergency number. Although the tears flowed from laughing at my bad jokes, Jodi and Peri were still crying after the bus left. I always miss Stacie when she leaves for camp, yet I'm also glad for her too, because she thrives there. The summer brings out an independent streak in Stacie. For example, most of her pals at camp are from the city, but Stacie's bus left from Long Island. Stacie had no interest in any of the girls on the suburban bus and chose to sit by herself. This is a kid who is constantly with friends during the year or talking to them online. It seemed a little out of character for Stacie. Stacie did not shed a tear but I sensed she would be lonely without Hillary or Peri. The girls are all so close. This was Stacie's first summer away alone and I hoped she would not get into too much trouble. It would not have surprised me if she had concocted a scheme for smuggling candy into camp because she loves candy. She had probably even brought along her Hammacher Schlemmer catalog, I imagined, and was calculating her first purchase.

Here is the first poem I wrote to Stacie that summer:

A bolt of lightning flashed across the sky
The sun was smiling, I wondered why

Not a cloud was in view
The sky was so blue

So why the lightning I asked Kendall she's my friend
She said you're silly I won't pretend

I cleared my glasses and looked again
Ten bolts more and ten little men

On broomsticks rising and falling
Screaming, Stacie they were calling

Was I dreaming or was I wishing
I looked again these men were fishing

Clouds appeared and one man departed from his broom
The cloud took shape and formed a room

Not exactly a room perhaps a dock
With flying chairs, umbrellas and a clock

And out of all the falling debris
A figure in glasses I began to see

I knew I'd seen the person before
Although certainly not in any store

He called my name as if he knew me well
He had a secret he needed to tell

Come fly with me on this starry night
Up in my galaxy it's quite a sight

You will pass waterfalls of tomatoes
And mountains made of red potatoes

It gets quite hot, very hot, even hotter
Come fly with me, even if I'm not Harry Potter

Love, Dad

Chapter VII

DID I FORGET TO SAY THANK YOU?

JUNE 26, 2001. HILLARY'S GRADUATION ceremony was last night. I was very happy that she graduated because her grades had been going down each marking period for the past few years. Once these girls get involved with boys the grades go out the window and it's party time. Hillary's high school experience was not the most pleasant, and although she had a few close friends like Carly and Meredith, most of the girls were extremely affected and made Hillary look like an angel. I remember one 'friend' who came over a few years back and referred to our house as a ghetto house because Hillary did not have a VCR in her bedroom. The same girl referred to another friend's mother whom she saw scrubbing the floor as someone resembling her maid. This girl was banned from my house and the other mom cast her out, too.

Getting back to the graduation ceremony, it was incredibly emotional. It surprised me that I actually did not cry, although I did fight back some tears. I'm really becoming a tough guy. My mother joined us and I was glad she was there, as this was a milestone in our family. My mother is aware that things are not always easy for me. She senses things, although not everything is openly discussed, and she has always been there for my girls for all the recitals, graduations, birthdays, even camp visiting days. The top three students spoke at the ceremony. The third ranked graduate spoke on mathematical and scientific formulas and it was rather boring, but good luck to him. He was quite humble in admitting mistakes he had made. I like people who can laugh at themselves. Next, the second top student and then the valedictorian spoke. Both students were very warm and sincere and I felt so proud for their families. I loved the enthusiasm the black students showed for each other. Such exhilaration is to be admired, especially when this energy is displayed as moving perfection on a dance floor, dancing us white folk into the ground. But like the clarity of a perfect white diamond reflecting its colorful hues, the melodic, flowing, soothing sounds emanating from the chorus resonated a joyous chord that sparkled within me. My Hillary was in that chorus. I could actually hear Hillary's voice when they sang and I was beaming. I was so proud and happy for all the children who won awards. I'm sure they worked hard for them. At first I felt a little sad that Hillary did not receive an award, but I know in my heart Hillary is a special, talented, spirited young lady. I know she loves me. And the award for "Capturing My Heart" goes to... Hillary.

I may have already told you this, but when I say good-bye to Jodi or the children I always say, "I love you," and it's something the kids have picked up on. It feels so good to have your child say, "I love you." That is how they end a conversation, too. Try saying it to your partner or kids. Eventually they will say it back and you don't even have to ask them to say it. I've got three teenage daughters and I will take an "I love you" anytime I can get one.

It's June 28th. I have been feeling pretty strong lately and I find myself in much better spirits. I went to the gym last night. I usually go twice a week and the workout is pretty

intense. It consists of about 1¼ hours of weight training followed by 30 minutes of stomach exercises. On Wednesdays
Lisa gives a half-hour abs class. It's a great workout. I may be
the oldest person in the class, but I keep up fairly well.
Considering the abs class is after the weight training, there is
something to be said for my endurance, also. The workouts
always put me in a good mood and I like talking to the people there. I met Hillary's friend James at the gym and we
chatted. I always like to hear what these kids are doing for
the summer and anything else they feel like telling me. It
would be an invasion of Hillary's privacy, but I would love
to ask her friends what Hillary is really like, not the Hillary
I know. I suppose if they were ever to talk about her in front
of me I would have to say (very timidly), "Please stop talking about my Hillary; this is an invasion of her privacy."
Anyhow, James told me he was working for his father in his
dry cleaning store in Brooklyn for the summer. It was time to
do another exercise routine, so this gave me a chance to think
of my next question or comment. We started discussing dry
cleaning bills and decided the average family must spend
around $50 per week. I suggested to James that he contact
a dozen of his friends and offer to do their dry cleaning for
the summer. If you multiplied that by ten weeks, it would
total $6,000. James would pick up the dirty laundry and
deliver the clean clothes. I told him his father would really
appreciate it. I rephrased it and said parents really appreciate
it when their children do thoughtful things for them. I hope
he took my advice. If you are a child out there, and after all,
we are all children, do something nice; go out of your way
and do something unexpectedly kind for your parents today.

Similar to wanting to know what Hillary is like when she
is not around me, I have this fantasy that I can go back in
time and appear in Stacie's class. I would be the new kid in

school and I could stay the same age as Stacie as long as I didn't reveal my true self and real age. Would Stacie like me? Would she let me hold her books? Would she include me in her group of friends or would she label me another dork? Stacie's mind travels in so many directions, would she share her thoughts, and more important, would she share her candy? Stacie loves candy, so I say to whoever buys our house one day: I cannot guarantee it will be delivered free of candy wrappers. I wonder if there is a checklist when you buy a home: no rats, no asbestos, no termites, yes to candy wrappers... we didn't like that house anyway.

Who knows what kind of treasures will be discovered when my house is sold? Perhaps my buried shoes from a past chapter of my life and a future chapter in this book will fly at unearthly speeds and their coordinates of time and place will crash, and flying out of my computer screen will be a footprint that reconfigures itself into the three dimensional lost shoe of the lost boy. And then I will write a book on how they were transported over a *datatimeline* thus proving my theory how refrigerators can travel not only through space, but also through time, thus proving time flies.

It seems as if another year has flown by, even though I last wrote yesterday. Yeah, you know what I'm talking about, *mmmmmmmarathon* time! It's Marathon Season and Jodi and I just found out our names were not selected to be entrants in the 2001 New York City Marathon. The selection process is by lottery, but it is common knowledge that if you know someone in the New York Road Runners Club, you're a shoe-in. Now, don't go calling the feds on the Road Runners because I'll surely never get a number. The lottery is legit, but they don't lottery off all the numbers. They save a few, or a few thousand, for people who write letters asking to run. Imagine that, you non-runners. We lie and write the tallest tale we can so we can punish our body and inflict torturous pain to every nerve ending in our body. Sick, absolutely sick! I can't understand why they turned me down when I was perfectly honest and told them my 121-year-old grandmother had miraculously regained her vision and her doctors in Russia agreed to let her visit me in New York for the running of the 2001 New York City Marathon. She even purchased her ticket and would have to decide if she would give up her medicine or her food for the month. I even sent a photo of Grandma, but first I crinkled it into a small ball so there would be extra wrinkles. Foiled again! The truth, you want the real truth? I wrote a letter and submitted pages from my manuscript and I thought the Road Runners Club would give me a number, but as of this date, no number. So for the first time in nine years I will not be running the marathon. If you believe that, you obviously do not know me yet, and I may have to drag you along for a training run. My training for the marathon has started and I have already completed my 15-mile run. I have also been injured and have been forced to miss a few days of running. Yesterday was my first day running in Central Park again. No external human force on this planet will keep me from running the 2001 New York City Marathon. Last year, when I was not selected to be an entrant, I contacted the New York City Runners Club and explained my story about how my wife and I have been running for the past several years and how this annual event is essential for my health, my marriage, and quite possibly my life. The Road Runners Club decided to allow me to participate in the 2000 marathon, and I would now like to thank them. It is my fervent hope that they again consider my request; they'd just better let my wife and me run! I have often wondered where Jodi and I rank as a married couple in our age group. As individuals we both come in at the top 20%

for our age group. Is it possible that our combined time classifies us as the fastest married couple in the New York City Marathon for our age group? I asked the Road Runners Club that question, but since running is an individual sport they did not have any statistics on married couples. Perhaps someday they will keep records.

Come on, *Newsweek*. You guys can make anything happen! Your sister company, the Washington Post, practically single-handedly overthrew a president. Let's get some stats on married couples running the marathon. Make me your poster boy for AIDS. Send me anywhere to speak except mountainous terrain, arctic conditions or deserts. Running on steep surfaces can lead to injuries, and temperatures below 20 degrees or above 80 degrees take a toll on my body. Or let me jog around the United Nations General Assembly chanting, "Let's get the medicine out there for all people and stop talking about dollars! And let's find a cure!"

Or send me to Washington. I pose this question to any fat cat senator who has ever once voted down funding for AIDS: How would you vote if your own child, a grandchild, a nephew or a best friend's child was HIV positive? Well guess what, I may not be that close to you, but somewhere out there is such a child, grandchild, nephew or best friend's child. I challenge all my readers to stand up to your senator and tell him your story and maybe, just maybe, this senator will never vote against funding for AIDS projects. Now more than ever, since the senate and country are in such a statistical dead heat, it is important for us collectively to voice our concerns.

It's so ironic that Bush won the Presidency and has been conducting his Presidency as though he won a landslide victory and the country handed him a mandate to fulfill his legislative agenda. Nothing could be further from the truth since President Bush did not win the popular vote. His party has lost its majority in the senate with Senator Jeffords' recent abdication of his Republican Party seat to become an Independent. Welcome to the 21st century, Mr. President. Millions of Americans do not fit into society's norm with regard to sexual preference, and many of us break laws regarding the use and abuse of alcohol, but we are all citizens of this land, and AIDS-infected people do not deserve to die any more than people with cancer or heart disease deserve to die. Why should we research cancer when so many people get cancer from smoking cigarettes and everyone knows that cigarette smoking is linked to cancer? The same is true for overweight people. You eat too much, you get fat, and you get a heart attack. There is a common denominator in all these diseases and that is they are partially genetic. Visits to psychologists will not change a person's sexual orientation. How many times have you seen a family where everyone is fat? And what about our Presidents? Even our current President's family seems to have a problem with alcohol. I'm sure the Bushes wish they never had this problem. There are people who cannot have a single glass of alcohol without becoming alcoholics, just as there are people who cannot puff on one cigarette without becoming slaves to nicotine. Yet we are a caring society and we must care about all people. We give aid to countries all over the world. What about Americans who are suffering? And what about all the children around the world who are growing up orphans because there was no money for medicine to save their parents? At least when my grandchildren ask me one day what I did for this cause, I'll be able to say I wrote a book, pleading to get the medicine out to all people; and I did this at the cost of subjecting my family to ridicule because their grandfather was bisexual.

Sometimes my goals seem lofty and sometimes they are very personal. Jodi phoned me to find out what I've done to get us into the marathon and I told her nothing. I need to do something because Jodi will not rest until we are officially accepted as participants in the 2001 New York City Marathon.

In case you are wondering, of course I ran the '98, '99 and '00 marathons. You need to be sitting down for this one. In 1998 my time was 3 hours 23 minutes 33 seconds. Yes, you heard right! In case you are not aware, that is an amazing time. My average mile clocked in at 7 minutes 46 seconds. I was sure this time was a fluke. I had just shaved 14 minutes from my overall best time in 1996. I could not even break four hours until my mid-40s. I was amazing, not nearly as amazing as the blind runner from the Achilles Track Club who whizzed by me. I remember telling Ivan at Midtown Realty who hardly ever had a kind word to say about me, and I think even he was impressed. Friends and relatives were congratulating me and I felt great. My mother was there and I really appreciated her being there. Maybe this year I will ask ten or fifteen people to cheer me on. Just because I've run eleven or twelve marathons, don't think they begin to get easier. Remember, I'm supposedly getting older, okay maybe better also. I always have my name printed on the front of my shirt with my expected time on the back of my shirt. People scream out my name and I feel like an athletic icon. In 2000, my time was 03:42 which really is not such a bad time for me at my age. My '99 time was 03:45 which was disappointing after coming off a 03:23 finish a year earlier. I have no goal for my time this year except to be the fastest I can be and to never quit trying my hardest. If I succeed in that goal then I will have won the race. If my time is below 03:42 I'll be happy; below 3:30 ecstatic; under 03:23 orgasmic; and if books could speak, get ready for the sequel, *Under 03:23*, and one super headache!

It's June 29th, 2001 and Stacie has been away for a few days. I think the break is good for both of us because Stacie and I are too similar. We are both strong-willed, stubborn and oftentimes we each must have our own way. This is the first time Stacie has been away while the rest of the gang is home, so I get a little reflective. I'm being extra nice to Isabel. Isabel is the family cat. Jodi and I are not animal people and we both decided we did not want any animals. A few months ago a stray cat whom we named Isabel found us. Isabel was deep, deep into her 9th life. We did not know her condition was quite that serious at the time, but she had a fever and the vet said if we had not brought her in, she probably would have died of dehydration. Jodi telephoned me at work and told me there was a kitten with a damaged eye that a bird had attacked. She asked me what she and Stacie should do. I told them to leave the cat as it was not our responsibility. I called Jodi on her cell phone a few hours later and asked her where she was and she told me she was at the vet's. The cat came home with them, but they promised me it would be gone in a few days when its fever returned to normal. I refused to look at the cat because I am the original softy and knew that as soon as I saw the cat there would be no way I could throw her out on the street. I actually held firm for about two days, but then I began to feel really mean because I wouldn't even look at the cat, especially since Stacie now adored the cat. Finally I broke down and peeked in on Isabel and the rest is history. For once I came across as a nice guy. Actually I'm really not that stupid. I realized the cat was staying, so there would be no point to my suggesting otherwise. Guess who my best friend in the house is now? You're right, Isabel. Isabel has taken a liking to me, but it's quite clear that Stacie is her favorite. Okay Stacie, you were right on this one.

You won't believe who I saw today: Mrs. Fishman, the French teacher! Jodi and I were jogging on the boardwalk in

Long Beach and Jodi said hello to someone. I asked her who she was speaking with and when I found out it was Mrs. Fishman, I had to turn around and say hello. Mrs. Fishman has been such an inspiration to Stacie, and interestingly enough, Stacie has been an inspiration to Mrs. Fishman. I thanked her for the wonderful year that Stacie had just completed. She also thanked us for raising Stacie so well. Mrs. Fishman adores all my girls and was hoping that someday there might be one more Brodsky girl to grace her classroom. She mentioned that Stacie says hello to all her teachers in French. Quite the petite mademoiselle, my little one.

I started thinking back to the earlier years and Kathleen Rubenfeld, an elementary teacher that all my girls had. What a terrific, enthusiastic, caring, likable teacher! My kids all had a great year with her. And then there was Dr. Kavarsky, a real fighter for Peri, who deserved to be in a gifted program but was somehow passed up. I wrote a letter to the local paper, the *South Shore Record*, and it was printed. It was titled *Getting Called to the Principal's Office:*

> I was always a good student... not a genius or anything, since I got good grades only by working hard. My behavior could have been a little better, although I'm told it improved as I got older. Then, all of a sudden, I get called to the principal's office.
>
> I never even spoke to a principal in my life. My attendance at school this year was minimal, and I probably wouldn't have recognized the principal if I saw him in the street. I didn't even know where his office was... and worse yet, I couldn't even remember one of those principals from another time. Another time? Oh, I forgot to tell you: I attended Lawrence Junior High 30 years ago.

If you haven't figured it out, I was called to the principal's office about a scheduling problem my daughter was having.

I won't bore you with the details. Suffice it to say, Dr. Kavarsky, the principal, and Ms. Tobin, assistant sixth grade administrator at Lawrence Junior High, turned out to be amazingly caring, concerned, real people.

They seemed to understand, appreciate, and take a sincere interest in my child. I could even imagine them knowing her by name if they saw her in the hall. I am absolutely certain no principal ever knew my name, or for that matter, 90% of the student body.

Dr. Kavarsky said we could stay in touch. He didn't say: call the department head or the executive assistant or special chairperson to such and such committee.

I actually left the meeting with a lump in my throat and a very special feeling that there are people out there who really do care. So thanks, Dr. Kavarsky and Ms. Tobin, for being part of the Lawrence school system.

When somebody does something nice and caring for my children or me, the world must know it. The *South Shore Record* probably has a circulation of only a few thousand, but when this book is read, many more people will realize Dr. Kavarsky is a fighter for the most important group in society, the children. Thanks, Dr. Kavarsky and Mrs. Rubenfeld.

I'm in a strange mood today, a mood to forgive people and a mood to thank people. Elaine, yeah, my sister-in-law. You have a very strong feeling for your family, your immediate family, and your parents who are no longer living. I remember you being a very caring daughter. I think we had some minor disagreements a lifetime ago and I hardly remember what they were, but I always respected your closeness with your family.

I've had the opportunity to work with some wonderful people over the years. Dawn has been my secretary for almost half her life. We have been through a lot, including about twenty-five operations to restore her broken face; her unbroken spirit carried us through this difficult time. This unwavering spirit was recalled and tested, but it would not die. We also endured about a hundred visits to the doctor for her son Nicholas. Nicholas is fine now, perhaps a little better than the average kid, because he knows the joy of not being poked at by a doctor anymore. In spite of Dawn's own challenges, she always offers a good caring ear for my family and me. Frank and Nelson, you guys are just the best and I'm proud and lucky to know two super fathers and friends. Dan, Greg and Karina have all always been there for me, creatively and as friends. Gary, we all miss you; you were the spark of the office in the old days. And not to forget Monica. Thanks, Monica, and all you guys.

The next person I would like to thank is a very good friend of Peri's, Jilian. Jilian and Peri are inseparable. Jilian has been there for all the good times and the not-so-good times. Jilian has a quiet reserve about her and honestly, I hardly know her, but if Peri likes her, so do I. One of my main dilemmas in writing this book is I do not want to hurt my family. Children can be mean and so can grownups. There will be people making fun of my girls because of me. I would like to think my children's friends will be supportive of them, but in Jilian's case I understand there may be family pressure to break up Peri and Jilian. First off, Jilian, even though I may have disagreements with your parents, I have never told Peri that she shouldn't be your friend and I have always been nice to you. Anyone who's a good friend to Peri is a good person and welcome in my home. Second, and this goes for anyone who has hurt me, we are all human and we all make mistakes. If anyone feels he has done me wrong, face it, apologize, and let's move on. My life is getting complicated, and with the publishing of this book, my family and I will need all our friends.

While still in a forgiving mood, I'd like to make amends with the Sesslers, a nice couple on my block whom I was annoyed with, but there are always two sides to every story and some things are not clearly black or white. I believe you may have been coaxed into saying some things that were later taken out of context and I overreacted. Let's move on, but not so fast. Since you readers have gotten this far into my book, may I ask you for one more favor? Find forgiveness in your heart. An unforgiving heart steals time and energy from one's capacity to love.

Maybe just one more favor. Can anyone get me a good deal on a room in Nantucket?

It's getting near that time of year. Jodi is planning our annual pilgrimage to Nantucket. It starts with Jodi calling every Bed and Breakfast, looking for a reasonably priced room for three or four nights. We never find that bargain because there are no bargains on Nantucket. My phone bill will confirm that, although I have to admit Jodi found us a decent deal this year. We are off for a five-hour drive in my Miata on July 4th. There is nothing like the anticipated, intoxicating, calming that manifests itself while driving in a convertible for hours on the highway, when your destination is a ferry which will take you to an island where you will step back in history to another era. Nantucket has no traffic lights. All the homes reflect the architecture of olden times. Every lane or alley is a picture postcard. Strolling about the town's ageless cobblestone streets reminds me of the late 1800s—a time my mind has journeyed to. The stores have all sorts of nautical motifs and alfresco paraphernalia. In the antique stores, you can imagine a fleet of masted ships docked at the harbor, unloading their cargo of treasures from halfway 'round the world. Each artifact from Europe and the Orient has a story. Of course there are local antiques from the island's own homes as well, perhaps from a seventh-generation resident who has decided to cash in on the island's out-of-sight real estate prices. The ghosts of his ancestors will creak and dwell in the canopy bed that was left behind where seven generations of Coffins or Gardners were conceived. The island boasts some of New England's best restaurants and the prices reflect the difficulty of bringing food and perishables to an island that is so often closed off from the rest of the world because of its fog and inclement weather. The unpredictable weather and a longing to be back in my past marooned days on the island conjure up romantic memories for me. Undoubtedly my fellow islanders have similar tales, as we savor yet another day of the familiar harbor scent. The harbor is filled with boats and yachts from around the world and the sunsets are just a little more beautiful than anywhere else. This Isle of Americana is known to hold scores of weddings every weekend. The local tradition of throwing a penny into the sea as you depart the island to assure a return trip is known to all. So come with me to my Nantucket, jog and bicycle, shop and browse, have dinner and an ice-cream cone, and take a picture of Jodi and me as we play away the weekend. If the ferries go on strike and we do become stranded on the island, I will be the next to last person in the world to protest and my wife will be the last.

Some of my better writing is done on Nantucket, whether it's a poem to the girls or a card to Jodi.

Dear Jodi,

I saw this picture as a child and wondered what it would be like to open the window and look outside and see what I could see. There was a magic potion set upon the checkered tablecloth that would allow me to see forever or see the most beautiful sight in the world. I chose quality, not quantity so I chose the most beautiful sight in the world. Would I be seeing the most decorative, ornate stained glass window set inside a cathedral that reached for the sky, or a bridge that stretched across the ocean, or a landscape filled with waterfalls set within rainbow-colored mountains with hues never before imagined, in a sunset that would endure forever as it reflected in a forest where all the leaves were turning pumpkin, crimson, amber, and golden yellow or yellow-gold?

I opened the window and to my surprise saw nothing. Then I turned to my side and realized the most beautiful person God ever created was lying next to me. Not only did I get to see the most beautiful sight, I also got to hold the most beautiful person for the rest of my life.

Love Richard

Jodi and I have been to Nantucket almost a dozen times over the years. We took the children three times and we captured the perennial, yet ageless spirit of the island on film. I remember our first visit with the kids. Jodi was 39 at the time and I wanted to do something really special for her 40th birthday, such as chartering a plane and hosting a surprise party on Nantucket. Our parents, brothers and sisters, and friends would be on board the chartered flight, and I would have a limousine drive us to the runway. Boy, would Jodi be surprised to see our children and guests aboard the plane! I thought chartering a plane would be less costly but I was wrong. The girls and I made about a dozen or so calls until we finally dropped the idea and decided to celebrate Jodi's 40th at a local Spanish restaurant. You may not believe this, but I managed to keep the secret and Jodi was completely surprised. I knew it would be more than a little difficult to keep the secret because I am never short on words, and asking me not to say anything... well, I guess you know me by now. Anyhow, I had to distract Jodi because we parked the car about 90 seconds from the restaurant and I was concerned Jodi would recognize our friends' cars. I decided to distract her by talking about her health. I'm convinced women live longer than men because they are so paranoid about their health that they frequent doctors a good deal more than their male counterparts. And sure enough Jodi began her medical discourse and she was totally shocked when she realized the 60 people inside were there for her birthday. The party was a wonderful success! We were disappointed that her parents, her brother, and her sister Patti could not attend, but we were thrilled that Suzie and Stu (Jodi's sister and her husband) drove in from Washington to share in our little fiesta. Thanks, guys. I wrote Jodi a special card for the occasion.

We have been journeying for many months through the Greek Islands, Italian Riviera, small towns on the Danube that haven't been discovered in decades, through meandering roads and streams that dot the Austrian countryside, and now we have arrived in France where an artist begs us to stay so he can paint your picture in the best light. We tell him we have no plans for we have worked hard for years and our only itinerary is love and reminiscing of days worth saving, almost as if to preserve time and our love and desire for each other. The artist gives you a blue hat which he goes on to explain is a Hungarian 'crown' from a beautiful princess who abdicated her throne to follow her lover around the globe. Her love and beauty are legendary and so, too, is everything about you, so by royal edict you will wear the crown.

We gaze at each other and upon the lake; materializing, setting forth in a blaze a skyful of colors, a procession of light waltzes upon the dribbling ripples of the lake. By a royal decree it is mandated that the colony of lowly ripples be uplifted and that henceforth they shall be elevated to waves. As if empowered by a divine right of their own, these waves majestically transform into a colorful pageant of green and gold and yellow and lime, melding to create a halo-like backdrop *coronating* your face and body. My eyes refuse to abdicate your regal stature of perfection as exemplified by you, and I become a prisoner of your timeless beauty.

We recall earlier times and wonderful vacations in Nantucket, Bermuda, or a stolen weekend or night without the children. The children are grown and one can only admire how beautiful, successful and loving they have remained. They all have your warmth and love, Jodi. Peri has your laugh and smile, Hillary has your looks, and Stacie likes to take care of me while you both fight in the kitchen over how to cook Dad's favorite dishes.

You've done wonders with the children and we are all better people for that. Your smile is remembered by all who know you and your love is appreciated, returned and very special to me.

Have the best birthday! *Love* Richard

It's Saturday, June 30, 2001, and I just completed a 14.5 mile run in about 02:20. If you do the math you will find that's between a 9.5 and 10-minute mile. So what happened to the 7-minute 46-second mile and who is this guy kidding! Let me tell you something about the human spirit and adrenaline. I'm sure there are scientific studies to prove that certain chemical reactions are occurring as you subject your body to a 26.2 mile run, such as increased levels of certain hormones being produced. For that you can read a science journal, and if you understand it, then try explaining it to me. I'd like to tell you about the human spirit as it relates to my marathon performance and how my body rises to the occasion and just says, "Forget about your training times. This is the New York City Marathon, the greatest marathon in the world, where the route is lined with tens of thousands of fans screaming out your name. I will not disappoint these people who have gathered to cheer 30,000 Olympians who are running a race in which the original marathon runner finished the approximate 24-mile run and dropped dead." This happened in ancient Greece, the cradle of Western civilization, a country I have visited and whose enduring warmth and beauty are timeless. I have a great deal of respect for the arts, architecture and history. Let's not forget that modern day Olympics originated in ancient Greece. So, how am I going to cut two minutes per mile off my time to get to 03:23? First, I may not get to 03:23. The odds are against me, but don't count me out. On the day of the marathon your body is pumped and ready to go. You are surrounded by 30,000 of your peers who all have their stories and have arrived from all over the world. Many are running their first marathon and many have run fifty or more, but everyone is equally excited about just being in this marathon. Each athlete has a goal, even if it is just to finish. Two weeks prior to the marathon, you begin to cut back on your mileage, approximately 20% the first week and another 20% the final week. I don't know how it happens, but the gun goes off, the race begins and I am off to a flying start. The first 10 miles I usually average between 7½ to just under 8 minutes per mile. Strangely enough, I never clock in at these times even when I do a 6-mile run, but somehow your body is electrified and your legs are charged to run like never before. About mile 10, I begin to slow down a little, or a lot; I cannot keep the pace up and that determines if I will run 03:23 or 03:45. The time I ran 03:23 I thought it was a fluke, but I had also run a 03:37 and 03:38 a few years back and, arguably, I should not have finished in those times either, but I did. It still is hard to fathom how a person can run 26.2 miles and how a person can run it at a faster pace than his training pace. One other point I would like to make on behalf of New York City: Central Park is the greatest training ground for the New York City Marathon. Its hills are pretty tough and a 14.5-mile run in the park just might be the equivalent of a 15.5 or 16-mile run on a level surface.

Today's run was not too bad for me, especially since I am coming off an injury. Usually I do a long run when I have taken a day off two days before, but now I have been running either on a treadmill or outside for the last six days. Add that to the fact that it was 81 degrees and humid when we started the run and the temperature must have risen a few degrees during the run. Actually, the trees provide a fair amount of shade in the park, and as long as you drink plenty of water and Gatorade, you should be fine. If you are not used to running six miles a day, then certainly you should not run fifteen on a hot, humid day. Jodi has run on warmer days, yet today was the first time I've seen her get uncomfortable after a run. She was actually feeling a little dizzy and nauseated, but after a little juice and water, she was back to herself in a half-hour. It's okay to push your body, but you have to learn how far you can push it. Jodi found out today and now she is off and about, doing her errands around the city.

We stayed in the city at our pied-a-terre last night. Our nest is in the West 50s on unquestionably the nicest residential street in the area. It's both tree-lined and completely residential, which makes this street unique for the area. If I were related to Pinocchio, my nose would be a mile long. I have been asked by everyone who has seen our apartment how I located such a great getaway. I must have lied a few hundred times and said, "I found it through *The Times*." That was only the partial truth. I knew the apartment was going to be put on the market because I had been with the previous occupant on a few occasions. It would have made great conversation at a family dinner to say, "Oh, funny you should ask, I was having sex with the guy." That reminds me of a great story I heard, and my reaction probably would have been similar to the reactions of the cousins listening to Min's remarks.

Min was married to my mother's first cousin, Sy. All the cousins were at my house in North Woodmere. These cousins were quite a group and I promise not to digress about them now. Anyhow, we had a split-level house and I was walking up the steps to the living room. There was an open railing so I could clearly hear the conversation. Min, who must have been near 60 at the time, said, "My husband hasn't had sex with me in 3 months so I masturbate." I immediately thought I'd better clean my ears! Every year or so, I recall that anecdote with my sister-in-law Liz, who was sitting in the living room with Min and a small group of cousins that day. If I were the husband I would find that statement to be so humiliating. However, I'm sure that when this book is published, I will have my own plethora of reactions to deal with.

Getting back to the apartment, I do not recall the tenant's name at this time, but he was renting it from an out-of-towner who could not continue to rent because of co-op regulations, or perhaps because she just wanted to sell. In any event, I knew the apartment was going to be placed on the market. I found this out the same week that Jodi and I were planning to buy an apartment. This was back in 1998 and I don't think I was keeping up with my writing at the time; that's why you are hearing about this now. I tried to contact the owner but could not reach her. Two days later the apartment was advertised in *The New York Times*. The price was within our price range. The apartment was in the only block I wanted to live on, so everything was perfect. There would be an 'open house' on Sunday; it must have been around early May. At some point prior to our seeing the apartment, I told Jodi how I had come to know about this place. I wasn't sure if her reaction was going to be, "I don't even want to look at it." I suppose there's something romantic about buying a home where two children were raised, and now one is a research doctor and the other works for a non-profit company in poor and destitute countries around the world, and the parents have been married for 53 years and there is a picture on the wall of their 50th anniversary, along with diplomas, citations and awards from Presidents, universities and charities. However, this was not the case. Jodi was actually pretty cool about it. She generally trusts my judgment on design issues, but don't think for a second my wife does not have a sharp mind and opinions of her own. I was aware she had seen very few New York apartments, so we made it our business to visit two or three other buildings that day. They were on streets that I would not consider, but I wanted Jodi to see some other residences and come to her own conclusions, even though I would be lobbying strongly for my choice. She quickly realized this place was really special. The apartment was a second floor walk-up, which was perfect for Jodi and me. The last thing I wanted was a doorman to know my business. I'm actually very private in that respect. I also don't like waiting for elevators and walking 200 feet down an unending corridor where there are from fifteen to thirty doors that look exactly alike. We submitted an offer the same day we saw the apartment; after some minor negotiations we agreed upon a price. I was ecstatic. Our new pad had three large windows in the living/dining area facing south and you could see trees. The ceilings were 10½ feet high. There were brick walls in the living and dining areas, and a working fireplace warmed the interior. It was my dream apartment except for one thing. It was not on the fifth floor.

I had this fantasy when Jodi and I were first married: we would be struggling in our fifth floor walk-up. Jodi would be cooking lasagna and I would come home to the whiff of garlic bread browning itself to perfection beneath my nostrils. Then... Jodi would throw open the front door and the hall would proclaim my wife's culinary talents as a chorus of mouth-watering neighbors eagerly, *busybodiedly*, and quietly unlatched their doors to inhale. We would dine at a small table for two by the window. The table would be dressed in a red checkered tablecloth and we would have a glass of wine and then have dinner. My wife never eats anything fattening, however, so that fantasy went right out the window. We were both thrilled to know that in a few months we would own a piece of the 'apple'.

I told Jodi I was not sure if we were overpaying for the apartment, as I hadn't had a chance to really research the market; perhaps we were paying 10% over market. We planned to keep the apartment for a long time, so 10% over ten years would prove to be an inconsequential amount, since everybody knows that buying real estate in Manhattan is a sound investment. By the time we got to closing I was more aware of prices and guess what, the Kid got lucky! I found out we had more likely underpaid by approximately 10%.

So now it was time to renovate the apartment. We had a limited budget although we never set a specific amount. The bathroom and kitchen were in pretty good shape and we were not going to put any money into fixtures and appliances so we left those rooms intact except for a granite countertop in the kitchen and new lighting. The living room, dining alcove and bedroom took on a theme that made you think you were in Nantucket. Floral area rugs and runners were laid over wood floors. The dining area featured a glass top balanced upon a wrought-iron base filled with silk flowers, designed so that when you had dinner you would see the flowers below the glass. Similarly, a coffee table in the living room had glass set atop an antique white, wrought-iron bird cage. The television perched itself in the corner, surrounded by a white picket fence. A granite slab near the foyer weighted itself on rustic looking, outdoor columns purchased from a nursery. A low wall unit with a limestone top and roughly constructed white painted doors concealed the radiators and air conditioning unit, thus providing storage fronting along the twenty-three-foot long perimeter. Atop the limestone counter two pergolas were constructed with glass shelves and lots of plants and flowers. A couch, two chairs and an ottoman were purchased for the living room. Track lighting, family portraits, and posters with floral, fence and window motifs completed the decor. You'd swear you were anywhere but a New York apartment. Clunky overhead storage doors were removed, the opening was retrimmed, and a window shade was hung. The shade was backlit and a bird hatched and nestled itself, likening the effect of a clerestory window

The bedroom was painted in shades of light blue. We bought a canopy bed finished in Nantucket blue. The canopy was dressed in loosely draped lace and a similar lace pattern beckoned its way to all the windows in the apartment. For the bedroom, old closet doors were removed and it would be 'curtains' for those not-quite-old-enough doors which just missed antique status. Instead of doors, lace backed by a blue fabric would conceal the closet interior. Both windows had granite sills installed and a similar one was installed next to the bed which serves as a night table, while a final sill was notched into a wall. The debilitated overhead storage doors in the bedroom whined and creaked, so they were discarded like an ancient, obsolete great-aunt who no longer serves a purpose. Nobody even remembered whose relation she was. Nobody claimed her or the doors so we were left with a void that needed a fresh face. Surgery was performed and the opening was framed with new arch-shaped mouldings. It resembled a Romanesque window from our aunt's time. Between the arch at the top of the window and the newly transplanted granite sill, an outdoor landscape mural was affixed to the wall. A Noguchi overhead, globelike light fixture was installed and the room took on a very romantic setting. Dimming the overhead fixture provided a moonlit, nocturnal feeling to the room. The lace canopy, a small chest and armoire, and candle wall sconces provided a safe haven for Jodi and me. We both love the apartment and it has become a Saturday night getaway for us, a chance to escape the pressures of our everyday life (although don't think for one second Jodi does not know where the kids are. The older two both have cell phones and Jodi tracks them incessantly).

Last night was Friday and although we usually go out for dinner only on Saturday night, I wanted to take the Mrs. out. We went to Trattoria, a cozy Italian restaurant on Bleecker Street between 6th and 7th Avenues. The food is delicious, the prices are quite reasonable, and the service is excellent. It's a nice friendly staff and since we are somewhat regulars, maybe we are treated a little extra special.

After dinner we went around the corner to Cornelia Street just to visit Michael, Nina, Donna and John. Unfortunately, John was away at a bachelor party in Las Vegas and Donna wasn't there. These individuals make up a warm, caring, and spirited group. Before I review their restaurant Po, I must tell you that the staff itself should be reviewed because they make the restaurant; the food is secondary. By now you know I'm a little nuts... okay, so that's putting it mildly, but I would rather be served a poor to mediocre dinner by a friendly server than a perfect meal by a rude one. In this case you get the best crew, the food is superb, and the prices are very reasonable. These people have taken waitering to an art form; they are truly artists. Where else can you go in New York and get a hug, a good meal and a conversation? If you find another such place, please invite me. Thanks, guys!

Chapter VIII

THE LIFE AND TIMES OF THE COUSINS

I STARTED TELLING YOU ABOUT my mother's cousins, Sy and Min, a few pages back and about the same number of days ago. Let me now introduce you to the rest of the family. My grandmother Beverly had three daughters: Ronnie, Gladys and Vivian. Vivian died at a young age. Beverly had a sister Eva who had two boys, Lester and Sy; Beverly's brother Eli had one son, Mickey; Beverly's other sister Esther had three boys: Hy, Alex and Eli. Beverly had two other brothers, Joey and Morton. Joey never married and Morton married a former Miss Oklahoma. The family was certainly diverse. I hear Joey was a really nice guy, although I never got to know him. These cousins were inseparable. They golfed together, went to cousins' clubs, partied at weekend outings, vacationed together regularly, and went out to dinner together. That is not to say they traveled together in a group of thirty, but more in varied size groups. For example, the majority of this group would be at the cousins' club. My parents used to go on vacations with Betty and Lester every year for the last five years before my father died. A few of the cousins golfed together. As a group they loved partying and having a great time. I remember a lot of liquor being consumed. Everyone would attend the annual tribal festival at Uncle Morton's summer home in Poughkeepsie. I recall Uncle Morton being around 70 and his wife about 25 years younger. The story goes she wasn't Jewish and after his parents died he married out of the religion. The exact number of years ago is unimportant, but I surmise it was more than half a century ago that my great-grandparents died. Back then Jewish people were more religious and my great-grandparents would not have permitted such a marriage. Permitted may be a little harsh, but I think you get the idea. So anyhow, back to the gathering. It wasn't just cousins who were invited to the reunion; it was also longtime family friends. I think some of the cousins came from a line of first cousins who married each other a hundred years ago. This bunch was a little wacky, and I wonder if that had anything to do with their wackiness. I remember hearing stories how two of these cousins' sons tried to pick up girls on their own wedding day! I also remember hearing some rumor about cousins or friends doing something of a sexual nature at the reunion. It was just a few people and every time I ask my mother or Aunt Ronnie about it, which is about every two or three years, I get sent to my room without dinner.

Uncle Morton's wife's name escapes me, and since I don't feel like asking my mother what her name was, she will remain nameless at this time. I imagine it was exciting being married to Morton. He was a famous surgeon who went by the name Morton Berson. I think he changed his name from Berezin to Berson because Berezin was too Jewish. Times have changed dramatically and while anti-Semitism is still prevalent, there currently are ten Jewish senators in Congress. Considering our nation is only a few percent Jewish, that's remarkable. In some respects a reverse phenomenon is going on. Non-Jewish people are proud to say their child married a Jew. After all, we live in relatively prosperous times so there is nothing to blame the Jewish people for. Read the book *The Warburgs*. It will drive home this point. It's my favorite book of all time about a prominent Jewish family dating back to the 1500s. From a historical standpoint, it follows that Jewish people become more politically involved and assimilated during periods of peace and economic stability. So with no war brewing on the family front, Doctor Morton Berson became fully assimilated as a Jewish-American upon his marrying out of the Jewish religion. Back then, Uncle Morton was a renowned plastic surgeon, a pioneer in his field, who had been decorated by the Greek government. My grandmother had a collection of articles about how he had reconstructed faces of wounded soldiers from World War II. He was also a tremendously gifted artist and I am fortunate to have one of his paintings that my grandmother gave me. Morton had three sisters. Morton's poor wife could never measure up to the sisters' standards. She probably blew them off and was glad when the weekend get-together ended. I just remembered her name was Evelyn. Evelyn, if you're around I'd love to hear from you.

In addition to one of Uncle Morton's paintings, I do have one other priceless objet d'art. It was brought over from Russia by my great-grandparents. If you, reader, are twelfth generation American, this story may not mean that much to you because you probably have an attic full of far more valuable heirlooms. But I wonder if you know the history of your treasures. At least we share something in common, and that is at some juncture in time and place our ancestors ventured forth across a sea of obstacles, and claimed their right to dream on American soil, and we are thankful they did. All past generations of immigrants struggled to make life easier for the next generation and the hardest part, I imagine, was saying good-bye to their relatives in the old country, oftentimes leaving a spouse or children behind to establish themselves in this promising new country, America. It was relatively new. Who knew if it would last? There were no guarantees. Think about it for a minute. Do you realize the sacrifices these great-grandparents made? Would you be up to a similar challenge? Do you think these people would like what they see of our world today? Sure, they would marvel at computers, fax machines, CDs, video games, but I wonder what they would think of the people today? I honestly don't know the answer. Would they think we're all lazy? "What's wrong with working a long day? Get out and play and get off the telephone!" Back to my objet d'art. I have a picture in my dining room of a passover seder. I've looked at it dozens of times and maybe a few times a little closer, but I've missed the details. One time I asked Grandma Beverly to tell me about the picture. It must have been valuable because in the old days families traveled very light when they came to America. Grandma showed me the blue box on the table, the few blue posters on the wall and a blue canister or two on the table and explained that the Russian writing on these items was from a Russian tea company. Back then you mailed a few coupons to prove you had purchased this brand of tea and maybe a few rubles for shipping via the 'Overland Siberian Express' and the tea company would *SibEx (overmonth)* you a poster. I would rather have my poster and this story than some painting worth thousands.

Heirlooms and objets d'art are memories of days gone by. But where are we today, Richard? Let me tell you about my favorite cousin, Steven, the dentist. Steven's grandmother and my grandmother were sisters. They hated each other for a hundred years, actually about 198 years if you add up their combined years before they died. Okay, so I exaggerate a little. They probably didn't hate each other for all those years. My grandmother Beverly died a few years ago at 96 and her sister Eva died about the same time at 102. Eva was survived by her fourth husband who was turning 103. Some of the arguments were so silly. It was fortunate they did not affect my mother's relationship with Eva's daughter-in-law, Betty. My mother and Betty were as close as sisters. I always liked Betty and her son Steven. Steven divorced his first wife and married Valerie. Poor Valerie. She got stuck with Steven's bad sense of humor. I think it's even worse than mine. I actually like Steven and Valerie quite a bit. Steven is our family dentist. He gives us price breaks and generally accepts the meager payments the insurance company allows. Steven and Valerie love nice houses and cars just like everyone else, but they also have a good sense of family. For the past four years I've stopped using Steven as my dentist. I would be morally and possibly legally obligated to advise him of my HIV status, and that is something I could not bring myself to do. I never for a moment wanted Steven to think I stopped using him as a dentist because I was dissatisfied with his professionalism. His jokes, however, needed work. Actually, if the truth be told, I am about to reveal one of our family's darkest secrets. Steven's oldest client was his grandmother, Eva. Can you imagine having to look inside your grandmother's mouth? I can't.

We were talking about my mother's cousins. The next story ripped the family apart. The closeness the cousins exuded was flickering out as the family's tide lowered and its bountiful cargo (its closeness) would be a treasure lost at sea. The lighthouse that navigated my great-grandparents to America's shores would no longer beacon its light on the cousins. And so the once unsinkable 'Ship of Dreams' would no longer set sail as its masts flapped aimlessly without guidance or direction. This once proud vessel that had weathered many a storm no longer had the desire to stay the course; navigating the cousins on their cruise through life now, would be an itinerary not fulfilled, a voyage dreamed of, a voyage unjourneyed. So what really changed *The Life and Times of the Cousins...* what else? Money, greed and jealousy... and my Uncle Joey. Uncle Joey had a nervous breakdown in his early 20s. Our pictures show a dashing young man dancing. The Berezin men and women were all quite handsome and beautiful. Their spouses were attractive and so were their offspring. Uncle Joey received a pension from his employer and lived frugally his whole life. Frugally would be putting it politely, but let's leave it at that. He always owned a car, and as much as I prided myself on knowing the year and model of all cars, his buggies were so old I didn't have a clue. I think they were just new enough for them not to be considered antiques. Uncle Joey neglected his health over the years. He was not the type to visit the doctor for his annual visit. He went to the doctor when he was sick or not at all. I suspect my mother and Aunt Ronnie must have dragged him to a doctor because they went to visit him often. I don't know if it was once a month or twice a month, but I remember they genuinely cared about him and they even liked him. One time Uncle Joey came to our house and presented Hillary with a five-dollar bill. That was quite out of character for him. It wasn't that he was cheap or unkind. The man had had a nervous breakdown and he lived his life differently, that's all. All the cousins considered him the 'black sheep'. Any time my mother wanted to share an Uncle Joey story, the cousins were not interested. He sometimes came by my father's place and my father would give him smoked fish, since he was in the business. I think my father had a soft spot for Uncle Joey. One day Uncle Joey was not feeling well. He must have been in his mid 70s at the time. My mother took him to the doctor, where he learned he had terminal cancer. He died a short time later. Uncle Joey, as I remember, left most of his money to my mother and a small amount to the cousins.

Uncle Joey was a class act, and all these cousins could have taken a lesson from him. At the time Uncle Joey died, my mother was a widow. When someone loses her soulmate for life, people should have a little compassion for the widow and show additional respect, kindness and consideration. Not my cousins. They felt cheated and accused my mother of stealing Uncle Joey's money. One thing I will say about my mother is she is the most honorable person you will ever meet. There is no way my mother would suggest to Uncle Joey what he should be doing with his money. Eva, grandma Beverly's sister and her son Sy initiated a lawsuit. I think they were further offended that Eva was not the executor of Uncle Joey's estate. She was, after all, the eldest. All the cousins left the lawyering to these two. The cousins wanted no part of the *legaljistics* except the money, should they win in court. So where did this leave my mother? Obviously she had to hire a lawyer. Most of the cousins were mute on the subject, but would they take her side when the case went to trial? Of course not. I felt really sorry for Betty, Lester's wife, who had been suffering from cancer for many years. The lawsuit put a real damper on my mother's relationship with Betty. Until then the two gals had been like sisters. I didn't think much of these cousins, but I always liked Betty and felt she was dealt a bad hand in life. Lester, her husband was no bargain. Her son Steven whom I mentioned earlier is a great guy, by contrast, and was very close to his parents. Finally my mother began speaking to Betty again. I might have had a minor role in this because I told my mother that Betty was a special person; my mother knew it, too. This was one of the few occasions in my life when I've felt that my family actually listened to me and took my advice. While I was growing up, my family repeatedly said I had 'book smarts' but not 'street smarts'. Maybe I was finally acquiring the latter or maybe I just felt sad for Betty because I imagined she needed my mother's support and love. Being deprived of any love, whether for a moment or a lifetime, is so unfair. In the end, Betty and my mother became close and we were all very sad when she died. I will always remember her as a fiercely independent, intelligent woman who fashioned her life around family, art, literature, theatre, travel and museums. She always had an opinion and never hesitated to say what was on her mind. I think she would appreciate my book and my honesty. She is the very type of person I would pursue for her comments. I never asked my mother what Betty had thought about the lawsuit. Perhaps they never discussed it because it could only cause a wedge in their friendship and in Betty's marriage. In her heart I'm sure Betty was happy when my mother won the lawsuit. I still have some vague recollection of Aunt Eva flying in from Florida at age 95. The plane had to make an emergency landing in Washington because Aunt Eva had fallen into a coma. All this for a few dollars. Miraculously she recovered and lived on for another seven years; almost single-handedly, along with her son Sy, she had destroyed the Berezin clan.

Writing this book has given me a keener realization of the importance of family. I feel a loss, not being able to share my writing with my mother who I know would definitely not approve. Mother, I'm sorry. I hope this book doesn't cause you too much grief. Surely you knew I was somehow destined to be a little different. You always said you were afraid to get up every day because you never knew what crazy idea I would have that day. Mother, I'm also a little sad because I wish I could show you this book before it goes to print, but I know you would discourage me. I don't know if I'm strong enough to write my story without family 'weighing in', but I'm almost 49; I can't carry this 'baggage' a day more.

Children. Do we ever really grow up and change and become adults, or are we just grown up clones of the children we once were? I don't think I've changed all that much. I remember being in a store with my mother when I was four. The store had a pyramid display of cans and I wondered what the reaction would be if I pulled the bottom can out. I knew the display would tumble. But what about my mother's reaction? What about the other shoppers? What about the owner? Each witness would be viewing the incident from a different perspective. Sorry, you'll have to buy the sequel to find out what happened... or maybe you figured it out. My mother hauled me out of that store so fast I don't think anyone had a chance to respond. Sometimes you can save your 4-year-old but you can't protect your 48-year-old son forever.

Ahhhhhhh... the age of innocence. Those days, another time, another life. At the age of six I used to draw pictures of houses and put them in my red notebook. From that time on I always wanted to be an architect. That's pretty fortunate, considering some kids never know what they want to be when they grow up, and most grownups never end up doing what they really want to do. Really, wouldn't all of us rather be race car drivers, professional surfers, ballplayers or ski jumpers? I think I'm partial to ski jumping because I have often imagined myself in flight. So now I'm an architect. Architecture is the ultimate art form. It's three dimensional and has a utilitarian purpose, unlike painting or sculpting, and architecture can also be quite sculptural. Unfortunately, my creativity has been limited primarily to architectural interiors. I've always had a strong interest in designing private residences or multi-family homes. When I interviewed with Skidmore, Owings and Merrill in Texas, the senior partner told me that the housing project I had designed in college was the best design he had ever seen. Unfortunately, I never got to work on new housing, so I feel as if I've been creatively deprived. Skidmore, the largest architectural firm in the country, and I were just not cut out for each other. One architect, Ralph, who sat near me, really got to me. He was the type of guy whose smirk you'd want to wipe off with your fist as soon as you saw him. Ralph and my brother Victor had been rooming together and had some disagreement. Ralph threatened to throw out Victor's luggage. In defense, I then menaced Ralph to return my brother's luggage immediately. I think I did this in front of 30 people, or at least within their hearing range. This was not the typical demeanor for a big prestigious office where the standard uniform consists of a navy blazer and whatever else goes with a navy blazer. So here I am with my creativity stifled and a need to get a reaction from people. Writing a book is creative, and somehow I think I will definitely get a reaction from this book.

One thing I've been doing a little different these days is not eating lunch. I prefer the feeling of being empty or a little hungry. When you are full your senses are dulled and you become a little lazy. I feel much more creative and alert when I eliminate a meal. You should try it sometime. It sort of helps bring things into focus and also helps you concentrate.

Chapter IX

A REVELATION, NOT ALL FUN AND GAMES, AND A TRIP TO NANTUCKET

ANOTHER SATURDAY NIGHT IN THE Village and dinner at Po. We like having late dinners because it works in with my schedule for taking medicine. It's also a little more relaxed at the end of the evening when the restaurant quiets down. The tables are all quite close at Po, so it's hard not to talk to the people at the next table or even one table beyond. On this evening we sat next to Ken and Michelle, a nice couple from Boston who were getting married in a few months. A more handsome pair wasn't in view. There was a nice chemistry between them and the young lady gave me her card and asked me to keep her informed about the book I was writing. I did not reveal the contents of the book, but I did reveal the title. Near the end of our meal we found out it was Nina's birthday. Nina, just think if this book sells a million copies everyone will know your birthday is June 30th. If everyone sends you a birthday card, as I am requesting they do to support finding a cure for AIDS, there will be a million of them delivered to Po every June 30th. I will contact the newspapers and television stations to come by and watch you open your cards. One other request I make is you send a card on a piece of paper rather than one purchased from a store. The card must also be hand delivered, no stamp or messengers. If my readers want to enclose a check for a few dollars to an AIDS-related charity, in lieu of purchasing a card and stamp, that's okay too. Nina, it was Michael, your fellow server, who told me it was your birthday, so you can thank him, too. In fact, I will volunteer Michael to sort out the checks and get them to the right charity. And if the book becomes a best-seller, I promise to be there on Nina's birthday signing my book, as long as you bring her a card. When Jodi and I found out it was Nina's birthday she was not in the room. I got everyone's attention in the restaurant, and told them it was her birthday and that when the piece of cake I ordered was served, everyone should sing happy birthday to her. Nina's birthday wish was especially sweet when she said, "I wish the Brodskys could be my guardian angel." This birthday wish brought a good smile to my face, and I wore my smile warmly all weekend.

The rest of the weekend was quiet, although I did hear from my friend Monica. I had given Monica an early draft of the first 55 pages for her comments. She found me to be self-ish and inconsiderate, and she had to put the draft down for a while. I think what bothered her most was my insensitivity to Jodi. Jodi needed to talk about my being HIV positive and other things that go with it and I selfishly would say, "I can-not talk about this because it gets me depressed." Too bad, Richard! It's not enough saying how much I love my wife. Why don't I do something for Jodi, like listen? What does Jodi want? I have to listen to my wife. Jodi has been seeing a therapist and has always asked me to go with her. I have always declined, until now. Finally I offered to attend a few sessions, but only because Jodi wanted me to, and not because I chose to. I was hoping Jodi would decide that if I didn't want to go on my own, then I shouldn't go just because she asked me to. I think Therapist Susan is dying to get her claws into me! Maybe I'm just flattering myself, but Susan must be wondering what I must be like since Jodi has not thrown me out after all I've put Jodi through.

Just when you are feeling good about things, something always pops up. Do you recall when I told you I was concerned about Hillary graduating? My mother even came to the graduation and I told you I did not shed a tear at the ceremony. That's 90% true, although walking to the car in the parking lot, I did drop a bucket or two when I told my mother I had been concerned that Hillary would not graduate. Hillary had contracted the worst case of senioritis ever reported. We had just gotten home from Po at 1:30 a.m. when Jodi found Hillary's report card in her room, five days after graduation. Apparently she had failed math and would not receive credit for the course. We were concerned this might affect her acceptance to the University of Florida, and Jodi and I were extremely upset with her. Hillary is a bright girl but chooses not to apply herself academically. As a result her grades have gone down over the years. Jodi and I started arguing because I had been telling Jodi all along that Hillary and Stacie needed to spend more time studying, but I was usually shot down. This was now a serious matter, given that Jodi and I had already invested time and money in signing a lease for an apartment and purchasing several plane tickets to visit Hillary at school. I began a chorus of 'I told you so's.' Jodi got very defensive because nobody likes to be proven wrong; moreover, the children's accomplishments and failures are a direct reflection on the parents. In this instance, Hillary's course failure was further exaggerated because Jodi had worked so hard to get Hillary to take the SATs one last time. Thanks to Diana, a very caring tutor, and a few bucks later, Hillary improved her score to 1150. But we turned down the full scholarship to Harvard! Just wanted to make sure you're not sleeping on me, but readers, we are talking about my daughter now; no skim reading here, please. Anyhow, getting accepted to the University of Florida had been a long shot for Hillary. Jodi is an alumna of the school and when Hillary got in, Jodi felt a little bit of herself had been accepted to the school, too. Before Hillary's final acceptance, however, came our confrontation with Hillary's math failure. Our arguing continued until four in the morning. I couldn't sleep, I was so aggravated and overtired.

This is a typical scene where Jodi and I react differently. Jodi is always there to protect her children and fight for them. Maybe things are different now but my mother never went to my school for me, although I never needed her to make her presence known. Every year I always had one bad teacher, but I dealt with it. Maybe it is also different with girls because supposedly they need to be protected more. Since Jodi raises the children, all I ever do is voice my opinion. Then Jodi does as she sees fit. Jodi's mind was racing. How do we get out of this one? Hillary has two best friends, Meredith and Carly. Meredith's dad is a teacher at Hillary's school. Jodi decided to phone Merdith's father, Norman. Norman is a decent guy and basically suggested that Jodi should contact the principal. This is exactly what Jodi did, although the principal was not available for a few days.

I peeked in on Hillary before I went to work today, July 2nd. She looked so sweet and innocent, sleeping. How could this darling child get herself into such a mess? Yeah, right! Did you forget who her father is? Even though I was mad at her, and Jodi and I were arguing a lot this weekend, mostly about nonsense, I could not help but love Hillary. I wanted desperately for this episode to pass. Jodi is always there to pick up after the girls and get them out of messes. My position is that if they get into a mess they have to learn to get out of it themselves; then they will stand taller. Maybe on this one occasion Hillary got herself in a little too deep, but Jodi is there all the time for the girls. I hope Jodi hasn't spoiled them too badly and I pray Hillary will be okay on her own. There will not be anyone to tell Hillary, "Be home by midnight because you have a test tomorrow." Good luck, Hillary.

Jodi finally did get through to the high school and even though she did not speak to the principal, the matter was resolved and Hillary did receive credit for the course. I spoke to Hillary a few times today and I think she really appreciates what her mother did for her. I hope she learned a lesson.

One thing I've learned from my mistakes is that I'm about as far from perfect as one can get. Here I am baring my soul and looking for acceptance and compassion from my family. At the same time I've listed a group of people: Martin and Hope, Sabrina and Nathan, Peter and Carly, Lisa and Jason, and Lloyd and Ivan. All of them have caused me strife in the past and I have not forgiven these people. Staying mad at these people no longer serves a purpose. I have commited far worse sins than these people have. If my family can find absolution in their heart for me, then surely I should learn from my wife and children and extend forgiveness to others. Everybody makes mistakes and everybody has reasons for doing what they do. Even if their reasons were selfish, my behavior was also selfish. The problems I've put my family through are much greater than what this group has done to me. What I'm trying to say is: I forgive these people. I do not want to be surrounded by negative feelings. I firmly believe that things happen for a reason. If the above named group brought out enough negative feelings that pushed me in the direction of writing, then it is this group that deserves my sincere thanks. And if any amount of money, no matter how little, is raised by a portion of the proceeds of my book, and even one life is saved, then please do not judge harshly any of the characters in my book.

Earlier I wrote about people who have disabilities and my thoughts that maybe God has a way of doling out disabilities and that perhaps these people are the true, chosen people. If there is some truth to that, maybe I can make a difference by making more people aware of AIDS, of humanity's need to find a cure and a vaccine, and of the necessity to provide enough medicine to those in need. I'm not trying to flatter myself but, to borrow a metaphor from Stacie, if I am a small part of the 'compass' that directs the modern day explorer towards finding a cure for AIDS, and if my family's love is another direction on that 'compass', then perhaps our stay on the planet will not have been for naught.

This book and chapter of my life should not be thought of as depressing, because even if I die tomorrow, I will know I lived to get a message out. There is some comfort about knowing your life had direction, other than to raise the most wonderful, loving family you could. That is how I view my family, and for that I am extremely grateful.

Jodi has been reading the book *Tuesdays with Morrie*. The book is about a college professor who is loved by a particular student. This student comes back to his dying professor every Tuesday to relive and celebrate his life even though he knows the old man is dying. Jodi recalled her mother's death from ovarian cancer a few years ago. We always prayed that Mom would beat the illness. We chose not to question how many years she had left, but rather what new medicines were coming on the market. We visited Mom at Thanksgiving, and somehow I think we all knew there was a good chance we would not see her again. Nobody said anything to my in-laws but we all faced the reality that Mom would not be with us much longer. Mom in her own way was brave and noble to the very end. She lived for only seven or eight weeks after Thanksgiving. Mom never asked the children to come down and hold her hand, and that part of her was admirable, but Mom also missed the opportunity to close out her life and bring closure to Jodi. Jodi never really had the chance to say good-bye to her mother and Mom never had the chance to tell Jodi just how special Jodi is and how much Mom loved her. Maybe a one-hour session of solid crying and hugging and really talking would have brought solace to Jodi. I think her sister Suzie needed this, too.

I think many parents favor one child over another. That's just how things work. I, however, have no favorites and even if I did, I would not share that with you because I would never hurt my children. I think with Joanne and Jules, Neal is #1, Patti #2, and Jodi and Suzie are tied for #3. Post publication of this book, however, Suzie will surely hold the #3 spot solo. Mom was a very complicated person. I will start out by listing her good points. First, she is the mother of Jodi. Second, as much as she loved golf, whenever the children or grandchildren came to visit, she never played golf. The closest she came to the golf course was giving the grandkids rides in her golf cart. Third, anytime a grandchild was born Mom was on the next plane to stay with her daughters or daughter-in-law for a week or two. She loved helping out when the babies were first born, making things easier on her children. But Mom had another side, one I will never forget. Once when Mom came up to plan Jodi's wedding, Mom spent an exhausting day shopping for bridal gowns. This bridal and wedding stuff was the farthest thing from her mind. I remember Jodi buying a small bouquet of flowers for her mother that day to thank her, only to find out that Mom was already flying back to Florida. She left without saying good-bye, and I think that is how she also died. This chapter of Jodi's life will remain forever open.

I cannot tell you how many times Jodi cried on the way to Nantucket, thinking about that story of Morrie and reading me passages from the book. Nantucket would obviously be a great chance for me to listen to Jodi. On one of our morning jogs, I asked Jodi a question and her answer surprised me. Sometimes when you are so close to a situation you cannot see the overall picture. The question I posed to Jodi was, "What is your greatest fear?" I thought Jodi would say one of the following:

1. You will not live a full life.
2. You will leave me.

Jodi's answer was truly Jodi in that it was so simple and easy. She said, "I don't live in fear. I only want you to be happy and not depressed." That response meant a lot to me and perhaps the preceding pages reflect my mood. Jodi is asking so little of me and her needs are so basic. All Jodi wants from me is to be happy. She is not moping around about my illness. To the contrary, she only wants to enjoy life. Sharing my life story has brought me a greater awareness of my family, world, Jodi and myself. I feel happy, lucky and proud. Perhaps this is precisely the time and place I belong in, although if a time machine ever were invented, no one would be more curious to test it out than I would.

People and places constantly change over time and my Nantucket is no exception. I told you earlier how much we enjoy Po in New York City. There was a similar restaurant on Nantucket that our family visited about ten times. The food, setting and staff were superb. The restaurant consisted of two small rooms with about five or six tables in each room. All the illumination flickered from candles and dim lamps attached to paintings. It was the most romantic restaurant in our world. It was called India House and was located on India Street. It was probably named after a trading company in earlier times. The structure was a typical Nantucket home on the outside with minor modifications to the interior. We dined there two years ago and it wasn't quite the same. The food and decor were off a bit, as the restaurant had been renovated. Last year, the place was closed as it was undergoing further renovations. Last night we walked down the street and found the restaurant gone! Someone must have bought the inn and restaurant and converted it into a home. It was kind of sad, like not hearing from someone for a long time and finding out he had moved, but no one knew where.

In other respects nothing changes on Nantucket except that the 125-year-old houses are now 126 years old, and more trees are beginning to win the battle of uprooting sidewalks. I try to imagine that some little boy planted one of those trees 125 years ago. If he could see that tree today, what power he would realize one tiny child had. Even if it's only a 75-year-old tree, surely a 70-year-old successful millionaire does not have such power because he will not live another 75 years to see his tree fully grown. Do you think the child is aware of his power? Do you know the answer? I know the answer because I am that child. I planted two trees where I grew up in North Woodmere. One tree was planted in our backyard neighboring the Goldmans' property. The second tree grew up just across the street at the Bassetts'. The tree in our backyard got cut down after my mother moved. Having loved plants my entire life, I was saddened when the tree was no longer there. But the Bassetts' tree? That tree is living and thriving on Park Lane adjacent to Eden Court. I am proud to say I planted that tree, and I'm not sure if my family even knows that. I hope the Bassetts never chop down *my tree*.

Yes, the Bassetts. I remember this family from my youth so well. Rita and Irwin were the parents and Clifford and Deborah were the children. They kept mostly to themselves but they were a solid down-to-earth family. I think one of their grand-mothers lived with them for years. Today Clifford is a success-ful doctor. Deborah bought a home six houses away from her parents and is a success in the garment center. None of this is any reason for me to mention these people. I suppose I could say that our Stacie and Deborah's daughter are good friends, but that still does not deserve a paragraph in my book. All this talk about the Bassetts is just an introduction to one of the nicest acts of kindness a child can do for a parent. In this case, it was buying their dad a new car for Father's Day, and I wish I could've been there to see his face when his kids presented him with his new wheels. The parents were nice people. The father had a severe limp most of his life and finally had sur-gery to correct his walk. Happy Father's Day, Mr. Bassett. Deborah and Clifford, keep enjoying your parents. You're so lucky to have both your parents around.

Today is July 6th and it's another delightful day here on Nantucket. Jodi and I started our day with a six-mile run and bought some bread at "Something Natural". Their bread is incredible. Then we went into town and spent about an hour at a florist. I feel very relaxed being around beautiful flowers, real or artificial, as long as they are of good quality and set off in a pleasing light. If there is a handsome man or attractive woman employee with a smile, I enjoy conversing with the staff about plants and flowers. I have a natural affinity to plants and flow-ers and can sense when others do, also. I once asked a pretty young lady: what flower could your boyfriend bring you that would enhance your already perfect smile? I don't recall her answer, but my favorite is ranunculus. I was surprised this young lady was not aware of the flower. It's sort of like a rose but fuller and tighter, more often found in upscale florists. However, I think its growing season is rather short. Next I met up with Stephen, a pleasant young man attending Yale. He patiently explained to me for about five minutes how to care for my orchid plant. I then found out he was majoring in history and English, the same subjects as Anna, a smart, friendly young lady I had met in a men's shop a day earlier. Since I thought both kids were sharp and had a lot in common, I told Stephen he should contact Anna. If the rest of today's youth were like these kids, America would remain on top of the world forever. I also discussed the book I was writing with Stephen. He seemed very interested and had some helpful advice. Any pointers I can get from people are appreciated. It was difficult to continue the discussion because he was working. I asked Stephen about another young employee in the store and Stephen told me she was attending Duke. I was impressed that the owner chose to hire such bright students.

Our next stop would be to visit Elizabeth, a very dedicated and caring woman at a health care facility. Jodi and I chatted with her for over an hour. Elizabeth seemed truly excited about Jodi's and my experience over the past four years. It was one of the few optimistic stories she had heard and was very positive and supportive of my book. We promised to stay in touch. I gave Elizabeth my card and said if there was anything I could do to offer encouragement to any of her patients, she should have them call me. Maybe I can make a difference before this book is published, I thought. We hugged good-bye with a mutual feeling of respect. Even Jodi seemed a little more relaxed about my writing this book after that encounter. Elizabeth especially admired and respected Jodi, and I think for the first time Jodi began to feel passionate about the book. Jodi spoke up a lot during our visit with Elizabeth. In fact, Jodi repeated her advice to me not to discuss the book with my mother who would not be happy about it and would do everything to discourage me. I am confident that in the end my mother will come around and be proud of me, probably prouder of me than she has ever been in her life. Thanks, Elizabeth, for an enlightening afternoon and your support. Hearing some of your stories about your patients left me shaking in disbelief about their state of depression. I now feel stronger than ever that I must finish my story and finish it sooner than later. There are too many people ashamed and hiding on the sidelines and their voices must be heard and not silenced out of fear. "We have nothing to fear but fear itself," said Franklin Roosevelt, and this is as true today as it was when our grandparents and parents sacrificed their lives so their grandchildren and children could be free. Let us not disappoint our grandparents and parents, but honor them by lifting our heads high and letting our voices be heard.

After visiting Elizabeth, we bicycled seven easy miles to Sconset, a beach at the tip of Nantucket, and then we pedaled back into a strong headwind. When we arrived back in town we stopped at an art opening and then walked around a little. Jodi made me promise that we visit Nantucket next year. Something tells me we may be back here sooner, but there are no guarantees in life except the love my wife and I have for each other and our family.

Today is July 7th and tomorrow we will be going home. Jodi and I jogged 15½ miles today and met up by chance with Carey and her family. Carey is a radiologist from Texas, living with her husband in Washington, D.C. She was visiting her in-laws here with her daughter and twin seven-year-old redheads. The girl is quite pretty and the twin boys are adorable. As a pair they are precious. It's a similar thing I tell my girls. Individually you are special, but collectively your star rises in stature, making you girls worth more collectively than the sum of you girls individually. Carey's in-laws are also interesting. They were thrilled to be taking care of the grandkids for a week while Carey returned home. I like these grandparents, Paul and Patti. They told me they split their time between Connecticut, Nantucket and Prague. All told, they have seven grandchildren. Carey also seemed to be a loving mother. Nice family!

We also bumped into David and Claire, an attractive couple we had met the night before. Claire is full of energy. Her father is Jim Lonborg, the famous Boston Red Sox pitcher. David told me that Jim once auctioned off a set of three baseballs signed by Roger Clemens, Pedro Martinez and himself for $10,000 at a charity function. All three pitchers were the only Sox pitchers to win the Cy Young award. I'd give anything to be able to sign my name and have someone fork over $3,333 to an AIDS charity. It's interesting how I spoke about my set of girls being a little more special collectively; I wonder if any one of these three pitchers' signature on a baseball is worth $3,333, but collectively they are each worth that amount. The same reasoning applies to people who are HIV positive or have AIDS. Separately, one person cannot make a difference but collectively, we can and we must.

Claire went on to explain how her father is now a dentist and does not miss his days as a pitcher. "Yeah, right," I replied. "David and I would be drooling to have the opportunity your father had." Imagine playing ball, being cheered and getting paid tons of money. We had a good time with

David and Claire and when we met them the following day, I gave Claire a big hug and she hugged Jodi also. David was a little more reserved, but I think if they ever get married they will be very happy together. David says she wakes up with a smile. What more can a guy want!

Do you remember I thought we'd soon be returning to Nantucket? Perhaps I was holding something back or perhaps it is a combination of things that I was sensing. Sometimes these timed events follow a path, and when several of life's episodes all lead in the same direction for eighteen years, there is bound to be an end result.

First, let me state that Jodi and I have a lot of money invested on Nantucket. When we visited the island for my 30th birthday we threw two pennies into the water to assure our return, which finally materialized about ten years later. Over the last nine or ten years we've invested almost a quarter of a dollar.

Second, Jodi mentioned to me today that she thinks she would like to buy a house on Nantucket, but that would depend on whether the girls would like to visit us there during the summers when they are home from college and later when they have families of their own. Maybe Jodi did not formulate the exact criteria for buying a home on Nantucket, but the seed was definitely planted and now it's up to me to harvest Jodi's dream.

Third, I am touched to have learned that the Nantucket AIDS facility has been enlarged. Money had been raised at an annual fund-raiser where families, friends and benefactors contribute generously. I hope Atlantic Beach, New York and the Five Towns will be as generous in their support of finding a vaccine and a cure for AIDS.

Fourth, I decided I might like doing design work on Nantucket, so I brought some pictures of my apartment in

New York which is designed with Nantucket in mind. It was told to me that Paul, the florist whom I visited yesterday, is on the Board of Directors of the Nantucket AIDS Network. So I decided to stop by and show Paul some photos of my apartment. Paul was with a customer when I arrived at the shop. After about fifteen minutes I peeked into the back area of the store after I sensed the customer had left. Then Paul invited me in. I showed him the photos and was expecting a polite rejection, but instead he seemed so interested that we discussed which ones most successfully illustrated my work. Then I left him with a few varied scenes. I was impressed with Paul's generous support of AIDS charities, so at this point I decided to tell Paul my story in a condensed ten-minute version. I also introduced Paul to Jodi. Paul listened intently and understood a lot in ten minutes. I had already learned that everyone on the executive board had lost a friend or someone close to them from AIDS. A common bond or brotherhood naturally develops. It's sort of like saying, "I'm so sorry... I know how you feel..." when someone loses a parent. Well, you don't have a clue how that someone feels unless you've lost a parent, yourself. The same goes for people afflicted with AIDS. As Jodi and I were saying good-bye, Paul gave us a package of note cards with his store on the cover of the cards. As I said earlier, I always feel comfortable around plants and flowers. This gift was Paul's way of showing warmth and affection and it was very much appreciated. Thanks, Paul.

So there seem to be many reasons that are drawing Jodi and me towards owning a home on Nantucket. In summary they are as follows:

1. We love the island.
2. We've established a tradition of family vacations there.

3. We feel accepted by the local gentry.
4. There is a good client base there.

This does not mean my family plans to abandon Atlantic Beach. This beachfront community has been home to us for the past seventeen years. Two of my children were born here, and we have developed some very special ties to friends and the community. Nor does this mean we plan to give up my architectural practice and our apartment in Manhattan. What it does mean is Jodi and I feel very comfortable on Nantucket and would like to spend more time there and make a contribution to the island. We feel we really do have something to offer Nantucket.

On the ferry ride back to the mainland I wrote Stacie a quick poem.

Dear Stacie:

The next time I go on vacation
Remind me to try another nation

The purpose of our Nantucket destination
Should have been for recreation

However Mom had to buy every souvenir
Nantucket was printed on her underwear

When she saw this live giraffe
She insisted on his autograph

She demanded that we truck it
Off the island of Nantucket

I said perhaps another day
Or maybe some other way

Even though Mom can be adorable
Her persistence can be incurable

Mom refused to be quiet
And started to cause a riot

Enough of feeling sorry for me
I guess this was meant to be

Mom can hardly wait to see you
That also goes for me too

You have always been a true delight
And I think about you every night

You always give us so much pleasure
My very special treasure

So now it's time for me to go
And Stacie I do love you so.

Love, Dad

Chapter X

THE KEYNOTE SPEAKER

TODAY IS JULY 11TH AND I'm beginning to formulate a plan for telling Stacie that I'm both bisexual and HIV positive and that I'm writing a book. I think a few months ago Stacie had an inkling about the bisexual part because she made a comment to her sisters about finding a gay magazine around the house.

I did not want Stacie at such a tender age to find out about my situation because I didn't want to burden her with my troubles, nor did I want to influence her own sexual development. But as I've said before, "We are where we are now." I have been feeling very positive about myself lately and I've always believed things happen for a reason. I would much rather live another 25 years and know my life made a difference than live another 50 years of an uneventful life. Although, don't count me out just yet for the 50 more years! This is how I honestly feel and will present my position to Stacie. I will tell her that she should not feel sad because I am not sad, and that I am determined to make a difference. I've got the best loving family a guy could ever have (and we got to party with Mikey Mike at the Sands Beach Club, besides!).

Jodi, Hillary, Peri and I were considering telling Stacie a few days before camp, but we agreed to wait until summer passed. Now our problem is that the family will be together for only one day before Hillary goes off to college. Stacie derives a great deal of strength and confidence from her sisters. Naturally I would prefer them being around to comfort her and for Stacie to see everyone still loves me. It will be Stacie's first day back from camp, but we'll just have to tell her then. I decided I needed to prepare Stacie, so I wrote her the following letter. In my heart I knew Stacie would find forgiveness and understanding, and not because of this letter:

Dear Stacie,

Today is July 11th and I feel bad I haven't been writing you as much as I would like to. I know we sometimes argue and I think part of the problem is we are both very head-strong, stubborn and set in our ways. I think you will find I am changing somewhat, but there is one thing that you must always realize: Mom and I love all you girls so much. Do you remember the first summer when Hillary went to camp and we all came up for visiting weekend? Do you remember how Peri cried her heart out for ten minutes before she could collect herself and tell us why she was crying? Peri suffered a tremendous loss that summer because she felt our family belonged together. I guess she missed Hillary a lot. Now it's your turn to be away and we all miss you so much. I'm getting a little sad because only one day after you come home from camp, Mom and you girls will be taking Hillary off to college. It seems like there is only one day we will be together and then everyone heads off in their own direction. Sometimes I wish I could climb up a giant ladder and find the clock that controls time and hold its hands forever or better still, turn its hands back.

Stacie, I've been doing a lot of thinking lately about our family and the lessons we learned as a family. It was so kind of you to save Isabel (the cat). Even though she has a disability with her eye I think she has a little extra warmth to her, especially for you. Maybe that's because you saved her life. Do you think Isabel is a little extra special? I do. I think the same is true of people with disabilities. I think these people can be somewhat more caring and maybe they don't view themselves as having a disability. I think they may look at someone with a worse handicap and feel very sorry for that person but not sorry for themselves. People with disabilities are sort of chosen and maybe God has a reason for giving a person a disability, and it is not to be mean. Maybe we can talk about it on visiting day.

Sometimes I run out of things to say so I ramble on. One of my favorite activities has always been sneaking into camp the night before visiting day. Do you remember the time Jim got on his World War I motorcycle and chased us off the campgrounds? If this were your last year at camp I probably would sneak in once again. I love it when all you girls look at us so lovingly. You kids are all so starved for a hug that even a hug from a friend's parent is better than none. My heart is always with you, and if I can see you one day sooner it makes me happy.

Hillary came into work with me yesterday and we had a major bonding session. She actually enjoyed my company and did not say to me, "You are so annoying," even once. Hillary and Peri are busy with a million boys and they are having the best summer. Mom has been great as always.

I love you, doll.

Love, Dad

An event occurred in the Brodsky household yesterday. Hillary and I bonded. It started out the night before in one of our typical conversations where I would ask her for something and her answer would be 'no'. I asked Hillary to come into work with me since she was not working that Tuesday. She declined, whined, *maybe'd*, complained she was tired, and said she'd let me know in the morning, all the usual answers that I knew meant 'no'. I then asked Hillary a totally unrelated question which she was glad to discuss. Anything was better than my badgering her to come to work. What Hillary did not know at the time was that my question was anything but innocent. In a family it's not just children who can manipulate parents!

I asked Hillary what the first thing was that she remembered about growing up. She struggled with the question for about a minute and I finally got her to think of her first-grade teacher, Mrs. Rubenfeld. Then she told me a story of her kindergarten days. I told Hillary I had some sketchy recollections of my own life from an even earlier age. Starting from around age nine, most people retain almost everything. I told Hillary, "Someday I won't be here, whether it's five or fifty years from now, and you'll remember the times you said 'no' to me and you'll wish you had said 'yes' and could savor the memories of one extra day spent with me." I concluded this little speech by saying, "I'm not saying this to make you feel guilty." I absolutely will not use that emotion on my children. Guilt and envy should be banned from all child-rearing books. Hillary processed this information in her brain. It surprised me when she voluntarily acquiesced to spend the day with me. Let's not get carried away. I didn't expect her to leave with me at 6 a.m., so I agreed she could take a 9:45 train that would bring her to my office by 11:00.

Hillary always has her own agenda, but she did arrive a few minutes before noon. Hillary told me she was late because she had wanted to finish reading my story. She found it very interesting and exciting. I was a little nervous about her reaction. There were some passages that dealt with depression, and even though that stage was in the past, such negative thoughts might have been difficult for Hillary to deal with. So we were off to a great start and basically the day consisted of conversations about Hillary's boyfriends, some light clerical work, a walk or two, plus a visit to the Steelcase (furniture) showroom, a hug from Arkady (a former employee at Midtown Realty), lunch, and a pleasant ride home where—you'd better be sitting down for this—Hillary asked me if she could come into work with me the following day.

Hillary dropped me off at the gym. When I arrived home that evening Hillary actually invited me into her room to recap the day with Peri, and tell me what her plans were for the rest of the evening. She even asked me to comment on her outfit. Quite a pleasant day in all. When Hillary informed me that she had made plans to go to the beach with friends the following day, I had no problem with that, for my memory of yesterday would last forever. My memory of our one day together was a dream come true; a memory that will carry me through for at least one semester of college. Or maybe even a lifetime, as I now have dreamed away all the mistakes I have made as a husband and father. And the Academy of Dreamers wishes to announce its unanimous decision for the recipient of the Lifetime Achievement Award. This year's *Dreamie* goes to... Richard.

I began to wonder what Hillary's life would be like at college. Closing my eyes I dreamed about her future and my future. How would society judge me?

Guilty as charged! Officer, please, you don't understand. I'm Richard, Jodi's husband. Jodi, you know the one that does the radio show about raising children and husbands. I'm on my way to give the keynote speech at the Democratic

Convention for nominating the President. Let me show you. See, I even have my speech written. It says Norma, Mike, Michael, George, Jayne and Louisa. Look, I even have my ticket to the convention.

All right, Officer. I admit to sampling the three dates in the supermarket and okay, so it's more like over a thousand dates, and I've been noshing on them habitually for the past several years. I'm Jewish. I can't help it. It's in my blood. We never pay retail. I kept tasting the dates. I'm sure I must have purchased a few over the years. Okay, so I'll even pay for the dates now, but I've got to get my message out. Officer, I don't like politics any more than you do. It's not even a political address. It's about people and how people make the difference. My message must be heard. I was selected to give this speech three years ago after I raised one billion dollars for AIDS research. A large chunk of the money came from advertisers whose products I agreed to endorse, but only on the condition that I believed in their product. Officer, who would have dreamed I could raise a billion dollars? I was only wishing my signature could raise $3,333 like Jim Lonborg's.

Officer, let me tell you about Norma, my girls' singing teacher. She's so full of life and energy! She always gives a little extra of her time and her generosity with Jodi and the girls. One time we went to her husband's restaurant. We hated the creep and vowed never to socialize with her husband (now ex) again. We never said anything to Norma, but I think Norma was embarrassed that he charged us for dinner, considering the thousands of dollars we had spent on singing lessons. Norma did something really sweet. The next time she saw Jodi she gave Jodi this short, sexy, black jeweled dress that she had worn only once. This was Norma's way of saying 'I'm sorry.' It wasn't necessary, though, because Norma always gives a little extra, and everything about her comes from her heart.

And what about Mike? Mike is the girls' tennis pro. Mike adores my girls and Jodi. Any time they want to practice indoors in the winter or any season, no charge. Mike has a tremendous amount of patience for my girls. He would have made a super father and Carey would have made a great mom. Mike, go get Carey back.

Michael, we love you even if you are losing your hair. Michael is the girls' piano teacher, although sometimes I'm not sure if he comes by just to hang out. After he's done sharing stories with Jodi and the girls, they do find time for their lessons, but if one of the girls has not practiced, there is no charge. The girls always kid me when I call looking for Mom and they tell me Mom is with her boyfriend. Guess what, girls! Mom could do a lot worse.

George. George was the first person Jodi and I turned to when we found out I was HIV positive. George and I have a mutual respect for each other. He does not lie and he has a saying: Be a Man. That says a lot. To me it means if you've made a mistake, face it and don't run away. George, we've had good times and disagreements over the years, and I hope you can appreciate that this book is about "Being a Man."

Jayne is one of Jodi's very dear friends. If there were a contest for 'Mother of the Year', it would be a tie between both these saints. Recently one of Jayne's children was involved in an unfortunate incident. I saw Jayne a few days later and tried to strike up a conversation. She was in such grief she could not look up. Jayne will do anything for her family of overachievers and has been a true friend to Jodi over the years.

And Louisa. You want a free cup of coffee? Go to Dunkin' Donuts and mention Louisa's name. If you go there and don't ask for her, she's insulted. I always ask for her and get a hug with my coffee. Louisa has a heart of gold. No one was kinder to Jodi and more considerate when Jodi's mother was dying. Louisa believes in prayer, so please stop and say a prayer for Louisa's recovery from cancer.

So Officer, please try to understand this country is about people, good people, not politics. Look Officer, look at my watch. It must be almost 8:00 and I have 30 minutes to arrive at Madison Square Garden for my keynote speech.

Then I looked at my watch, which was as real as the nose on my face, except that my watch was gone. I turned to my side and saw the most beautiful sight in the world, my wife lying beside me. I gave Jodi a big hug, and who knows? Maybe dreams do come true, I thought, as I gave Jodi an extra hug.

Chapter XI

LEARNING FROM PERI

TODAY IS FRIDAY THE 13TH. I visited Susan, the therapist, this morning. My skin is still intact, given that she is a pleasant lady without claws. I think I was expecting a woman a few years older and less attractive. The session was just a summary of where my family and I are now. I even agreed to see her another time and probably will continue to do so, although I don't think I need to see a therapist.

If I haven't made it clear in the last chapter or two, I will restate how I feel now, if someone will provide me with a long enough ladder because I'm up on this cloud, kind of looking down on the world below. Everything looks so small and buildings appear to be the size of pencils. I can barely see movement on the ground and the only time I can distinguish people is when they are grouped together in masses. It seems as if one person standing alone is invisible. Get the picture? Or do I have to hit you over the head with a bolt of lightning? I have never been happier. I love my family as much as any other person has loved his family. Mine has chosen to forgive me and accept me for the person I am, and I adore them a little extra for that. In fact, you'll have to excuse me, because I would like to write a poem to Stacie at this time.

***

Dear Stacie:

It seemed like just another day
But I continue to miss you being away

I needed someone to calm me down
It's hard with you out of town

I placed a picture of you beside my bed
And another of Mom and me the day we wed

I think that's what I did that night
In the bright glow of the evening's moonlight

I started wondering and my mind was racing
My legs were tied as I was chasing

The questions and the solutions
Of many of life's illusions

Where did the moon go every day
And how did it know it couldn't stay?

When the sun came out and took center stage
Did the moon get mad and fly into a rage?

Back in my room I began to wonder
And then a scream or was it thunder?

Was I sleeping for an hour or two
Or was I awake thinking of you?

Why couldn't I tell if I was sleeping
And what other secrets God was keeping?

Why was I given such a good life
With you girls and my wife?

I opened the window and looked outside
And then I thought I'd go for a ride

Not in my car, not for a drive
Tonight I was feeling really alive

I wished for you and you suddenly appeared
I knew you'd be there, I knew you cared

You looked at me and held my hand
It was nice you always understand

I was sure you didn't doubt me
And you wouldn't go flying without me

Not even in the golden balloon
That danced across the moon

The balloon began its descent
It really was quite an event

As the balloon got closer I could feel
This was no dream, this was for real

I reached out the window and jumped twenty-three feet
This was not easy for me to complete

I threw you a rope and you held tight
I pulled you into the balloon that star-filled night

The balloon went up, sideways, back and forth
Traveling east, west, south and north

We traveled across the Atlantic Ocean
You and I were causing quite a commotion

Birds were flying so very near
It seemed they had lost their fear

The sky seemed brighter than ever before
This I knew, I knew for sure

After awhile we flew higher and higher
And this is true, I'm not a liar

The balloon and the moon were two miles away
This day was like no other day

We began to gaze upon the moon's land
Oh what a sight, it was so grand

It was a sight I knew I'd never see again
This I realized, I knew just then

The balloon began dropping and sinking
And all the while I was thinking

About the wonderful exciting flight
And your expression of pure delight

I held you tight as we embraced
This was one moment that could never be replaced

The balloon was falling fast
I knew this trip couldn't last

I saw our street a mile below
And knew that soon we'd be saying hello

To family, relatives and friends
Of course this all depends

Who will believe our journey in the heavens above
Of two people who share a special love?

And then I looked at my bedside
And there was a photo of you and my bride

But the sky seemed brighter than ever
And this I was sure I'd remember forever and ever

Love, Dad

Saturday, July 14th. As I was telling you yesterday I have never been happier in my life and I believe my story will raise tons of money for AIDS, as people become more aware of where we are in the battle against AIDS. We are losing, and even if we find a vaccine and a cure tomorrow, we still have lost. 22,000,000 hearts have perished and each heart has its own unique story. What about all the children left without parents? What about a mother who had to bury a son or a daughter and wonder what they died for? Did they die fighting to preserve freedom for their country from internal or foreign forces? Did they die rescuing an infant from a fire? These hearts died for nothing. We cannot prove to the surviving families that we have done everything we can to rectify the situation, because we have not made the commitment as people, as corporations, and as governments to find a vaccine and a cure. As far as corporations go, Mazda, you'd better call me because I have an ad for your company. I know exactly what I will say and I won't be cheap, either. 100% of my fee will go to AIDS-related charities.

I've been singing a new tune lately. It goes something like, "There's a place for us, somewhere a place for us." Jodi tells me it's from *West Side Story*. I started to explain to Jodi why I've been singing this old song, but then I can't get the words out. Tears start streaming down my face, only these are joyous tears. I know this sounds crazy, but if I were given the chance to wake up one morning and erase the last four years of my life, and relive them, I would still choose to be in the position I am in now. I finally feel I can make a difference in this world. I'm not afraid that I may live only 5, 10, or 20 more years, because my family will have the memory that I did something with my life. I've only begun to realize this in the past few days and when you can look death in the eye and not blink, you are 99% or more cured of any disease. Do you remember how I used to be overly depressed because I couldn't go one hour without thinking about my illness? Well, guess what! That one hour has been reduced to thirty minutes, and that's because getting my story out has become my passion.

To anyone who believes there is no justice in the world, this book will shout volumes you are wrong. My quiet wife, whom I've always considered to be one unique person on this planet, will now get the recognition she deserves from her family, relatives, friends and the immediate world. I've been kidding Jodi that they will recruit her for a talk show about raising children and husbands.

I feel like I belong on a game show called "Will the Real Richard Please Stand Up?" I think I can finally rise and be counted. It feels great! But you know what feels even better? The acceptance I get from my children and their friends. A few evenings back Peri had about five guys and her friend Ashley over. They're a nice bunch of kids. Peri even allowed me to participate in the conversation. I held my own and they loved hearing the story about the Bassett tree.

The following morning I went for a walk on the board-walk with Peri. What a great, well-adjusted kid! Do you remember some chapters back I told you that Hillary's ex-boyfriend was threatening to expose my illness and we were not sure how to deal with it? You know what? We forgot to ask the 'Solomon' of tribunal affairs what to do. Peri knew instinctively what to do, as a similar situation was launched via communication lines. A friend of Peri's telephoned her and asked if I was HIV positive. NASA got dozens of calls that day about a UFO resembling a local teenager who had last been seen on planet Earth, talking to Peri. Peri had really blasted the kid! How dare he ask such a personal question about her family! And who is he to Peri to be asking such a question? He was actually one of several guys that liked Peri, but she told him just how rude he was. The conversation continued and the young suitor apologized, but my girls are tough. Peri repeated how annoyed she was and when the boy asked if he could call back another time, Peri replied, "Maybe, but I am really upset, so probably you should not call back." I even thought Peri was a little tough on the boy, but my girls are very protective of me. One thing the world had better understand: you do not say anything bad about us

Brodskys, or collectively we will come down on you. My girls love me very much. I think I am a good father. I think there are worse fathers and better fathers, but there is one thing I can say with certainty. There are no better mothers than Jodi, and if you think I'm the only one who thinks so, then let me read you the following card that Peri presented to Jodi on Mother's Day:

Dear Mom:

Well... since today is Mother's Day... of course I went to the card store to buy a card for you like every other year... but this time it was different... all of the cards there would-n't be able to express what I wanted to say to you this year. I guess I grew up a lot this year and became more thankful of what you have done for me. Every week when I go to Susan... I can go on for hours about how I have the best mom. Mom... I'm not just saying this... it's the truth. I go on about how you go around the world and back for me, Hill and Stace. You not just do what a mother is supposed to do, you go far and beyond that and times that by a million. When you always ask me if you should get a job, my answer is always no. I don't know if you know it, but the hardest job in the world is truly being a mother. I don't care if you work at the highest paying job or anything... because your job is 24 hours, 7 day a week... which is no one's hours... A mother's job is the most important of all... You've taught me the most important lessons in life... You've shown me the best examples from just watching you and Dad... You showed me how to be happy with everything you have... see... in general... people tell me I'm a happy kid... and that's true because I learned it all from you... you always walk around with a friendly smile and never get upset over anything... you're the happiest person in the world... and I consider myself the second because you're my mother. There are many things in my life that I am happy about... but the best thing I will ever have in my life is you... Mom, you're the greatest and no one can compare to you... I can't even explain what you mean to me... You're there to listen, you're there to talk... You're even there to scratch my back late at night when you come into my room just to talk... When you always ask me where I want to live when I get older... the answer is... wherever you are... I will never be able to live more than five minutes away from you... I love it how you call me right after school to see what I am doing or just to hang out. Many mothers don't want to have anything to do with their kids... but with you it's the complete opposite... anyway... the purpose of this letter is to wish you a HAPPY MOTHER'S DAY... but I wanted to tell you what's on my mind... I hope you enjoy this day because you should know you deserve only the best... I love you more than anything and I hope we become even closer... even though that could be hard... because I think we're about as close as mothers and daughters get... I also want to thank you for EVERYTHING you've done for me, EVERYTIME you went out of your way to make things good for me...

Mommy... I LOVE YOU

Happy Mother's Day

XOXOXOXO

Love always, Peri

Now do you see why I feel like the luckiest guy alive? Peri is such a super kid! I think my children get a strong sense of confidence because they know their parents love them so much. All those hugs and "I love you"s cost nothing but paid off big-time. What a great feeling to grow up knowing your mother is the best mother in the world. What a feeling of security! How many children can honestly say that about their mother? I know I'm not the best father in the world; I'm not the best husband either. But even before I broke my vow to Jodi I wasn't the best father in the world. There are some fathers, like my brother Victor, who are not interested in going to a gym. Maybe he does a little exercising at home but he would rather spend as much time as he can with his daughter. That's not me. There were times I would be tired when I came home from work and I might have been short with the girls. None of this means we love each other any less. They may recognize my faults, but my girls know I love them, and I know they love me. If you were to ask them if I was the best father in the world, I would expect them to say 'no', but I've been wrong before!

Chapter XII

MY GREATEST FEAR

AS I READ BACK ON what I've written I realize life has been exceedingly good to me. I've even openly stated that I would not trade the last four years of my life. I don't want one teenager, married guy, or whoever you are to think for one second, that this guy you're reading about is leading a great life and that being HIV positive isn't so bad, so why should you practice safe sex? You're a fool if you don't educate yourself and find out exactly what safe sex is. Obviously the same goes for women and probably more so, since guys can be pretty persistent when it comes to sex. For those of you who have not had sex, trust me: things progress very quickly and in an uncontrollable manner during passion. Don't think for a moment that you can control a sexually charged situation.

At present my HIV status is being held in abeyance, but there is no guarantee my immune system will hold up. 80% of the people taking medicine have side effects including vomiting, nausea and diarrhea. Sounds like fun. There are all sorts of diseases I am prone to. My life can be shortened at any time and more than likely will be. Before we went public with my story it might have been helpful if Jodi and I had known a couple we could get close to, a couple we could confide in to share our story. Instead the opposite occurred. Do you know how many times we told friends we could not meet them for dinner at 8? We always made some lame excuse. The truth was an early dinner didn't work for my schedule for taking medicine. Why do you think Jodi and I dine alone at Po and have dinner at 11 or 11:30? Actually it's not that bad, because my wife and I feel like we're dating again and we prefer each other's exclusive company.

I think of myself as family oriented, but family dinners have been cut back some. As much as I would like to celebrate my brothers' and their wives' birthdays by going out to dinner with them, we rarely do that anymore. The illness can take its toll on you socially. All these events get tied up in your emotional well-being, and this leads to stress, which I believe is the ultimate killer, whether you are HIV positive or not.

If I haven't convinced you to practice safe sex, go to your local AIDS center. Maybe they will allow you to sit in on a session when someone comes in to visit and is very depressed. Or go to a hospital and ask to speak with someone who is dying from AIDS. There's no shortage of these people around. If that doesn't convince you, arrange to meet a mother who has had to bury a child who has died from AIDS. The school system might be wise to take a similar approach, and I don't mean through a 15-minute film. Yeah, get out and visit a hospital. Take a group of students to watch an AIDS victim being buried by his parents. I'm crying just thinking about it and I guarantee even the toughest kid will cry, too. Our schools and the education system at large is a topic in itself, but my belief is that school systems must be creative and challenge their students. Shock the kids. Get a reaction, or you will put the kids to sleep. We've all been there, in a terribly boring classroom, but in more complacent times.

One last point. I've given blood about three times in my life. Stop worrying. The last time I gave blood I can't even remember, but it was probably before I was married. It really doesn't hurt, you know. I felt good about donating blood because I was helping someone. The Jewish religion teaches you the highest form of charity is when you give to someone who does not know you are the donor, and you do not know who the beneficiary is. I'm not sure I believe that, though, because ever since I became HIV positive I've had this fear that a friend would ask me to donate blood for his child and I would have to decline. I would feel depressed that I had let a friend down. Don't let me down. Do not get this illness because it won't just be your life you will be affecting; it will also be the lives of all those who love you.

I'd like to move on and maybe get onto something cheerier, like telling you to put this book down for a few minutes and touch the person next to you; maybe just be grateful that this person is part of your life. Give him or her a hug and before you continue reading, say a prayer for the 22,000,000 people who have died from AIDS and promise them they will not be forgotten. To make this prayer really meaningful, write a check for $1 or $1,000, but promise me you will write a check to an AIDS-related charity at this time. I'm counting on it and so are the 22,000,000 souls that have been taken.

"THEY CANNOT SPEAK BUT SOMEHOW THEIR VOICES WILL BE HEARD FOREVER"

We cannot forget. In addition to your contribution, make your vote count in the next election and vote for the candidate who will make a difference. Buy products from companies that are supportive of AIDS victims and charitable towards AIDS foundations.

Wouldn't it be great if Mercedes came out with a new luxury convertible model without a power top and said, "This model is $2,000 less, but it's only available in a limited edition. Instead of $100,000 you will pay only $98,000, but you must write a check for $2,000 to an AIDS charity." This limited edition might have a logo or something so the public knows the owner chose to donate $2,000 to an AIDS charity. I'd be more impressed by that vehicle than a $120,000 car. Perhaps BMW would offer a $3,000 discount for a wheel cover that was less fancy, but the wheel cover would be synonymous with the fact that the owner had made a major contribution to an AIDS charity. I would certainly find that car and driver more appealing than the car with the super fancy rims. I would be willing to appear in that ad also and gladly donate 100% of my fee to an AIDS charity.

Actually, I'd like to see an automaker hire Stacie to design a grill for the front end of a car. This limited edition would have a concept similar to the chrome rims or manual top, and Stacie's payment for services rendered would be a college scholarship. I just love the concept of a limited edition. It's hard to come by and you just have to have it. Did you ever stop to think what product has had the most sales resulting directly from advertising? It's obviously the automobile. Most of us have a more expensive audio system in our car than our homes. Most of us settle on fabric for a chair in our homes and we'll keep that fabric chair for ten years. But for a car, it's leather, even though we'll probably trade in the car in three to five years.

Getting back to that college scholarship, I sure could have used it. If you haven't figured it out yet, I paid for my entire college education. I also paid for my first car, a new 1970 LeMans convertible, and yes, Hillary paid for her first car also, which makes us very proud of her. I think Hillary is even prouder. I was a very independent child. I delivered newspapers to nine houses in the neighborhood when I was only eight years old, and I have worked ever since. I remember my mother used to fold the newspapers and put rubber bands around them. If there was one cloud in the sky, she would drive me, just in case the clouds opened up. Anyhow, I think this independent streak was a good thing then, but our world seems so different today. Maybe boys are more independent than girls in general, or at least in the early years. This all goes back to raising the kids. We already know Jodi pretty much decides how that is done, even when we disagree. Jodi has a way of being intuitively correct 99% of the time, so it's hard for me to argue. After all, that leaves just one chance out of a hundred that I'm right, and I'm sure that doesn't surprise you. Is it possible I'm just wrong?

So why am I always wrong... and when did my Age of Enlightenment begin? I might ask my friends, relatives and readers to weigh in on the subject, but my mailbox is not large enough. Maybe my mother was right; I had 'book smarts', but not 'street smarts'. Did I ever have street smarts? How was I as a child? Boring.

I think I need to visit my old neighborhood in Brooklyn. I'm not exactly sure why. I remember Flatbush Avenue was a few blocks away from our apartment at Kings Highway and East 41st Street. I wonder if any of the stores are still there. I vaguely picture a Chinese restaurant with a red storefront. The story goes I bit the waiter's hand because he ran off with my won ton soup before I was finished. I also remember getting haircuts, and I can *distinktly* smell and feel my hair being plastered down with "green gook". I suppose today they label it gel. It came in a rectangular-shaped bottle that went straight up about 7" and tapered to a round cap. Back then I don't think they had to put ingredients on bottles, but it was definitely 110% grease. I saw the man in the back of the barber shop boiling it down and then he added another 10% to the bottle. You sort of gave up washing your hair because you never could get the gook out of your hair. My hair style or lack of it became my calling card. In kindergarten I was placed in front of a potted cactus plant when they took the class picture. You couldn't tell where my hair ended and the cactus plant began. Luckily, it was a decent looking plant, so it was one of my better pictures. I wonder what else I might remember if I visited the old neighborhood. Computers, what do they know about neighborhoods? The computer is telling me I misspelled Flatbush because it doesn't recognize the name. Flatbush is the soul of Brooklyn. If I write in 'Beverly Hills', I'm sure the computer will recognize that.

Moving from Brooklyn, my next stop on the 'bus of life' was North Woodmere. Maybe I'll take my girls to visit my house in North Woodmere. I could show the girls my room and maybe some of the plants that I had grown. Then I'd sit down on the ground at the Bassett tree and write a poem about the tree and me. I thought about these last few things when I was jogging this morning. It's a good time to either clear your mind or let your mind run off in all directions. You should try jogging. Start out walking fifteen minutes and increase that a little each day and then try a one-quarter mile run and increase that a little each day. You will definitely lose weight, and the aerobic exercise is a lifeline for your heart. Speaking of losing weight, I saw Lois Weinstein the other day and I know she was about to tell me I had lost weight, but decided not to. This woman is truly a beautiful, caring human being and should be listed in the group with Jodi and Jayne for Mother of the Century. I know I look better a few pounds heavier and have dropped around five pounds in the past six weeks, but I like being lighter for the marathon. Besides, marathon runners are supposed to be gaunt and my gaunt look has nothing to do with my being HIV positive. Years ago I told an older friend of Jodi's she looked good. She had no wrinkles. She replied, "Fat people don't have wrinkles." I didn't realize it at the time but it is true. Have you ever looked at a photograph of yourself where you don't like how you look? (That's because you're probably ugly.) Just kidding. At least you haven't fallen asleep reading yet. Thanks. Save the photo. I guarantee in six months you'll like the photo and you'll only wish you could look like that now, since you have aged six months. You've aged, not me. I'm getting better and I hope to prove it by beating my marathon time.

I have told people that Jodi and I were not selected to be in the marathon this year. It's decided by lottery and has nothing to do with the number of times you've run the marathon in the past. There is absolutely no way Jodi and I will not run in the marathon. Even if we don't get a running number we will run. I will have Jodi and me surrounded by 30 legitimate runners and there will be no way the officials on the sidelines will be able to pull me out of the race. Imagine the headlines,

DYING HIV POSITIVE ATHLETE PULLED OUT OF THE RACE OF HIS LIFE

The course of my life appears before me like a quarter-mile race. I am coming out of the last turn and heading for the finish; focusing, gathering momentum and sprinting to achieve my goals. This may sound strange, but I think I like myself more now than at any other stage of my life. I look at my high school yearbook picture and it's a pretty nerdy picture I see. At nine I was playing the accordion; at twelve I was planting flowers in my backyard; at fifteen I was mastering bridge. Sounds pretty exciting.

But I was good at some things. Trouble. Trouble was my middle name. It started when I was four. The story goes something like this, although I honestly don't remember that much except for the part about the cars. I used to park a few of my toy cars in the hall that went to the bedrooms. My father told me not to park the cars there, but I did what I had to do; I parked all my cars there and told my father to get out of my parking lot. I got smacked, but I would get even. Outlining Stuart with a crayon as he always tucked himself tight under the covers was my next favorite pastime. Ouch, smacked again. Back then almost all parents hit their kids. I said something like, "You have no right to touch my skin." I was really mad and got even by taking a dump in the closet.

Closeting myself for the next 40-some-odd years might have solved all my problems. You don't have to agree so fast!

I wonder if I felt safe in the closet back then. If only I had known when I was about to do something stupid, I could have gone into my closet and whiled the time away until my 'stupid episode' passed. Sounds like a good television series that I could write the script for. I'd have no shortage of material to draw from: And now 'Stupid Episode Time', featuring Richard in 'Not Exactly a Shoe-In'. I must have been about five when my parents found out I needed corrective shoes. It hurt them more than me. They used to have to fork over $30 or $40 for shoes, which was probably triple compared to regular shoes. Then we moved to North Woodmere. My friend and I used to play pirates and travelers on a field of empty sandlots. Yeah, I guess you figured it out. The shoes were only a few days old when they got buried and we never found them. My friend Mark was a smart kid, even at that age. He had buried his sneakers, which back then cost only a couple of bucks, but of course he found his sneakers.

Then there was the time Aunt Ronnie left her new Cadillac convertible at our house for the weekend for my parents to use. I don't remember if Aunt Ronnie said or implied that I could drive the car. In any case I got into this new convertible and... Oh my God, here we go again with my obsession for convertible tops. The top goes down automatically when you push a button, and you know I have a thing about power tops. So I push the button and the next thing I see is the glass completely shattered in the rear window. My parents had left their golf clubs in the trunk where the top was supposed to go, and even though physics wasn't one of my better subjects, I did remember that two things cannot occupy the same space at the same time. In this case the golf clubs won out.

I was blamed for the glass breaking, but at the time I felt it was my parents' fault for leaving the clubs in the trunk. Perhaps I thought about it a few times during the next decade and I still felt I was right and my parents were wrong. Another twenty years have passed, and now I don't think it was anyone's fault. Things just happen. As par for the course I got yelled at then. I still hate getting yelled at. That reminds me of the time I tipped the golf cart over at the Downingtown Inn, but I'm getting tired of talking about all the things I did wrong. Getting back to the convertible, Aunt Ronnie was really nice about it and said her insurance company would cover the damage. I wonder if there was a deductible and she was just a being a sport about it. Honestly, I will never ask her. I prefer to think there was a deductible, but that in the spirit of family, my aunt could not ask us for the money.

There was a very unique, unusually close relationship between my parents and Aunt Ronnie. I became aware of it a few years before my dad died. My father worked five days a week at this stage of his life. Prior to that it was six or seven days. Financially my father did quite well the last several years of his life. One week he would work Monday through Friday, then the following week he'd be off on Friday and Monday, but he worked Saturday and Sunday. It was on those

Fridays and Mondays that my parents and Aunt Ronnie were almost always together. As sad a loss as it was for my mother when Dad died, Aunt Ronnie also lost a very dear friend, and she had to grieve for her sister as well. I'm not sure if anyone really understood how deep the loss was for Aunt Ronnie.

Aunt Ronnie's husband, Uncle Joe was a good man in those days, as he is to this day. I owe him a tremendous 'thank you' for the many things he has done for my family over the years, too numerous to mention. He is a very private person, so we will leave it at that. Uncle Joe religiously bought Aunt Ronnie exquisite jewelry and fancy cars, but my father did something which I will never forget. The year was about 1979. My father was buying my mother a new car and my uncle was also buying Aunt Ronnie a new car. Back then Cadillac was the 'in-car'. Foreign cars were barely making an impact in this country. Of course, Uncle Joe bought Aunt Ronnie a Cadillac; so did my dad for my mom, but the top-of-the-line model. My father loved my mother very much, and as I said earlier, they had a great marriage. His love was equally returned by her. My mother hates me saying these things because everything is so private, even the good stuff. Mother, your steadfast commitment to marriage and family is perhaps the best lesson I learned from you and Dad, and now is as good a time as any to say it: Thanks, Mom and Dad. I love you both.

You must be wondering how I managed to complete any assignment in school. I'm all over the place. This book doesn't need a "Table of Contents": a road map would suffice. But you don't need a map for my next stunt, just your Nikes and your running gear; I need a cheering section of sweaty runners. Mazda, here's the Miata commercial I promised to deliver: It would be a race between me (in my sweaty shorts and tee shirt after running six miles) and a suit and tie executive to see who could put our convertible tops down faster. Since mine is manual and takes only a few seconds, I would win. The executive would lose and his glass window would break because he had forgotten to remove his golf clubs from the trunk.

Ready for another Miata commercial? It starts out very innocently. Jodi and I are leaving a friend's wedding, waiting for the car attendant to pull our car up. I am wearing a tuxedo and my wife has never looked more radiant. It hardly matters what she is wearing because her eyes are alive and there is a smile on her face. Friends of ours, Walter and Andrea, are also waiting outside. Jodi is admiring Andrea's shawl and Andrea wraps the shawl around Jodi and says, "It's yours." Jodi insists that she cannot accept the shawl and Andrea is even more insistent. She says this gives her much happiness, so of course Jodi accepts the gift and gives Andrea a hug. I love hugs, so I manage to get in on the action, too. (So far the story is true.) Next, the car attendant delivers my Miata and some famous actor's expensive convertible arrives at the same time. It starts to pour. My top goes up manually in two seconds, while the actor is sneezing his brains out and getting soaked waiting for his power top to go up.

Thinking about Andrea and the shawl reminds me of a card that I sent Jodi in another lifetime.

Dear Jodi,

Wouldn't it be great if someday soon you and I could go on a vacation in the French countryside? Picture it. We get lost in the meadows and hike down the valley until we find an abandoned country house, steal a bottle of wine, make love and fall asleep outside. Upon awakening, we dress in our finest clothes for dinner. As we stroll about the town, passing its many patisseries, gurgling fountains and flower markets, the townspeople come out to look at you. This town is off a main road and isn't often toured. It is mostly visited by the French who have migrated from towns bordering Belgium and Luxembourg. The intermarriage of people from these three countries has produced some of the most attractive people. The town seems spotless and completely at peace. The townspeople are coming out for dinner and the merchants are closing shops. The sun has almost set and a flower vendor hands you a rare white flower. The vendor is not known for his generosity, so naturally everyone turns to admire you. It takes but a moment for the crowd to realize why this rare flower that took twelve years to bloom was given to *you*. The townspeople begin to applaud you and the vendor. The vendor begins to explain the flower required an extra five years to bloom, and then he apologizes for his grumpiness over the last few years.

Guys with cameras snappily appear to immortalize the moment as a sunset of colors flash before my eyes; colors never before seen, presenting you in a light never before imagined. We proceed to a candlelit table overlooking the river, with waterfalls and mountains in the distance. The dinner is wonderful. We meander back to our hotel room which overlooks the town square, fountains, church and gardens. Nightingales and faint music lull the town into a serene peace. Our room is filled with flowers sent by people who saw you today and admired your beauty. There are rich mouldings, marbled walls, wood floors, antiques, and a canopy bed facing the oldest fireplace in the town. It has been said that its flames have burned for centuries, never stopping for a moment; never will the fire go out as long as there is love in this room. Tonight the fire is roaring brightly as I hold you in my arms and we make love again. I realize I am the luckiest man in the world to have you for a wife.

We awake in the morning and I tell you of my dream. Was it a dream, or does everybody constantly admire you? Were we together in a lifetime before, and was our love so perfect that we were destined to find each other again and again and again?

Love

Richard

I spoke to Stacie at camp this morning. She received my letter about disabilities which she thought was strange. She also read the letter to her counselor. The girls often read letters to their counselor so I thought 'sure, it's okay.' Stacie repeated the story to her sisters and described the letter as weird. What really touched me was that Stacie's counselor said she could not wait to meet me and get a hug from me. If my book is successful, maybe we can do a hug session instead of a book-signing session. Maybe the counselor's reaction was exactly what I was looking for. People need to express affection towards other people. What better way than a hug or a poem? Stacie, this one's for you:

Dear Stacie,

I sat down in a chair and began to write
Grabbing a cup of coffee, perhaps I might

Dream of a place where prayers are heard
And love is spoken without a word

A smile, a touch, a warm face
Was universal in my imaginary place

I thought of Stacie in my heart
It's always hard when we're apart

I held Stacie's picture close to me
Isabel jumped up and had to see

She smiled I think she knew
How much I really loved you

Isabel and I closed our eyes
And something appeared like a surprise

Not a person, furniture, just a voice
It said follow me you have no choice

I tried to stand but my feet were tied
I wished I had you by my side

And then I saw you and held you near
But I was here and you were there

And the chair began to grumble and couldn't sit
In this same spot for one more bit

It moved sideways - up and down
And next I knew I was cross-town

We squeezed between lanes of cars
Underneath a sky blanketed with stars

I made a wish on this starry night
That I could fly and see what might

Be a golden meadow beneath the tallest tree
Something beautiful I needed to see

And then the chair rose two feet
I held Isabel, wow was this neat

Higher and higher the chair was soaring
The stars, the meadows, forests we were touring

We passed a waterfall in the sky tonight
This I'd remember night after night

Something was missing I wanted more
Someone to hold, someone I adore

The chair began falling
I heard you calling

So did Isabel and the chair
We were not scared, we had no fear

And then the chair glided down
To the most picturesque little town

Not nearly as beautiful as the next sight I saw
It was something my eyes could not ignore

I held you tight
And squeezed you with all my might

My dream came true
I guess you knew

Love, Dad

July 17th. Happy Birthday, Dad! I love you and miss you. It seems like yesterday you were here. Dad, you would be proud of Mom, Jodi and the girls, and if you were here, I know you'd be proud of me. Can you think back to when we used to go for a walk around the property every spring, looking at how much the shrubs had grown? I cherished those walks. Dad, I can still picture you and Stuart, Uncle Bernie, Steven and Ira planting burlap-wrapped shrubs and maple trees in front of our house. Mom was upset that you had spent $167. Dad, revisiting those times makes me both happy and sad. I'm happy that I can remember those days and sad that you are not here, so happy and sad that I'm crying. Dad, I have the most beautiful shrubs in front of my house and I wish you were here to walk around my garden once. Imagine if I had a chance to see you for five minutes! I do miss you a lot. More then seeing my garden, you would have loved seeing my girls. You were fortunate to meet Jodi. I want you to know she has been the perfect mother and wife who has kept our family together.

It's probably an appropriate time to introduce you to a good friend of our family. Dad, you would have liked this author and his wife (whom I will refer to as Fred and Dolly). I've known them for over twenty years. Fred has a sharp, creative mind and even though I see him only every five or so years, he's the type of guy who will always be there. I had sent Fred the first hundred pages of this book and was anxiously awaiting his comments. Finally, we spoke. I hung onto his every word and felt so grateful that Fred was giving me his advice. I think writers in general and Fred in particular have a tremendous amount of intensity. And I very much enjoyed our dialog.

Fred and I discussed the fact that I had a need to inform a select group about my illness. This group consists of people who like and respect me. It's for a combination of reasons that I need to relate my story to these few. First, I need encouragement and acceptance because I am scared, and second, these people think I am an excellent father and husband; I am living a lie to those people and I cannot continue lying. There are others who think I'm okay, not great, but not terrible either, so to this bunch I'm not living as much of a lie. Fred was helpful when I told him I had a need to tell Aunt Helaine about my illness. I then explained to Fred that when I told my mother, she became convinced that bisexuality was a passing, curious stage for me and that it was over. I'm stronger now than anytime in my life, but I didn't have the strength then or even now to reiterate again and again to my mother that I had become HIV positive because I had been with a man who was HIV positive, and that I now continue to be with men. Fred explained the only way to deal with this older generation is to tell them from the start that I am still involved with men. I agree with Fred but...

Fred said for the book to sell, the public needs more honesty, and that includes how I feel when I'm having sex with a man, and whether or not I am still having sex with my wife. Before I respond, I want to tell you about a family dinner we had for my mother's birthday last year. Her boyfriend Herb was there. He is a sweet, kind man who at 80 still works and plays golf. Stuart and Liz, Victor and Susan, and Jodi and I were also at the dinner. Stuart was steering the conversation in a sexual direction to a point where it became clear that Herb would have to respond as to whether or not he and my mother were having sex. Jodi and I did not want to hear what Herb was about to say. We were cringing. Victor was more demonstrative and put his hands over his ears and said, "I don't want to hear this." Another incident comes to mind. When I was 45, I asked Hillary at what age she thought people stopped having sex. Her reply was 45. Children cannot imagine their own parents having sex, so if I sell a few less books because I choose not to go into sexual details, then so be it.

I will, however, answer the second question. Yes, my wife and I still have sex, although I must use a condom that will protect Jodi from contracting the AIDS virus. I have children and that is all I feel comfortable saying.

I will say one other thing and that is: homosexuals are no more promiscuous, and probably less so, than heterosexuals. When I meet someone who is gay, he usually does not want to become involved with a married man. His major concern is breaking up a marriage. If we manage to get past the married part, the next topic I mention is I'm HIV positive. I suppose I come with a lot of baggage.

Chapter XIII

VISTING WEEKEND

July 23, 2001

JODI, HILLARY, PERI AND I visited Stacie at camp this weekend. Visiting weekend is probably my favorite time of year. Come along; you're invited, too. Celebrate 'Father Nature' with me. Bring some Kleenex along.

I'm going to ask you a question, but before you answer, think about your answer. Maybe ask your lover the same question. What is the most beautiful sight you've ever seen? Was it a stained glass window in a cathedral in France, a beautiful landscape, a perfect sunset overlooking the dunes where you first made love to your lover whom you allowed to escape from your life, or perhaps your spouse on your wedding day, or was it the look in your lover's eyes the day you both decided to spend the rest of your lives together? My answer to that question is: the image of my girls walking arm-in-arm. For me, this is the most beautiful sight in the world. Similar views are available to many but visible only to a select few. This scene is the reason I cried three times that weekend: once from seeing my girls, once from telling my wife how I felt at that moment, and once from reliving the moment all over again with my girls.

I will probably be criticized for my thinking in the next few paragraphs, but first I would like to say I am truly blessed by having three daughters who are so loving, especially considering the fact that I am bisexual and on the gay side of the spectrum. I have taken the liberty to include Stacie at this time, because if she does not agree that this book should be written then you will not have read my story. I am further appreciative that people like me are not usually biological fathers. The few who are probably do not raise their children in a typical married setting, so this places me in a unique position in fathering, one I am extremely grateful for and do not take for granted.

I stated earlier that I think gay people have been willing to explore a sexual side that has not been accepted by society. I also believe there are very few 100% gay people or 100% heterosexual people, and that we are all a combination of the two. If the range weighs in at 50/50, then we are truly bisexual. If we fall in a range of 25/75, we are probably still in a bisexual range. I think there are a lot of people who are afraid to explore their bisexual side because society says it's wrong. Consequently, married or not, a lot of people are living with repressed feelings to some extent.

On the other hand, a bisexual or gay person has taken a step toward breaking society's standards. It takes a certain amount of courage to deal with this issue. Just admitting you are bisexual (even to yourself) means you are guilty by society's rules. You are even guilty in the eyes of the gay community. Check out the movie *Chasing Amy*, if you don't believe me. Society has also judged you guilty if you're gay. To be willing to face the world and admit that you are a nonconformist and that you are gay or bisexual takes more confidence, sensitivity, and creativity than the average sexually repressed person has for such a task.

I touched on this earlier, but it goes back to: Why do you think there are so many more gays involved in music and the arts than in Wall Street and the Law? So the question arises:

Are gay people more creative than heterosexuals? While I don't think it's true of every gay person, I think as a general statement you can say a higher percent of gay people choose artistic and musical careers as compared to straight people.

So here I was, this bisexual or gay person, thrilled to be witnessing this arm-in-arm confirmation of sisterly love. At the beginning of the summer and for about the first 12 years of Stacie's life, I never expected to see such closeness because Peri was always a touch intolerant of Stacie. If Stacie coughed, she didn't cover her mouth; if she breathed, she breathed too loud. Peri always loved Stacie, but maybe didn't like her up until about a year ago when gradually Peri began taking Stacie's side whenever Jodi or I criticized Stacie. After Stacie went to camp, Peri wrote Stacie every day, sometimes two or three letters a day. She began to miss Stacie terribly and couldn't wait to see her and bring her presents and candy wrapped in baskets laden with ribbons. Hillary and Peri really went overboard, and I know Stacie appreciated it a lot. So now all three sisters have become each other's best friend. That is the most beautiful sight in the world for a father to see. I am saddened by the fact there are so few fathers who get to witness a similar scene.

The cameras are rolling and the scene replays itself before my eyes as I see Jodi's love, guidance and hugs over the years. My vision is clear; there is nothing obstructing my view and from my vista I observe my girls learning to negotiate life a little more triumphantly each day. Their ability to deal with issues is evident even in their disagreements and in the manner they resolve their problems. They repeatedly display for me how much they are developing, growing and maturing, sometimes taking one step back, but always two steps forward. Seeing this past weekend how they have arrived at such a perfect, harmonious state and seem to be in such an incredible state of equilibrium, I wish they could stay in their current mindset forever.

The love, the caring and the need to protect each other are as real and clear and timeless as the ageless pines framing a cloudless sky that one dreams about. And the dream becomes reality as the girls snuggle under their protective canopy at their summer home. I know there will always be fights and disagreements, but they have reached such a level of maturity and love and respect for each other, that even the disagreements will be resolved and forgotten quickly. Jodi, these girls are the most fitting tribute to you. They are a priceless gift, and just one more reason why I believe there is justice in this world.

Is anybody out there listening? Does anybody understand where I am coming from? My girls are the three girls you see in the painting, frolicking in ankle-deep water in the ocean. It's the watercolor that costs between $5,000 and $8,000. You know, the one you see when you go to Nantucket or whatever resort area you go to. It's the scene you would love to have and place above the fireplace in your living room, but you just don't want to spend that much money. Your excuse is easy. What would I do with the portrait of grandma and grandpa that's already hanging there? Or I'll take a photograph of my kids at the beach and hang that photo instead. The vacation ends and you completely forget about the picture. A story comes to mind when Jules was in New York for Stacie's Bat Mitzvah. Jules' children decided to have a family portrait taken. The picture came out great and Irene, his girlfriend, figured out the perfect place for it: Jules' Orlando home above the fireplace, so 'we' would have to take down the image of Jules' mother watching over us. As far as the 'we' goes, count me out. I'm surprised you didn't read about it in the newspapers. Don't you read?

MAN STRANGLES GIRLFRIEND AS GIRLFRIEND REMOVES PICTURE OF MOTHER

It wasn't quite that bad. Irene suggested the picture of Grandma Helen could slide further down the wall. Can you imagine suggesting to a Jewish man to remove a picture of his mother?! Maybe Irene was pulling a Richard-move and was just trying to get a reaction from Jules. That's the type of thing I would say, then cover my mouth because I was laughing so hard, and doing this all just to get a reaction. I used to do that with Grandma Beverly in her later years when she was beginning to lose it. I would mention her sister Eva and she would remember arguments from half a century ago. It's kind of like when people get old and their hearing goes bad. They hear and they know everything. There's nothing you can say that they haven't heard before, and they're tired of hearing whatever it is that you have to say. What can you possibly tell them that will make them happy once they've already reached their final, preliminary resting home? Next stop, cemetery. I can just picture Grandma saying, "That's okay, this old-age home smelled the day I got here." Actually in fairness to my mother, Aunt Ronnie, Jodi, Hillary, Peri, Stacie, and to a smaller extent myself, everyone gave tremendously of their time and love to make Grandma Beverly's final years in the nursing home a little more pleasant. No one acted like better daughters than my mother and Aunt Ronnie. If Grandma Beverly sneezed there would be a carton of tissues delivered within minutes. The two sisters had and continue to have a very close relationship. There was never any talk of 'it's your turn to do this for Mom.'

Since you got me started on Grandma Beverly, just one more story. Grandma lived until about 96. She never exercised a day in her life and her diet consisted of whatever was not nailed down. Herring and cream sauce and chocolate cake would suffice for breakfast. I remember the time I was in college and Grandma was recuperating from some kind of operation and had lost about fifteen pounds. I didn't think she needed to put the weight back on, but maybe for medical reasons, she did. Papa Al, Grandma's husband, must have been close to 80 and he wasn't going to be taking care of her. Besides, he was working for Joel and me at a cozy eatery that we operated on our college campus. So it was decided that Grandma would stay at my parents' house where my mother could feed her a few extra meals a day so that she could gather back her fifteen pounds. Someone forgot to tell Grandma she didn't have to gain the lost weight back in three or four days. Nobody was exactly running away with Grandma's lost weight. Grandma devoured everything but the kitchen sink. Then one day Joel came over for lunch. We had our bite to eat and put our glasses and plates in the dishwasher. When my mother came home later that afternoon Grandma started complaining about the mess I had left in the kitchen. The reality is it was her own mess.

That reminds me of my own mess that I'm in right now. We were talking about visiting weekend and somehow we began discussing girlfriends being strangled and grandmothers chasing after lost weight. All I ever wanted was to spend time with my family. On that visiting day the whole family seemed to bond in missing Stacie. We had been inhabiting our house, but Stacie's spirit and energy were absent. Maybe I missed her the most. I found it odd that the camp my girls attended was filled with people from an economic stratum that I clearly did not belong to. There are four economic classes in this country: lower, middle, upper and then Point O' Pines. Point O' Pines was the camp my girls summered at. Hopefully the camp owners, Sue and Jim, will cash my deposit check for the 2002 camp season so Stacie will be granted a 'stay' and we will not lay claim to the only campless child in 'our world'. Visitors spend hundreds of dollars doling out jewelry, cameras, hats, stuffed animals, shoes and candy to the 'deprived' campers. Even we got caught up in it to a lesser extent, but I brought something that I don't think any other parents brought their child: flowers. It was a last minute thing, picking a fresh bouquet from a meadow while I was waiting to chauffeur 'La Passenger'. I think Stacie appreciated the gesture because it's something that money can't buy. If you miss your chance, you can't take it over again. Actually, the camp scenery (and here I include the owners) is quite beautiful and interesting. The land juts out into Brant Lake and water is visible from most areas of the property. Tall pines dot the waterfront. We take a family portrait every year on the second floor deck overlooking the lakefront. From this deck you can see the water-skiing area, private beach, and a beautiful lake that stretches at least seven miles. The site is majestic in its beauty and I am thrilled to be able to send my kids to what might be the best camp in the country. Even the food is good. The owners Jim and Sue have owned the camp forever. All the mothers hate Sue. It's great. Sue doesn't care if you are showcasing the $2,000 handbag. In fact, I can just imagine her telling these mothers, 'No, I will not add the 20th cereal because 19 is enough.' That comment would be a typical response if one of the mothers said, "My princess doesn't like any of the 19 cereals you serve." Sue, this is not intended as a put-down, but I think I'd get off on it, too. Poor Sue, we are relatives by style. We both express our thoughts honestly for the betterment of those voices often heard, but more often silenced: children and those suffering from any ailment or disability.

And, I, the darling child, hear stories of what these mothers say and I would respond in kind, except I would be snickering as my parents and I bid a tearful 'good-bye', wondering whether Sue and Jim would receive my parents' deposit for next year's summer season by September or October.

Otherwise they'd be stuck with me for the summer!

Why is it that people with money always think they are right or they are entitled to something extra? Some things you cannot buy and good manners and respect are two of them. I love when my daughters say 'good-bye' and 'thank you' and then ask me if they should give someone a hug. My answer is always 'yes', although by now that should not surprise you.

The rest of the weekend is filled with scrumptious breakfasts, lunches and dinners. The camp lunch is my favorite. Each year I look forward to tasty barbecued steak, fried chicken, salads and heaping trays of brownies. Fresh fruit bowls are hauled out by two Russians. Coffee is continuously available as you dine, or rather picnic, under this canopy of pines. The terrain cascades down to meet the water. The lawn forms a plaza and it is surrounded by rustic well-kept buildings, slate patios, potted flowers in full bloom, and a few Adirondack chairs to remind you that you are partaking in exploring one of the most unspoiled areas of our country. If you drive around the entire lake, you swear you are in some European country on a meandering road. Maybe the lure of the area is that it is so undiscovered, a modern day frontier; my hunger to be a modern day explorer is what draws me to the area. I'm getting hungry again, so let me tell you about "René's". It's a great place and they are famous for desserts. Usually it's a treat just to hear the seven or eight desserts being offered for the evening, but this year we were anxious to complete the meal and head back to our room. A typical dessert might be warmed blueberry ice cream laced with shavings of raspberry-infused white chocolate with mango cream, *garni* with a citrus glaze.

If your culinary palate is not satisfied by gorging on a rich dessert, or even sampling a smidgen of a portion of such, then let me tell you about breakfast. Breakfast begins with a pleasant greeting from Judy and Carl and fresh orange juice and coffee. Then you move on to succulent fruit, quiche, French toast, blueberry or blackberry pancakes with local maple syrup, and homemade muffins, coffee cakes or whatever else Judy conjures up. You sit around and dine at a formal dining table set for ten hungry breakfast-people. The *brekfeastians* are all friendly. I think that's the nature of folks who prefer the charm and coziness of a family-run inn to the austerity and anonymity of a large hotel. I can just imagine staying at the Sagamore, the fancy hotel where the majority of the campers' *mealtickets* go slumming! I'd ask to speak to the owner who, of course, nobody would know. Perhaps it's a corporation. Maybe the company president was in town by chance for the annual corporate golf tournament. They would ask me if I would like to speak to the President and I would say 'yes, thank you.' I'd give him a big hug and tell him how much I enjoyed staying at the Sagamore. Somewhere in the middle of the hug, five golfers would be screaming for the police. 'Get this nutcake out of here!' Happy to oblige, I prefer the Landon Hill, anyway. Besides, Judy gives a mean hug. I love our room, the Adirondack Room. It's something you wouldn't expect at a Bed and Breakfast. The ceiling is all wood and one side is all windows. The other two sides have about ten feet of running windows. Maybe the room was once a screened-in porch. The view from the room consists of walls of trees that are so dense, it's impossible to see the distant road beyond. And right in the middle of the yard is the best kept secret in Chestertown. There is this mammoth, beautifully shaped evergreen that is so overpowering it's comparable to the Rockefeller Center Christmas Tree. I think it might even be taller. Jodi and I enjoy Judy's and Carl's hospitality so much that when we heard they were planning their first trip to New York City, we insisted they stay at our place. When we saw them this weekend we invited them back again. Judy, if you read this book I must apologize, because it seemed as if Jodi and I were rushing the entire weekend. And, Judy, I want you to know that Hillary and Peri also appreciated your warmth and hospitality. By the way, if we forget to tell you, we will be staying both Friday and Saturday night next year.

So what really was the highlight of the weekend? If the three sisters walking arm-in-arm isn't enough for you then I could tell you about our passenger, but I won't. The mother of a friend of one of my children asked for a ride up to the camp. When someone asks for a favor, I don't like to say 'no', even though I highly value my private time with my family. We had some interesting conversations about my book and life in general. However, since the passenger was merely an acquaintance, her knowledge of my family was very much limited to what we discussed in the car. The passenger introduced us to instrumental jazz music and we all agreed this was pleasant music to listen to while driving. Under normal circumstances, I'm always fighting with the kids. They don't like my music and I don't like theirs.

Do you remember a few chapters ago I was talking about visiting my old neighborhood? Maybe I'm trying to find out something about myself from when I was younger. I'm really not sure. Maybe it's like a police drama on TV where the detective finds an accordion, and inside the case there is a key, and through some clever deduction he can trace the accordion to a specific year. The serial number on the accordion proves it to be the sample model and the 85-year-old salesman still remembers the man who purchased the only accordion the salesman had sold that day, only because he worked in a piano store, and someone seeking an accordion is not all that common. And the key is now traceable to a safety deposit box in a bank that is now defunct, but it had cost too much money to remove the vault, so the vault had been left in place.

I purchased that accordion during visiting weekend and you must be dying to find out what the key opens. It's an imaginary key and maybe it will open something up about my past. Even if it doesn't, the accordion is a beautiful instrument, except I never got the hang of it. I took lessons for five years before 'calling it a day'. I was terrible. I had no sense of rhythm. Ask my kids who the worst dancer out there is. If they had a website address www.worstdancers.com I would pop up on your screen. On the other hand, nobody has more fun dancing than Jodi and I do. I promise that if this book is successful, I will have the biggest 50th birthday party on August 29th, 2002 and Mikey Mike will be the DJ. I don't care if he has a wedding booked for that date. The bride and groom will just have to change their date.

Chapter XIV

THE TREE AND ME

LIFE'S A BUMMER. I'VE BEEN sitting on this bench in the Village facing Bleecker, Cornelia and life, writing for the past forty-five minutes, and it's pretty hot. I am protected by an awning in case it rains. Damn it, rain already! Unfortunately, there's not a cloud in the sky and the sun is low, so the awning does not even protect me from the heat. I would love to sit here and write when the sun goes down in the early evening, but by that time I will have run out of things to say, or opt to leave and go to the gym. You can kick yourself now for having wasted your time reading this paragraph.

Did you ever wish you could make time stand still? For how long? A second, a year, an eternity? An eternity, count me out. How depressing to look at my messy hair, day in and day out, forever. Why is it that I and the rest of the world must always wear a watch? Wouldn't it be great not to worry about time? Is it time for dinner, is it time to play, is it time to go jogging, is it time to go to sleep? I can't even take an afternoon off and do my writing without thinking about what I'll be doing that evening. Great, the sun has finally set. I still haven't decided if I will stay in the city tonight or go home. I have a feeling my kids appreciate me a tad more when they don't see me for a day. They seem to tolerate my sense of humor and are more likely to let me chill with their friends for thirty or forty minutes.

I still am very much concerned about my children and how their friends will deal with my being bisexual and HIV positive. I have given an early draft of my story to friends and relatives, as I need to get some feedback. I've never written a book before. Somehow I think you figured that out chapters ago. Anyhow, one friend said, "Your friends will be your friends and they will stick by you; you are the same person you were yesterday." I want to believe that is true and I do believe it for a few reasons. First, I believe in the human spirit and that people are understanding and compassionate. I also know I haven't hurt anybody. I am guilty of not having been honest with people for some time, but in the end, it was only myself I was hurting by not being honest. To test your own truthfulness, ask yourself how many secrets you are hiding because you want to protect someone. Second, I am basically a confident person. My story is proof that you can take a negative situation and make something positive out of it. And third, I believe in friends and family. I know my family and Joel, my closest male friend, will always be there for me. My head is not totally in the clouds despite what you may think, even though there were references made in an earlier chapter of me looking down on the world from the clouds above. I know there are people who will make a federal case out of my poetry, 'my life and my wife', and there may even be a comparison to 'Bill and Hill'. After you have read this book and if you think anyone would feel negative about my wife after hearing our story, then pass this book on to dispel that myth. Sure, I'd prefer the world to like me, too, but as long as I'm loved by my family, that's the important part of my life.

Please don't underestimate my wife. Think about what options she really has. Jodi is a beautiful, caring, kind, personable, passionate woman who could surely have found another husband. Financially I offered Jodi whatever she wanted. Somebody recently told Jodi that she should have given me an ultimatum to stop being with men or else get out. After all, Jodi is still young and could go on with her life. I was there and heard the hurtful remark. It was clearly addressed to Jodi, so it was not my place to answer. Jodi's answer was pure Jodi. It was simple, direct, and spoken from the heart. Jodi said that she never asked anyone's opinion because she had no doubt how she wanted to live her life. I was the one she wanted to live with for the rest of her life. Great answer! That's just one of the reasons I love her so much. Jodi always knows what to say and how to say it. If you met Jodi for the first time you might think she was a bit simple after a ten-minute conversation. But after an hour you would realize Jodi sees things very clearly and there are no problems, only solutions. Friends who have known Jodi for years recognize her wisdom. These friends will be surprised and shocked by my bisexuality and HIV status, but they will not be shocked by Jodi's commitment to me. Jodi's commitment is based on the type of person she is and the type of person she has molded me into. I'd like to think I have matured over the years into a kinder, more caring individual, largely because of my wife.

July 26, 2001

Do you ever find yourself making a promise to your child that is impossible to keep, but because a promise is a promise, you have to keep it? One of my girls told me a story that I cannot repeat here. Even if I were to modify the story and change the names and places, it would be obvious who I was talking about. I would just like to take time out now to address this evil man who was hurtful to my child this past week and let that person know he really did the wrong thing. My daughter won't let me approach this individual directly, so all I can say is this person is a total jerk. I feel sorry for him and would never print even a fictitious version of his story, because he's just not worth it, and besides, the purpose of this book is not to hurt anyone. It's a funny thing. I can forgive people who have hurt me in business, but I can't forgive a plumber from 20 years ago who hurt my mother, or someone who hurt my child last week. All these people need to do is say they're sorry. Is that such a hard word to say? Some people can't find the word in their vocabulary. Too bad for these people. In the long run, it becomes their loss.

I did promise you a poem about the Bassett tree, so here goes:

THE TREE AND ME

I went to visit you the other day
You smiled as if you had something to say

A tree cannot possibly talk
So I thought I'd clear my head and go for a walk

Perhaps you had secrets you needed to share
With someone who loved plants who really would care

So I ask you Mr. Tree, what makes you glad?

You replied, "a lemonade stand and a child on a sunny day
And lots of children coming out to play

I love providing a place for the children to play in the shade
Or a baby in a carriage whose eyes are beginning to fade

Sometimes the children come out and turn on the hose
All hell breaks loose and anything goes

And then they spray water on my bark
That keeps me cool in the evening when it's dark"

Mr. Tree, what are your dreams?
"Hearing the clamoring of hammers it seems

Would be a good reason
In a warm season

To think that a tree house might be erected
On my very limbs if they'd be selected"

Mr. Tree, what do you know about pain?
"When I hear the words prune and maintain

I hate when the gardener thinks the plants need a trimming
It's his brain cells I think that are probably dimming

What really hurt me the most
I felt your spirit I saw your ghost

Your scream I felt in my trunk
I felt a sadness and I shrunk

And trembled as I felt your grief
And then I realized there would be no relief

For the tree that you planted across the street
Would no longer be able to repeat

A moment of shade for a little boy of eight
Whose life was now ended by a very sad fate

An ax felled the tree
It was a horrific sight to see"

Mr. Tree, what do you fear?
"When people listen but no longer care

I fear the wind on a summer night
A strong gust and anything could happen tonight

If my leaves were to fall and my branches were bare
This is something I dare say I'd fear

Who would want to find shade
Below a leafless tree that was made

Bare and barren in its prime
I'd be left behind for another time

But one more thing I really fear
And this is something you need to hear

When the children grow up and move away
I will miss the day they are not here to play"

Mr. Tree, what are your favorite seasons?
Can you explain all of your reasons?

"I love the fall when my leaves turn gold orange and red
Or perhaps the spring instead

The smell of freshness in the air
And the children playing without a care

I do my best growing in the spring
One year a rope was hung for a child to swing

My limbs became very weary
I was afraid for the child for it would be scary

I braced myself for the occasion
And through some inner persuasion

The rope held firm and did not break
Thank God, oh for goodness sake

A child falling and scraping his knee
Is something I just hate to see"

Mr. Tree, what advice do you have for me?

"Always be loving and strong
And be willing to admit when you are wrong

Remember don't forget the number five
        (Family members total 5)
This will keep your spirit alive

If this is something you don't understand
Then you are as helpless as an arm without a hand

I cannot tell you what you don't know
It's something you found thirteen years ago"
        (Stacie is 13 and always on the go)

Mr. Tree, tell me the secret of life

"You look at a bird in flight
And you think for one second you might
Soar through the sky and fly throughout the night

Or you look at me and admire my height
And wonder what dreams I might have for tonight

My limbs reach for the sky and the stars
And the bird might fly to Mars

But you have a great dream
Believe in yourself, others and it will seem

That you've found the secret in life
Along with your wonderful wife

Go forth and follow your heart
I will allow you one more question before we part"

Mr. Tree, when will I die?

"That is such an easy question for me
It's really quite clear it's plain to see

You die when you no longer continue to grow
This is something you already know

And even if you weren't aware
This is why you've chosen a new career

You're strong and your story must be told
Be kind, be caring, go forth and be bold"

Chapter XV

IF YOU HAVE A DREAM MAKE IT HAPPEN

July 28th: MY PARENTS' ANNIVERSARY. I had a long talk with my mother today. My mother feels I should be telling Victor about my illness. I promised her I would tell him by the end of the summer. If by chance you think my mother awoke at three in the morning and said, "I can't sleep. I'm going to phone Richard and initiate a conversation about his being HIV positive," then obviously you don't know anything about Jewish mothers. The definition of a Jewish mother is: sweep everything under the carpet. Keep those family secrets buried. Our gabfest was initiated by me when I asked my mother why she never told her boyfriend Herb about me. She said she felt it would accomplish nothing, as Herb always speaks so highly of her children and their families. She believes Herb would have to start clarifying his statement about one of her sons. Ouch! I guess that's supposed to hurt, but you either become numb after a while, or you decide to write a book. Mother, even though we just had this conversation, I'm still the same man I was yesterday and I'm still your same loving son. I'm also the husband and father I always was and will continue to be. Actually, the fact that you wanted me to tell Victor or could even openly discuss the topic was a bit surprising.

I was continuing to wonder what my mother would think about my forthcoming book. Would she trash it or praise it?

Why couldn't I formulate her reaction? After all, I'd known her for almost 49 years. Was there something in my past that held the answer? Perhaps I could learn something about my past from a photograph. Have you ever looked at a family having their portrait taken and noticed one person looking very impatient with another family member? Sometimes the photographer captures the less than tender moment on film and the 'proof' is quickly tossed. Looking into our family's hourglass as the sand passed through, I sifted through my mother's albums. I thought I might find a grain of truth as to how I got into the position I am in now.

Telephoning my mother and suggesting that we review the family albums to see if I was hugged and held closely, or sneered at, was not the type of conversation I was looking forward to. I didn't exactly lie but I told my mother I was interested in seeing pictures of the relatives from years ago. She took me quite literally, but as the saying goes: Be careful what you ask for, you just might get it. That's exactly what happened. I got to see a collection of relatives from twenty or thirty years before I was even born. After about a half-hour, that was it for me. I wasn't sure if my mother even knew the babies whose names she was rattling off. I sensed my mother being both sad and impatient; I was prying and intruding into her past. Even the great-grandparents seemed to be frowning at me. Why is it these ancient ancestors never smiled? Was this banned in the Magna Carta and when was smiling finally tolerated? (Maybe they didn't have laxatives back then, or they had too many kids and were straining to remember all their names and birthdays.) Anyhow, the photo review session was going nowhere and since my mother was feeling uncomfortable, there was no reason to continue.

So how could the 48-year-old Richard find his answers in the past? Could the 48-year-old Richard have detected a glimmer of his current life and predicament by examining the four-year-old version of himself? I decided to travel that road and I invited Jodi along for the ride.

We visited the old neighborhood yesterday. We saw my apartment building, my grammar school, and Flatbush Avenue from one end of town to the other. Quite an interesting way to view Brooklyn. The neighborhood and landscape constantly change until you see the skyline of Manhattan. One thing left me rather depressed. Meyer Glick, the man who gave me my scooter, would be so sad if he were alive to see his house today. He once tended a magnificent garden, but now it was uprooted by an ugly two-story, brick, tenement-looking building. Meyer's garage door was in shambles and obviously was not even operable. Other than that, the old neighborhood sort of had a quaint charm to it, and I was glad I had made the visit. But the purpose of my trip was to find answers to my past. To that end nothing was gained.

Since there were no answers to be found in my past, I realized it was time to relocate back to the present and assess where I now was. Jodi and I were still fumbling around trying to find an agent for my book. I hardly had a clue as to what to even ask an agent. I was afraid of coming across as a dummy with a great story. Jodi and I had discussed my book with Louisa who said it was a great story and that I'd be on *Oprah* someday. That seed was planted in Jodi's brain. Soon Jodi suggested we really take our story to Oprah. 'What a great idea! Let's get on television and have agents clamoring to meet us.' So I wrote a letter to Oprah. I had already written the introduction to my book which I sent to Oprah, along with the epilogue that Jodi had written, plus a few excerpts and a poem.

Other than that the only news for the day was that Jodi and I jogged for three hours in Central Park and we both felt it was one of our best runs. That clocked in at about 17 miles for Jodi and 18 for me. We still have not been granted our acceptance to the marathon, so I may be asking for an army of volunteers to protect my wife and me from being pulled out of the race.

July 30th. I'm scared. I've known for a long time that I'd be writing my story, but there were other issues going on in my life. Hillary will be leaving for college the very next day after Stacie finds out about me. After Hillary leaves, nobody will be there when I walk into her room at eleven at night. I will miss our late night talks. No one will be asking to drive my car and there will be no Hillary to yell at for the 1,000,001 things she does wrong. But mostly there will be one less person to give me a hug every day. We've gotten a lot closer since I decided to write this book, and it will be very difficult for me when she leaves. I'm crying as I'm writing this, and I wish she could be here to share in my happiness when my story is finally told. I will miss you terribly, Hillary.

Dear Hillary,

There are so many thoughts I'd like to share with you that I hardly know where to begin. It's getting near that time when you will be going off to college and you will have to fend for yourself, so why am I crying? Does that mean I have to fend for myself, too? I've come to count on you a lot more than I realized. We both know we've gotten so much closer since we decided that I had to be honest and tell my story.

From the day Mom and I first discussed having a child we were scared like most parents, but we knew that children were what we wanted more than anything. About a year later you were born; you were named for two very special people who would have adored you more than anything in the world. The years passed and we were blessed with two other children. Peri became your best friend, and more recently, you have found a second best friend in Stacie.

Hillary, you have no idea how many times I have replayed the video of your bat mitzvah. Your beauty and poise and command of the day were all breathtaking.

I know the high school years were difficult. They were difficult for me, too, as I relived your pain. My situation did not help any, although I know we both feel that after going through so much, we are stronger and more loving now and have never felt closer to each other.

Hill, sometimes it's just the little things I will remember: spending a day with me at work, letting me hang out for a few minutes with your friends, or just holding me, or maybe the 1,000,000 conversations we had on the telephone when you said, "I love you."

I'm so proud and happy for you that you have afforded yourself such a positive self-image this summer. I know you will have an exciting year in Florida. I wish I could be there to share it with you, but that's exactly what will make it exciting for you. You will be independent and free to make your own choices. I pray the majority of these choices will be the right ones. Always look to your heart if your brain tells you it's a tossup. You have a good heart, and even if you make wrong decisions, your mother and I will always be proud of you.

I'm sorry I was harsh with you when you wouldn't end things with *Brucifer*. I never could have thrown you out and I hope you know that. You're a part of me and if ever I lost you, it would be like cutting off my arm. Hill, I'm also sorry for not being the perfect father and for having to put our family through so much. If I wrote everything in my heart that I'm feeling right now, I would be rewriting my life story, which I have just written.

There is no easy way to say good-bye to a child who is setting off to live her own life and fulfill her dreams. In many ways it will be harder for you than it is for me, but always remember in a weak moment or at a time when your spirit is soaring, I love you and our family so much!

Love, Dad

August 4th. What a difference four years make. It seems like a lifetime ago I was faced with telling Jodi I was HIV positive. We talked about it as we jogged in Central Park today. I was glad we had scheduled only a 14-mile run because it wasn't an easy run for me. I started to feel a shin splint coming on from the beginning of the run. After a long run, it's nice to take it easy, so I finished David Sedaris's book *Naked*. Michael, from Po, suggested I read the book. I think he finds my style similar to Sedaris's. Since I am but a novice, I am flattered by the comparison. However, I think I lack the consistent sarcasm that David has and I found myself wondering if all David's stories were true. I found the reading very entertaining. The words and pages flow, even though nothing he says seems overly important or relevant. I actually mean that as a compliment. If the writer can sustain a reader without a powerful love story, exotic setting, or a plot to blow up the world, more power to the writer. One gets the feeling David woke up one day and said, 'Nothing good on TV today, it's drizzling outside, I have enough cigarettes, so let me put my letters together and buckle down and tell my story.' David then proceeded to knock out his story in a day or two, being the masterful storyteller that he is.

Since I have my children to reflect on, I seem to have more material to draw from. Peri has changed tremendously this summer and has developed a marked confidence in herself and her sense of style. She is also way beyond her years in knowing what is important in life and what isn't. One, good grades are important. Two, steady boyfriends are definitely out, since you expend too much time and energy on them and somebody always gets hurt; besides, it's more fun going out with different guys. Three, fancy schmancy cars. Forget them. You can't count on job security from employers. Four, good friends are important. Friends who have been traveling to Europe, California, upstate New York and elsewhere check in with Peri almost on a daily basis, because everyone loves Peri. However, Peri's biggest lesson learned has to do with a job that she had for the summer. I started to mention the story in my July 26th entry and there are three reasons why I am now going to tell you the story. The first reason is: nobody who hurts my child can expect me to remain silent. The second reason is, and I need a drum roll for this: this is the one time out of a hundred I was right and my wife was wrong. The third reason is: nobody makes a fool of my wife, even if Jodi's judgment was wrong this once.

Peri worked in a local coffee shop in the spring. The owner paid Peri a few dollars per hour and Peri made a few more dollars from the customers' tips. If the owner didn't pay a salary, the job would not be lucrative and he would be without a waitress. Peri informed the owner she would like to work full-time in the summer and the owner said he would work her into a schedule, but could not be specific as to whether it would include days, evenings or weekends. Peri started working two or three days, but soon the owner told Peri he had a lot of college students returning from last year. Peri wanted to work more. She knew full well a lot of these kids would call in sick and go to the beach on a sunny day. Also, some of the kids left early for college. Peri knew she was extremely well-liked by the local gentry. She also always arrived at work promptly. Naturally she figured that if there were extra days to be had she would get those days. This did not come to pass.

It all started when Peri became upset after the owner told her that she would not be receiving any salary from him for the day that she had worked. The owner told Peri that she had not done a good job and that was the reason she would not be getting paid. Peri was so outraged that a few days later she went back to the coffee shop and gave the owner a piece of her mind. The owner gave Peri the few dollars that were due her. Peri told him that it wasn't about the money, but the principle, and gave it back to him, money and all. She wanted nothing more to do with this deadbeat. It was at this time that Peri finally agreed to let Jodi and me speak to the owner.

In a flash, Jodi and I went down to the coffee shop and I, too, gave him a piece of my mind. Peri is an excellent worker, and from what I had witnessed, was working harder than the other girls. I explained to the owner I had employed many people over the years and that if I was not pleased with their work, I would give them a few warnings. If after that they did not change, I would fire them. But there was never a situation where I withheld their salary, even if they had made mistakes that cost me money. Then the truth from the owner came out. During the summer, the tips were much better than in the spring; this I had already known. The bottom line was: even without a salary the waitresses made more in tips in the summer than they did with a salary and tips in the spring. The owner never mentioned to Peri that the summer workers were not getting a salary and the owner resented having to pay Peri a salary. From the owner's point of view and from a business point of view, he felt it unnecessary to pay a salary if he didn't have to. That's all okay, except when you make a commitment to give a sixteen-year-old a summer job. If you have no intention of paying her a salary, it is your obligation to tell her so. Then the owner started rambling on about his family's personal tragedies. Even though his story was quite sad, he knew that I had been previously informed of his story, so to me it was old news. Perhaps he should write a memoir, or if that's too painful, an autobiographical novel. I think that the levels of depression he must have sunk to, his feelings of hopelessness, and how he chose to negotiate life and go forward would make an engrossing story. Learning how to deal with tragedy and growing from it and developing compassion for others is what life is all about. I don't think the owner ever found daylight at the end of his dark tunnel. If he had, he would not have treated Peri as if she were some child laborer in the 1800s when 'kindness' and 'caring' were foreign to the English language. If the story simply ended like this, I would not have told it, but here's what really bothered me. Even though my child did not lose one bit of confidence in herself, my wife lost her edge for knowing whether or not citizens are being honest*Abel*. The owner seemed to be feeling very sad and apologetic. He volunteered to telephone Peri, but as of this date he has still not called her. Jodi walked out of the coffee shop after our discussion, feeling a little better. After all, hadn't the owner shown such remorse? I didn't buy his story at all, because what he did was clearly wrong and not telephoning Peri was just further proof that he was not sorry. Trying to find a job at that time of year when all the summer jobs were taken was a job in itself. Peri has not been able to find another job and that is mighty frustrating for a hard-working, ambitious kid who is saving for a car.

Jodi and I are very much aware of how important it is to raise strong, confident children. We both have issues from our own upbringing. We did not get the confidence that we needed to stand tall and strong. In my mother's world, I am a good son and am to be respected as long as I keep my secrets buried. But I can't live like that. I know my kids will be teased by a minority of children who will say their father is a fag. It's very important for Jodi and me to know that our children are confident that we love them dearly and that we are proud of them without any 'buts'.

I'm sorry for being so miserly about putting pen to paper now. You see, I've become my own one-man public relations firm, trying to make this book successful. Jodi has been helping me in this direction and we bounce ideas off each other. Promoting my book, training for the marathon, and practicing architecture, which I still need to do to support my family, all take up a good portion of my waking hours. My theory is: if I can get some rather well known people to publicly recognize the potential benefit of having my story told, this will give my story a good deal of credibility. From this I can hope it will then be less likely for children to tease my children. I have written Oprah Winfrey to see if I can get on her show. However, I'm convinced Oprah gets thousands of letters a day which are probably screened by some summer intern, so I'm going to find out who her makeup artist and hairdresser are and bang out letters to them, as well as to her creative and marketing directors. I've also drafted a letter to Bill Clinton asking him to speak at Lawrence High School or to pen a brief foreword for my book. I even know someone who knows Donna Summer. I would love her to rewrite the words to "Somewhere, There's a Place For Us" from *West Side Story* and dedicate the song to me. I tried contacting Elton John and Elizabeth Taylor, but you can't reach these people directly. I will also be sending a letter to Hillary Clinton. Jodi wants to drop a line to Mary Fisher, an AIDS activist whom Jodi finds to be very inspiring.

Besides doing this for my children, I am, to be perfectly honest, doing this for myself. As I've said earlier, children at any age need the love and acceptance of their parents, and Jewish kids may need it a little extra. What will my mother be able to say when I tell her, "I'm writing my story, but I can't talk to you about it now because I'm late for a meeting with Bill and Hillary, I'll be on *Oprah* tomorrow, and Donna Summer and Elton John are singing a duet dedicated to me"? Even a Jewish mother would have to forgive her son for that.

Okay, Richard, let's get real. If you get even one positive response from the above group, you know you will be thrilled. That may be true, but don't forget the introduction:

IF YOU HAVE A DREAM MAKE IT HAPPEN
AND DON'T LET ANYONE KEEP YOU DOWN

Chapter XVI

SPEAK LOUD, WE HEAR YOU, NOT JUST ON THE GROUND

I've been carrying this manuscript
And people look at me like I've flipped

It's kind of like a woman and her pocketbook
Sometimes I need to have a second look

To make sure my characters and commas are all in place
Like a woman checking lipstick on her face

I placed the manuscript on the table by my side
And gave a kiss to my lovely bride

And closed my eyes and all seemed so calm
Surely a night with no cause for alarm

I could feel myself drifting off to sleep
And tucked in my brain would be another day's memories to keep

My brain was getting overstuffed with new thoughts
From childish pranks to villages and seaports

And so many characters to think about
And if I forgot one they might cry out

So off I drifted into the darkness of the night
Deeper, withdrawing for hours till the next daylight

I felt such a warm inner glow
As though I was sleeping many years ago

I knew the moment was right for me to dream
Everything was perfect or so it would seem

I dreamed of my recently purchased accordion
That was something you would have adored me in

And then my scooter from forty years past
Oh how I wish my scooter did last

And then I dreamed of the characters in my cast
Their personalities and styles were so vast

What would Oprah say to Elaine?
What would George Bush say to Jane?
Perhaps you could visit my father in Maine

Bill Clinton and Monica would make quite a pair
Championing causes they both felt were fair

Holly could make dresses for everyone in the book
No, too much satin, I couldn't stand to look

Aunt Helaine would make veal balls for all
That's perfect and I have one more call

Jules can get tickets to any place in the land
By getting on a chair and taking a stand

And Louisa could serve hugs and doughnuts
And Uncle Joe could send a platter of cold cuts

And then right before my eyes I saw
Walter and Andrea, I saw them for sure

I asked them what they were doing near my bed
They explained the house was full so instead

Of going home they were looking for a place
A pillow a blanket and perhaps a canopy of lace

Enough, enough, I said, is this a dream?
I'm sorry I didn't mean to scream

But I'm tired and if this is not real
Please go out and let's end this tale

You haven't greeted even a single guest
I agreed and said I needed my rest

What guests and how many are there?
Downstairs forty or fifty all without a chair

Well who are they and how did they get here?
You wished for them and then they appeared

I don't remember sending a single invitation
Nor receiving a single confirmation

You are correct, now open your book to any spot
Don't think about why, how, where or what

Count to three and I promise you a surprise
Of ballet dancers before your eyes

There's Aunt Helaine doing a pirouette
This is not the Aunt Helaine I met

And Alice doing cartwheels four feet above the ground
Perhaps a bottle of liquor I had downed

But I was awake and I knew this was real
It was not a mistake, this is something I could feel

I flipped through the book that was next to me
There was some text that I had to see

I found my dad, I stared at the word
I was so glad and then suddenly I heard

The light penetrating through my room and my soul
There was a four foot square hole

Cut through my bedroom wall
And the light had a voice and the light stood tall

It said, 'follow me and bring your bride too'
And in a flash the light fell on cue

And the wall sealed itself tight
And left not a memory of this night

I arose and looked outside
And then I remembered and tried

To recreate in my mind the magical balloon
That Stacie and I had traveled in to the moon

And then it came to me to see
Departure: Heaven, Arrival: Bassett Tree

I hurried to get dressed
And told every single guest

To meet me at the Bassett tree
For something in my soul needed to be free

I closed the book and Alice and Aunt Helaine
Dutifully folded themselves into a plane
Of two dimensions and did not complain

I woke Jodi and told her I had a promise to keep
And my story was long and filled with memories that would reap

An understanding of my past
Something I would find at last

But Jodi, you must trust everything that life has taught you
And especially the good life that God has brought you

You will see things in the stars tonight
That you will remember night after night

We gave the girls a gentle kiss on their face
And headed out the door in a race

We floored the car and off we went
Into the night our moments would be spent

Searching the heavens above and the stars
From Mercury to Pluto and Mars

For that bright balloon in the sky
And my answers to the question why

And there appeared before us above
A brilliant shining star and a single dove

Gliding the star down to our planet Earth
Perhaps to see if our life had worth

And then the car seemed to travel on its own
This was right, it's something I'd known

The car refused to stop for a single light
This for me was a true delight

I felt a power, I had no fear
This is something I really needed to share

I could find meaning in all God's magic
And understand why he caused things tragic

Or if you look inside and say this is final
Then you have as much substance as a cloth that is vinyl

But if you dare to dream and feel alive
You will grow and your spirit will survive

So come with me now for one more stop
Hurry 'cause the spaceship is about to drop

Assembled here are all the characters in my book
Who invited you all, I asked, and took a look

And then a gust of air rustled the leaves of the tree
And the tree would speak one last time to me

Richard is scared he has done many things wrong
I am here to help him and make him strong

Richard planted a seed, gave me life and watched me grow
This is something you all should know

From each of you Richard needs love
Forgiveness, kindness, a hug, a song
All of the above

Alice spoke first and said something very amazing
She was talking about me as if she were praising
A perfect person without flaws
I thanked her profusely because
She set the tone for a night without blame
Where perhaps I could dwell without feeling shame

Aunt Helaine dropped eighteen years
She hugged Uncle Ernie amidst eighteen cheers
They spoke from their heart
'Richard, we loved you from the start
We will not be wrong
We forgave you all along'

Elaine said, 'I love family and you know it is true
And that includes you, that's something you knew
Be kind to your family they adore you
I love you Richard, please know I'm always for you'

Louisa gave me a hug and a squeeze
It felt so good down to my knees
'I love everything about you
Please don't change, the world would not be the same without you'

Norma promised to write me a song
A chorus of friends would be required to sing along
'You are loved by many and I sincerely pray
Be strong, be healthy, and be here a long time, okay'

Andrea rose to her feet and spoke
She said, 'come here, come close all you folk
No one has a wife with a more radiant smile
And that comes only after a long while
When someone professes a love that is incurable
I think Richard is absolutely adorable'

Mike said if he had a brother
I would be his choice and no other
And if he was ever to have a daughter
He would look to me for the type mortar
That makes our family so tight
And makes our world seem so right

Jayne could not sit anymore
'We all love you Richard, we're not keeping score
You've always been a friend
Someone to count on and always depend
Please look to us at a time of need
You planted this tree from a seed
And it is the tallest one I see
Congratulations, you fathered a tree'

Joel was next and he had the kindest words to say
'You may be different but perhaps better in a way
If you weren't so kind your wife would not be here
She loves you, adores you and she really does care
It's that quality that I found in you
That will keep you my best friend too'

Patti looked at me and we both knew
'In this world there are only a select few
Who are blessed with happiness in their heart
And this is something my sister and you had from the start
And nothing can take that away
It's forever in your heart and there it will stay'

Lois got up and made quite a speech
She said I was kind, always within reach
Not distant, not evasive, but always there
With a kind word and always eager to hear
She wished me well and gave me a kiss
And said 'stay around a long time, it's you that I'll miss'

Rabbi Ginsburg got up and I was scared
This was a man that nobody feared
But I had sinned and broken a vow
Could he find forgiveness for me now?
'Richard, I blessed you three times in the past
This blessing I pray will last and last
I cannot say you live without sin
Life is not as simple as lose or win
It's about character and choice
I admire your strength, style and voice
Make a difference and make us all proud
God be with you, I say this quite loud'

There were numerous other visitors on the ground
Many would not have a chance to utter a sound
But they all came with a kind thought
Or a loving memory that they brought

And then this zeppelin-shaped spaceship landed
And something told me I would never again be abandoned

The passengers began to walk the steps down
And soon their feet would be touching the town

But there were no steps that I could see
And then I realized this night would be

A once in a lifetime event
That would be worth a lifetime spent

For there before us after their long journey
Dad, Meyer Glick, Uncle Ernie
And in the rear with a perfect tan
Grandma Beverly and Joanne

My mother and Aunt Ronnie saw Grandma Beverly
The three of them were such a sight to see
They told Grandma they loved her so much
And Grandma said, 'enough, enough
Don't make me late
I've got a game and they won't wait'
Some things will always be the same
Grandma found her corner in heaven in a card game
The sisters could not have asked for anything more
I think they've come to adore
Their mother even more than before

Jules found Joanne and his dream came true
He wanted to hold her one more time before his time was due
They embraced and held each other
And then realized there was a special mother
Who also needed to be held tight
Joanne and Jules held Jodi with all their might
And Joanne said, 'Jules, we did something right'
It wasn't like Mom to say I love you and all that stuff
But Jodi knew this was more than enough
Mom hugged me too and said 'I already know
I made my decision a long time ago
Go forth, be strong and speak in a loud voice
This is for humanity and we have no choice'

Elton John and Donna Summer were serenading the crowd
To a song I often sing out loud

"Somewhere, There's a Place for Us"

Something told me it was now or never
I reached for my father, I'll remember this forever and ever
My father said, 'be strong
Nothing you've done is wrong
I too am a father and I am proud of everything you do
This is something I think I learned from you
I know all about AIDS and I've seen its curse
There is nothing in this world that could be worse
Than you keeping quiet and not making a sound
SPEAK LOUD, WE HEAR YOU, NOT JUST ON THE GROUND
I love you and always have and always will
Now bring in your family 'cause I can only stay until
You, your family and mother are sure
What you are doing is right for finding the cure'
And then Hill, Per, Stace, Jodi and my mother
Gustofliably embraced one another
Thus beginning a marathon hug session
And ending with something I'd like to mention

Thank you all for being part of my life
My parents, children, and especially my wife

Chapter XVII

STACIE, THIS ONE'S FOR YOU

August 17, 2001

IT SEEMED LIKE ONE OF those endless summers that you read about. You know, the perfect wave, sunset, lover, beach that you accidentally stumble upon when you are at a turning point in your life and there, just beyond where the eye can see, the beach takes a convex turn and... I felt it and so did Jodi, Hillary and Peri. Maybe our lives were taking a turn and we couldn't quite make that turn without Stacie. We all needed Stacie home in the worst way. Stacie is such a likable, bubbly kid, gushing buckets full of sensitivity. We couldn't wait for her to be part of our life again. I have this intrinsic need to apologize to Stacie for keeping my secret from her.

We picked Stacie up at 1:45. The bus was a few minutes late. You could spot the Point O' Pines mothers in a second. Trim, fashionably dressed, the perfect handbag and their hair a mess. Put that mirror down, Richard! We are talking about the elite, not you. The passenger as referenced in an earlier chapter avoided Jodi and me, but that was okay as I did not feel like talking to her, either. So how do you go about telling your thirteen-year-old daughter that you are bisexual and HIV positive? Unfortunately, this is not one of those neighborly situations where you ring the bell next door and ask to borrow a cup of sugar, and then proceed to say, "By the way, from your experience, how do you tell your thirteen-year-old that you are bisexual and HIV positive?" Ouch, somebody just slammed the door in my face. It's not one of those contests where you pick the winning number, collect a prize, and we all live happily ever after. I am taking this seriously and I do have a plan, but if I were to lose my comedic side, hmmm... let me think about that, you might even like this chapter more. On the other hand, you've stuck it out with me this far, so why change flying balloons while I'm already up in the clouds?

After a good round of hugs we told Stacie what the surprise activity we had planned for her was. It wasn't a visit to the BMW showroom to buy a new car, or a private concert with the Backstreet Boys, or a personalized tour through Willie Wonka's candy factory. It was even better. We were going as a family to Hammacher Schlemmer. For those of you who do not live in New York, Hammacher Schlemmer is 'the store' you go to for buying anything from an electric toothpick to a self-cleaning automobile. I don't believe the store is currently carrying either of these items, but maybe you will see them in their catalog next year.

As soon as we found a parking spot, the first order of business with the four girls was, as always, to have a snack, a drink and to go to the bathroom. Good-bye thirty minutes. We decided it was time to tell Stacie. Having Hillary and Peri there to express their thoughts, feelings and optimism about my health was extremely important to Stacie. Her initial reaction about my being bisexual was insignificant as she was concerned more about my health, and tears were welling up in her eyes. If Stacie didn't cry she wouldn't be normal. I was scared she might hate me, but she didn't. We talked a lot that day about the book and how most people up until now have been very kind and supportive, but that there will be people who will make fun of me and tease her. I asked her how she will deal with this. This is a difficult question for any person, let alone a child. We talked about my speech at Stacie's Bat Mitzvah, where I spoke about how the Jewish people had been oppressed for centuries and how proud I was when Stacie stood up for some child and proclaimed his innocence in a classroom. Stacie had studied the Holocaust in Hebrew School and so understood my parallel: that if her grandfather could have done something to help the plight of the Jewish people, Stacie would have been very proud; if her father could make a small difference in the battle against AIDS, she would likewise be proud.

I told Stacie if she starts feeling a little depressed, angry, ashamed, betrayed, confused or whatever, she should talk to her mother, her sisters, me, relatives or friends, but not to keep these thoughts to herself. We could also schedule a session with a social worker. Stacie seemed accepting and loving, but mine is a shocking story to tell anyone, much less a thirteen-year-old child. I suspect her initial reaction might change, yet if I were to use one adjective to describe Stacie, it would be compassionate. She got that from Jodi of course, but you know what? She also got that from me.

So back to the main event. Enter the Brodsky family into the world of Hammacher Schlemmer where all you have to do is dream of a can opener that serves as a knife and a lighter as well, and presto, they will market it. It doesn't even have to sell as long as it is unique. We have all made our wish list pending the success of my book. Hillary and I both have opted for the electronic massage brushes, pads, rollers, and accessories, after having compared all the effects of the various equipment. Of our top choices, one was fantastic and the other was a little better. Peri got caught up in a bed that molded her body to the mattress, while I snoozed in the neighboring bed.

Stacie found an electric car. I don't recall if Jodi had any interest in any item. Jodi was just thrilled we were together as a family.

Following our imaginary shopping spree at Hammacher Schlemmer we went downtown and had dinner at Po. All told it was a very pleasant evening and we were delighted to have Stacie back home. Jodi had a lot of packing to do for the trip to Florida. Hillary's friends kept dropping in to say good-bye. Jilian and her boyfriend came by, too, so the house seemed like it was back to its old self again. Even my mother came by to say hello to Stacie. Somehow Jodi managed to steal an hour or two of sleep before it was time to drive Hillary to the airport.

The next few days are going to be very difficult for me, as my entire family has left to take Hillary to college. Between prepping the house for Stacie's homecoming, coping with the emotions of telling family members about my book, packing Hillary up for school, and whatever else Jodi does, the available hours remaining for sleep have been minimal.

I am now going to tell you the worst flaw of the Brodsky family. We are always late. The girls just made their flight today. It was so hard saying good-bye to Hillary. I cried just a little. You must realize by now that I don't see anything wrong with a man crying. These joyful tears were a celebration of my happiness, realizing that Hillary will be off to find a new life for herself. Although she craves independence, she is oftentimes inseparable from Peri and to a smaller extent, Jodi. It's taken me eighteen years to realize that Hillary needs me, too. She seems to have an easier time confiding in me than in her mother, although I am constantly asking the girls, "How do you feel, knowing you have the best mother in the world? Does that give you a little extra confidence when you go out and face the world?" There were also tears of sadness for the emptiness I felt in my heart. It's hard to imagine that for eight whole weeks I will not be able to hold Hillary or even talk to her face-to-face.

You must be getting tired of this book by now. I am not a great architect, politician, actor, poet or writer. Thank God for copywriters, editors and agents, but I have something that nobody else has. It is the heart of Richard. This heart is as singular on the planet as is the heart of Irene, Lisa or Gary. All of us have our own special heart, how we feel and see things and how we dream. We all have our own unique story. I challenge any of you to write your story. If you can help one million, a few thousand, or just one person, then a very caring heart is your prize. And I, too, applaud you, for you have made a difference; you care.

I asked for forgiveness from Jodi and my girls, and not only did I get forgiveness, but I got to achieve a closeness that I couldn't have made up or dreamed of, even if I tried. Thank you Jodi, Hillary, Peri and Stacie.

To my brothers and sisters: I know this news has been shocking to some of you. Some things were said to each other hastily and then withdrawn. It has been a roller coaster of emotions. I have always believed in family. Family forgives and I still believe that. I love all of you, whether you have been against my writing this book or passionate that my writing this book is the right thing to do. But most of all, I thank you all for your caring and your love.

To my mother: I know this book has not been easy since you are such a private person. Your generation is different from mine and my children's generation is also different. No generation is right or wrong. Perhaps each generation is right for its era. Mother, if it is wrong for you to write the story, *Herbert, The Greatest Love Story Ever Told*, then you should not write it. If it is right for Richard to celebrate life, and author

Jodi, The Greatest Love Story Ever Told, then Richard has an obligation to write it. I still love you, but you could no longer stop my story from being told than you could stop me from loving you. I understand your concern is for my children, but guess what? So is mine, and by the time you read these pages, I think you'll agree that we have the same concerns. There will be a small minority of people that will find me unfit to live on this planet, but you know what? I wouldn't want my children associating with those families, and it will be my family who will be turning our noses up at such people.

To my father-in-law Jules: You have given me the greatest gift of all, my wife, and I cannot thank you and Mom enough. We have had our differences over the years and it is now my turn to say I'm sorry. My story was not meant to hurt you. I know you and Mom do love your children and grandchildren very much, and for that I love you, Dad.

And to all of you with whom I have shared my story: from Holly to Suzie, Dawn to Louisa, Claude to Diana, the world is a better place because people like you inhabit it. You are always there. You are the infinite, eternal silence and stillness of the air we breathe and take for granted. It is you who nurture our souls and are the source of everything beautiful and good on this planet. This book is dedicated to Anyone and Everyone whose heart is beating with a kind thought for Jodi and my family.

To my mother-in-law Joanne: We all love you and miss you. You would be very proud of your four children and their partners. As I stated at your funeral, I know who your favorites are: Jared, Jessica, Kari, Hillary, Peri, Stacie, Alexa, Marissa, Erin, Bradley and Michael (your eleven grandchildren).

To my father: Dad, it hasn't always been easy growing up. It takes some people longer to find their way and purpose in life than it does others. My purpose continues to be: to raise the most loving family I can, to love my mother, brothers and sisters and their families, and to always find forgiveness because I am farther from perfection than anyone in my family. But, if by some remote chance I can turn my curse of being HIV positive into a gift by truly making a difference, then let me be thankful and try to help in any way I can to find a vaccine and a cure for AIDS. And if my contribution is telling the story of

JODI, THE GREATEST LOVE STORY EVER TOLD,

then let my story be told. And may God grant me the strength, passion, courage and voice that will make you and Mom proud of me. I love you, Dad.

EPILOGUE

THE STORY YOU HAVE JUST read is about my life with my husband. It's one that we could not have invented. It is absolutely true. I know that this experience has been an incredible journey for our family, but through it all we have stayed very much there for each other. We understand that we are not in a popular place, but if our story can help even one person or family feel more comfortable with their situation, then this will all be worth it.

We chose to live a very quiet and secretive life for four years, but after much thought and soul searching we realized that this story had to be told. None of this, of course, has been easy. It's never easy to stand up and speak out for what you believe in, especially when you are taking a stand on a very controversial subject. I feel very proud to have been courageous enough to speak out on this issue; I hope I have paved the way for others to speak out as well. As Richard said, I never wavered in my decision. This is because I knew in my heart from the very beginning this was the right decision for me. After Richard's initial diagnosis, I became very well educated about HIV and the choices we had for Richard's treatment. The first few weeks were spent talking to people on hot lines and interviewing doctors in New York who specialize in AIDS, trying to see which one would have the best treatment and be the most encouraging. At first, Richard thought that because he was healthy, he could fight the virus on his own. We (the doctor, Richard's mother, and I) were able to persuade him that the best way to fight the virus aggressively was to start the anti-viral drugs immediately. Combavir (a combination of two drugs) and Viracept have been the three drugs that have worked great for him from the start. His viral load at present is undetectable and his T-cell count is in the 750 to 800 range, an acceptable number for a person who is not HIV positive. Richard is extremely diligent about taking his medicine to within one hour of the scheduled time. I feel that this has been critical to his healthy medical condition to date.

I'm sorry if this story hurts or irritates anyone in either of our families. This was not Richard's intention. True feelings and situations were described to try to make the reader understand Richard's emotional and mental state while he was going through these trying times. I hope that my role in this story convinces each of you that you are strong enough to take on anything that life throws your way. I have learned an incredible lesson about love and inner strength, and that the first step in dealing with any challenge in your life is to say "I can."

I also hope that our good friends and family will forgive us for keeping this secret for so long. It's something we felt was too heavy a burden to share. I now realize that people are genuinely caring individuals; the recent outpouring of understanding and love has been extremely gratifying.

I feel so fortunate to be able to have such a wonderful husband and family. I've always known that Richard and I have a very special bond. Together, through our deep caring for each other and for our children, we have been able to survive and triumph. Never take for granted any day each of you has to live. Each day is just one more day to show others how much you care. I'll never stop appreciating the life I am living. I realize how truly blessed we are.

While recently telling our story to family and friends, many people commented how trying this must have been for my girls and me. We have emerged from this experience and have a keener appreciation of life and what is truly important. The lessons learned about love, compassion and family will last us a lifetime. As Peri says, "I (Peri) have learned more about compassion and love in my sixteen years than most people learn in a lifetime."

The road ahead will remain bumpy because we know going public with our life will incur a wide range of reactions. I'm not even sure what the future holds for us since we live in such fast changing times. I could never have guessed I would be writing the epilogue to such a story. But other parts of our lives have never changed. We still feel as happy today as the day we first met, even though the road we've taken is far less traveled. Having you share our journey has meant a great deal to Richard and me. We are no longer alone, as we had been for the past four years. May you, too, never be alone, especially in difficult times. And whenever tragedy rears its ugly head, rise to the occasion; it's just another of life's challenges for you to overcome. This will make your triumphant times that much sweeter and more joyous. Try to appreciate everything about your lives as Richard and I do. We all have so much to be grateful for.

FIND PASSION IN THIS LIFETIME
BECAUSE A LIFETIME
WITHOUT PASSION
IS NOT WORTH LIVING

AFTERWORD

THE NEW YORK ROAD RUNNERS CLUB denied Jodi and me running numbers. Numerous appeals had been made to the New York Road Runners Club for acceptance into the marathon; all were denied. I had forwarded the Road Runners Club my introduction to *Jodi, The Greatest Love Story Ever Told* along with Jodi's epilogue and a cover letter. However, I was not successful in pleading my case; granting us numbers for the 2001 New York City Marathon would remain a voyage dreamed of, a voyage unjourneyed. Depriving me, a native New Yorker, of my right to passage through the five boroughs of New York City was heartless, an unforgivable act that saddened me to no end. Maybe the story of my 121-year-old grandmother was a better story than trying to raise money to save lives!

If Jodi and I did not run the New York City Marathon because of some minor technicality like not obtaining running numbers, what would you, the reader, think of us? I couldn't live with your answer because mine would be similar, only magnified ten times.

Enter the world of the New York City Police Department as they once again come to the rescue. The NYPD was kind enough to permit Jodi and me the privilege of running with them, even though we did not have running numbers. It was an incredible experience, a privilege I will always remember, an honor I will never forget. For one day, they allowed my wife and me to be a part of their family, and that memory will last a lifetime. God Bless the NYPD and their families.

Richard completed the 2001 New York City Marathon unofficially in 03:55.

Jodi completed the 2001 New York City Marathon unofficially in 04:30.

These times are unofficial. Only those with bona fide running numbers are permitted to run into Central Park for the final quarter-mile and experience the 'Olympic' spirit of the crowds cheering you on to the finish line. I was not permitted to enter *my* park... I'll be back.

BEFORE I SAY GOOD-BYE

I have wished a bird would fly away,
And not sing by my house all day;

I have clapped my hands at him from the door
When it seemed I could bear no more.

The fault must have been partly in me.
The bird was not to blame for his key,

And of course there must be something wrong,
In wanting to silence any song.

Robert Frost

IMAGINE IF ONE OF MY flying balloons just landed on Earth. Disembarking from the balloon would be students from another planet. Their mission would be to see if there was life on Earth, and if so, what lessons they could learn.

We might start off by giving them a tour of the airline industry and explain how our government had just spent 15 billion dollars to bail out the airline industry, but had allocated only a fraction of that amount to finding a cure for AIDS. Anybody want to volunteer for that job and sound convincing? Remember, those extraterrestrial creatures are here to learn!

We could teach them about Congress and how the Senate voted 90 to 7 in favor of funding domestic AIDS projects for 2002 and the House of Representatives voted 393 to 30 on the same legislation. This legislation was passed just before Congress recessed for 2001. We would feel obligated to tell our space travelers that the pressure was on Congress at this charitable season to provide AIDS funding for 2002.

"If this plague has caused so many deaths, then why wasn't the vote unanimous and why wasn't more money allocated?" questioned *Neptoranus*.

"Anybody care to field that question?" I replied.

"Let me try," volunteered Senator Oldersmont. "The President requested a smaller amount to be budgeted than the amount that was finally appropriated. He flipped-flopped a bit during the year on his commitment to AIDS. The President believed private institutions should be picking up the slack for charities, yet this has never materialized. Actually, the exact opposite has come to pass after September 11th. People have been very charitable to the surviving family members of the World Trade Center disaster, so much so, that other charities have not fared well at all."

"Don't you people have governments and world bodies that are elected by the people to solve problems on your planet?" asked *Plutomar*.

Another senator jumped in. "We have the greatest highway system in the world and the most sophisticated intelligence network on the planet. Our military is second to none. But all this comes at a price. So we skimp a lot on our contribution to world health and we contribute a smaller percentage of our gross national product than our European counterparts do."

"So your governments don't really serve the people who are most in need. What about people? Can people make a difference?"

No one answered. I replied this time. "I've written a book which I pray will make a difference. But over the past year there have been studies concluding that certain strains of the AIDS virus are not receptive to current medication. This is extrememly frightening. However, I still believe that living a healthy lifestyle and taking some medication will keep AIDS sufferers living a longer life, as opposed to those who take a defeatist attitude. No one knows the results of positive thinking more than I do. It is positively more crucial now than ever for government to take the lead role in eradicating AIDS, mankind's greatest curse. For once, let us look upon our nation's leaders as representatives whom we can be proud of, and say, 'I voted for that senator.'"

Space traveler *Vernocury* got up to speak. "Do you punish your representatives when they don't vote for the benefit of humanity?"

"That's an easy one," I shot back. "You just don't reelect them. You also write books and publish their names. For example, the seven senators who voted against funding domestic AIDS projects for the year 2002 are as follows: Allard, Feingold, Fitzgerald, McCain, Nickles, Smith and Voinovich. All of the above senators are Republican with the exception of Feingold, whose past record has been favorable to AIDS legislation. Fitzgerald and McCain have not been the staunchest supporters nor have they been active detractors. The remaining four, however, are more consistently against AIDS legislation."

Spaceman *Juposat* rose and concluded. "It is time for us to return to our distant star. Our home is millions of miles away. You can't see it from here but we know the way. If we have learned anything form our journey, it is that you people have so far to go to complete your trek." And the balloon flew away to visit other heavenly bodies.

We can only pray that we have realized the mistakes of our past. Then, and only then, can we firmly redefine our existence by acknowledging our misguided values. Then we can stand tall and proud on planet Earth, and be proud our brain has worth.